COSCOM ENTERTAINMENT

Also by A.P. Fuchs

Blood of My World Trilogy

Discovery of Death
Memories of Death
Life of Death

Undead World Trilogy

Blood of the Dead
Possession of the Dead
Redemption of the Dead

The Axiom-man™ Saga
(listed in reading order)

Axiom-man
Episode No. 0: First Night Out
Doorway of Darkness
Episode No. 1: The Dead Land
City of Ruin
Of Magic and Men (comic book)

Other Fiction

A Stranger Dead
A Red Dark Night
April (writing as Peter Fox)
Magic Man (deluxe chapbook)
The Way of the Fog (The Ark of Light Vol. 1)
Devil's Playground (written with Keith Gouveia)
On Hell's Wings (written with Keith Gouveia)
Zombie Fight Night: Battles of the Dead
Magic Man Plus 15 Tales of Terror
Undeniable

Anthologies (as editor)

Dead Science
Elements of the Fantastic
Vicious Verses and Reanimated Rhymes: Zany Zombie Poetry for the Undead Head
Metahumans vs the Undead
Bigfoot Terror Tales Vol. 1 (with Eric S. Brown)
Bigfoot Terror Tales Vol. 2 (with Eric S. Brown)

Non-fiction

Book Marketing for the Financially-challenged Author

Poetry

The Hand I've Been Dealt
Haunted Melodies and Other Dark Poems
Still About A Girl

Go to

WWW.CANISTERX.COM

&

WWW.UNDEADWORLDTRILOGY.COM

Book Three of the *Undead World Trilogy*

REDEMPTION OF THE DEAD

by

A.P. FUCHS

COSCOM ENTERTAINMENT
WINNIPEG

The fiction in this book is just that: fiction. Names, characters, places and events either are products of the author's imagination or are used fictitiously. Any resemblance to actual events or persons living or dead or living dead is purely coincidental.

ISBN 978-1-927339-21-3

REDEMPTION OF THE DEAD is Copyright © 2012 by Adam P. Fuchs. All rights reserved, including the right to reproduce in whole or in part in any form or medium.

Published by COSCOM ENTERTAINMENT
www.coscomentertainment.com

Text set in Garamond; Printed and Bound in the USA

COVER ART BY GARY MCCLUSKEY
INTERIOR "ZOMBIE HEAD" ART BY A.P. FUCHS

For Keith Gouveia, fellow writer, editor,
but most importantly, best friend.

Book Three of the *Undead World Trilogy*

REDEMPTION
OF THE
DEAD

BOWELS

Prologue: Completion 1
1: Devil Rising 4
2: The Arrival 11
3: From Hidden Places 17
4: Taking Chances 27
5: Hang Ups 34
6: You Can't Die in Hell 39
7: Sleep 45
8: Between Worlds 47
9: Loners 53
10: Grassy Hills, Evil Beasts 61
11: The Window 68
12: Escape from Chinatown 72
13: Rock Bottom Heartache 80
14: The Cottage 85
15: The Safe House 91
16: Two Roads 96
17: Crystals 102
18: Meet Up 109
19: Mirror, Mirror 115
20: Honesty 121
21: The Lie 126
22: Rooftop Gathering 131
23: Elevators 136
24: Spill It 142
25: Demons 151
26: Leaving 159
27: On the Street 163
28: New Place 169
29: The War Begins 173
30: Getting Out 178
31: It's About Time 185
32: Retreat 191
33: Battle of the Angels 196
34: In Hell 202
35: The Past 207
Epilogue: Alterations 213

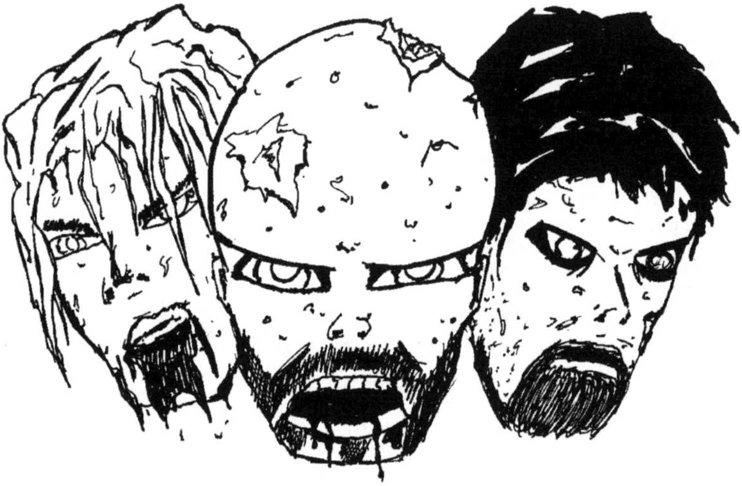

PROLOGUE
COMPLETION

*O*NE YEAR AGO, *outside of Time...*

The demon Bethrez moved quickly through the rocky tunnels of Hell, the news he had been waiting for finally about to become a reality.

As he emerged into a cavern at the end of a long corridor, he came to a sudden stop atop his reptilian feet. His commander, Holgrack, stood before him, with dark eyes the size of eggs and rough scaly skin that made even Bethrez's own appear smooth by comparison.

"Is it true?" Bethrez asked.

Holgrack simply nodded.

"Are you certain?"

"I would not have summoned you if it wasn't. The master had called a meeting and I was in attendance. The whisperings are true: all is ready."

"And the converter?"

"Come, this way."

Holgrack led Bethrez through another long corridor lit by the ambient light from the great lake that burned with fire beyond its walls. At the end of the corridor, they turned left and emerged into a sunken room made of stone. Toward the rear wall was an oblong frame carved out of the ancient stone from the bed of the fiery lake itself. Along the frame's border was the master's name in every known tongue, both presently spoken and extinct, even in the languages only known to those of the unseen realm. Written within the characters of the master's name was another phrase: "To merge, to change, to die, to live in death."

Bethrez asked, "And it works?"

"You will soon see, my friend, but take pride in this moment for what stands before you is the fruition of your labors."

"But it was you who brought it to the council and was appointed overseer of this project."

"Though true, it was still your idea, your genius. I foresee great exaltation for you should this operate as you suggest."

Bethrez inspected the structure. "It seems properly put together. The last two had flaws, even just in the characters written. One out of place mark and it will not work as planned." He gazed up at the frame.

"What is it?" Holgrack asked.

1

"Which chamber are we in?"

"Cave D-S-Seventeen-Lateral-J."

Bethrez muttered the name back to himself. "This is in the wrong location!"

"How dare you raise your voice to me!"

"And how dare you and your men once again go against my instruction."

"You are in no position to tell me what to do, underling."

"I might not be, but I know someone who is." Bethrez pushed his way past Holgrack and headed into the dank corridor beyond the room.

A sudden force knocked out his legs from under him and he hit the stone ground, chin first. Flipping over onto his back, he put his arm out to block Holgrack's fist as it came down on him, and instead was able to deliver a swift blow of his own.

"Get off me!" Bethrez shouted.

The shouts of other demons a few passages over echoed throughout the corridor.

Holgrack removed his sword and brought its jagged blade against Bethrez's throat. He applied so much pressure that Bethrez's esophagus was collapsing against his vertebrae.

With a grimace, Bethrez lashed out with his claws and cleaved a chunk of flesh from Holgrack's face, tearing away scaly skin and sending a spray of black blood into the air. It was enough of a distraction for him to grab Holgrack's wrist and push it and the blade away from his neck.

He struck his commanding officer again and got out from under him.

"I will kill you!" Holgrack shouted.

Bethrez simply shook his head. His commander has never been bright, but had been chosen to lead after centuries of being one of the finest warriors in all of Hell's ranks. What Holgrack didn't know was Bethrez was also highly skilled, though it was something he never showed to his kin and only unleashed on the battlefield when going up against those blasted angels of Heaven.

Holgrack lunged into the air, angled the blade, and brought it down into Bethrez's shoulder. Bethrez turned away, then swung back with a backhand to Holgrack's head.

"Fool," Bethrez said. "You just gave me your weapon." He pulled the blade from his shoulder, ripping out scaly flesh and gobs of stringy blood in the process.

Holgrack moved in and Bethrez feigned to bring the blade in from high up, then switched hands and brought the blade from down and low, plunging it deep into Holgrack's chest. As Holgrack reached for the blade, Bethrez swatted his commander's hands away, removed the blade and jumped over him. Once behind, he brought the blade down into Holgrack's skull. His commander dropped to his knees, then fell forward, the blade still stuck in his head.

Holgrack's fate was sealed. Despite being immortal, his evil spirit would leave his scaly body and be forever chained to the fiery lake, never to escape again.

REDEMPTION OF THE DEAD

Bethrez spat on his commander's body then stormed down the corridor just as other reptilians emerged from the tunnels.

"What have you done?" one of them asked him.

"Go see for yourself," he said, and went off in search of Vingros, the very one Holgrack answered to. "It must be tested. The portal must work."

1
DEVIL RISING

THE PRESENT...

Sharp bits of jagged glass pierced Joe's lips and cheeks as the truck spun upside down across the pavement. Billows of dust blew against his skin like coarse sand, scratching across its surface. Eyes squeezed shut, mouth the same, he could barely breathe through his nose, each tiny breath a miniscule sip of dirty air. He shoved his hand back against his mouth, trying to filter out the debris flying around inside the cab. Tracy was somewhere in here with him. A couple of times he felt her body knock against his as the howling wind outside tossed the truck around like a beach ball.

Ear piercing, nails-against-a-chalkboard screeches wracked Joe's hearing. It came from right beneath him, the cab's roof scraping across the cement as it slid along pavement.

He wanted to call out Tracy's name, but when he opened his mouth, a thick puff of dust managed to get past his hand and dump into his mouth. Scraping the filthy paste off his tongue, he spat it out as best he could, most of it landing against the hand in front of his lips only to get shoved back in his mouth again as the truck moved.

The finely-tuned *ping-ping-ping* of dusty debris raining against the truck's hull grew louder as a huge gust of wind blew the truck off its roof and back onto its side. It rocked a couple of times before the sound diminished and the truck finally stopped moving.

Coughing, Joe slowly moved his hand away from his mouth, using the other to brace himself against the steering wheel, his elbow caught by the gearshift. Spitting, then swallowing gobs of mucky dust, he hacked them back out, his stomach sick with pronounced nausea.

Coughing again, he finally managed to bark out Tracy's name.

No response.

"Tracy," he wheezed as his breath caught; he coughed out another gob of wet dust. He blinked his eyes open. The entire interior of the cab was coated in light brown at least half an inch thick. Beneath him, the dust was even thicker—several inches—so much so that his leg, which had gotten itself parallel to the front seat and hung down by the passenger side, was covered in dust up to his ankle.

"Tracy," he said again. Joe pushed against the steering wheel and straightened himself as best he could before having to adjust to get his elbow free from between the gearshift and ashtray. Glancing over to the passenger side, he saw her body upside down, her knees up against the passenger seat, the rest of her torso hanging over onto the cab's floor. Her head was mostly covered in dust and gravel. "Tracy!"

Joe scrambled to lunge his body forward and get himself in a position to pull her up. Able to get beside her and keep gravity's pull at bay by pressing his knee against the radio, he grabbed her by the waist and pulled up and back. Her head was so far under the glove box that he couldn't hoist her any higher lest he risk smacking it against the box's underside and possibly complicating any injuries she had sustained.

The passenger window was blown out; glass mixed with the dust and gravel littered the cab. Stretching past her, he reached up and grabbed the edge of the passenger window's frame and pulled his body up. With a quick bend forward, he was able to shift his weight and climb out of the cab like climbing out of a pool. Now on top of the cab, knees against the truck bed, he tried to open the door. The handle moved, but the door only budged a half-inch and no more, and it wasn't gravity keeping it down. The entire door mangled, the metal and plastic crumpled, part of the cab side was ripped and bent over the door, acting like a mini latch. He tried to bend it upright so as to free the door, but he wasn't strong enough.

Wiping the sweat from his forehead and coughing out some more dust, Joe straightened his body, got as close to the open window as possible without losing his balance, then brought his knees back up under him. He reached in slowly so he wouldn't tip, and once again put his hands and forearms around Tracy's waist.

"Have to get her head free," he said, straining. *She'll suffocate, otherwise.* "Come on, Tracy." He pulled against her, this time able to have the leverage to pull her away from under the glove box before dragging her up.

Joe got her upper body free. Her arms and head hung limp. He quickly debated checking for a heartbeat, but thought better of it and decided the best course of action was to just get her free from the truck.

"I won't let you die. Not you, too."

April had died at his own hand, but she had already become one of the undead creatures before that. Despite the wall he'd put around his heart since that day, he found his kinship with Tracy had penetrated it enough for him to care about her.

5

He quickly adjusted himself so he sat on the truck door, his legs now dangling inside the cab. He reached low and readjusted his grip on Tracy before pulling up with everything he had. Her body turned in his arms, her legs dropping beneath her. He held her tight and with a heave, pulled her up hard enough so he could momentarily let go and get his hands and arms under her even more securely. He did the same thing again, and was able to jerk her body up so her upper half was now across one thigh, her legs hanging between his.

Gravity no longer an issue, he put his fingers to her neck and listened for breathing.

She wasn't, and with the hollow moans of the giant undead floating on the air from downtown distracting him, he wasn't sure if he felt a pulse either.

"Tracy!" he said and shook her. He forced her mouth open, pinched her nose, and pressed his lips against hers. He breathed out, hopefully getting enough air in her lungs to jumpstart her breathing. He listened. Nothing. He yanked on her harder and got her out of the truck even more. He pressed his palms hard against her chest and pressed down three times. He breathed into her again and pumped her chest once more.

Joe kept up the CPR, whatever it took, however long.

Please, God, no. Don't take her. Not Tracy. I need . . . ". . . I need her."

He breathed into her mouth again, pumped his hands against her chest, waited a moment, then resumed trying to resuscitate her. Screaming, he cursed at the sky and got back to work, the heavy dust lingering on the air not helping him any.

Once more and . . . Tracy wheezed.

"Yes, yes! Breathe! Breathe!" He leaned in to give her air again and about halfway through his breath, she coughed wet dust up into his face and started to gag. "Yes, yes! Cough. Get it out."

Invigorated, adrenaline pumping, he hoisted her into a sitting position and tapped her firmly on the back several times. Tracy kept gagging and coughing as she let out wads of wet dust.

Somehow in the middle of all this, Joe clearly heard the word, "Ow." He stopped slapping her on the back.

"You're . . . hurting . . ." She coughed and yacked out some more moist dirt. "You're hurting . . . me."

He stopped and wanted to hit her on the back again to ensure she got everything, but stopped himself.

Tracy coughed some more before finally getting in a deep, long breath. She exhaled then panted hard and fast.

"You're alive," Joe said. "You're alive." He couldn't believe it and the emotions flooding through him caught him off guard and sent his thoughts into a whirlwind. Barely able to concentrate, but so happy she was okay, he reached around her and hugged her tight. "You're alive, Tracy. Thank God."

"Joe . . ." was all she said before coughing again.

Body shaking, every muscle weak from strain, Tracy held onto to Joe as tight as she could as he piggy-backed her away from the truck and further from the city, the aim trying to clear the cloud.

She had nearly died. There had been many close calls since the dead began to rise, even since meeting Joe, but she had felt herself go to that place of darkness where any thought and idea of herself and her body was gone. All she remembered was a strange sense of awareness that she was on the edge of being transformed into something new. Whether something good or bad, she didn't know. Just some kind of transformation. Yet there was also an extreme heaviness, one not physical, but almost spiritual.

That was all she could recall.

She closed her eyes and rested her head against the back of Joe's shoulder.

"You okay back there?" he asked.

"Mm hm," she said.

"Hey, Tracy, you okay back there?"

"I said yes," she said louder.

"Didn't hear you."

The dust eventually began to clear. They were in the suburbs, a fairly modern neighborhood that looked to have been built in the eighties, one they passed when driving back to the city.

Finding shelter under a large pine, Joe eased her down. When she landed on her feet, she wobbled and fell against him. Joe grabbed her and slowly lowered her to the ground.

"Is it . . . is it okay here?" she asked.

"I think so," he said. "While trying to get away from that dust cloud" —he coughed— "I saw the shadows of a few of them, but made sure to keep away. Didn't see any in this neighborhood, though."

"Do you have your gun?" she asked.

Joe's eyes went wide as he patted himself over. His expression sank. "I gave it to you." He started to get up as if he was going to take off back to the truck, but stopped himself mid-stand and squatted down again. "Do you?"

Tracy couldn't feel the solid security of a weapon resting anywhere against her. "No, I'm sorry." She saw the disappointment in his gaze.

She took a deep breath and coughed some more. It would probably be a few days before she expelled all that had built up in her lungs during the accident.

"How are you feeling?" he asked.

She was sore all over, especially her gut and chest. She didn't think anything was broken, just strained. "I'll live."

"Wonder what caused that dust storm?"

"I don't know."

He was running through a mental checklist, she knew, because she was, too. "It's sheltered enough under here, but nowhere near safe. Why don't you rest here for a bit then we'll get up and take it from there?"

She nodded, her head pounding. A rest sounded amazing.

To greet the devil.

Nathaniel's words were all that lingered in Billie's mind ever since he said them.

She was in the woods, the angel having lifted her and Hank, a man with a few screws loose, into the air and set them upon a thick tree branch four or five stories from the forest floor. A lake separated them from the other side where hordes of the undead had gathered, some from within the forest itself, others having traversed the bottom of the lake before climbing up onto the shore.

The lake stained with gray rain looked like liquid clay. Already the stench of the dead had wafted across the lake, causing Billie to ensure she only breathed through her mouth. Nathaniel stood between her and Hank.

"This going to happen like you said?" Hank asked the angel.

"Yes, it will." Nathaniel's voice seemed strangely calm.

"How's *what* going to happen?" Billie asked. "You said these things are going to greet the . . . the devil." Though she had never been a church-going girl, she, like almost everyone else, had heard of this master of evil. She just never believed he was real, and even now wasn't sure what to think of what was about to supposedly happen.

"He will come when he is ready and will claim dominion over those gathered to greet him. From there . . ."

"He's gonna take over the whole planet," Hank said. "He's a bad boy. Very bad. I don't know why he's so bad but he is."

"Iniquity was found in him long ago," Nathaniel said, "and he caused a great war in Heaven. Him and a third of his brethren were cast out."

"To Hell?" Billie asked.

"To the Earth."

"What? Is this what this is, that casting out?"

"In a manner of speaking, but the downfall of Lucifer happened before the world began."

It made zero sense. How could the devil be sent to the Earth before the Earth even was? *This is the exact reason why I avoid religion*, Billie thought, turning her attention back on the shore across the way. The undead stood in ranks even despite their usual disorientation.

"The Earth existed before the one you know," the angel said.

"You're still not making sense." She bit her tongue, forgetting for a minute *who* she was talking to. "Sorry. I mean—"

"Do not be afraid, Billie. You can talk to me, you can be honest. I won't harm you." The gleam of his golden robe dimmed then morphed into a gray turtleneck and jeans. Nathaniel's brilliant visage dimmed as well and he took on the features of a young man no more than thirty with dark brown hair and stubble across his cheeks.

His gleaming blue eyes drew Billie in, and she thought better of herself when her first inkling was to be attracted to him. *He's an angel for crying out loud!* She cast her eyes downward.

"If I may," Hank said, his voice suddenly taking on an attempted British accent that was both terrible and stupid. Billie cut him a break though. The poor guy, she gathered, couldn't help it. "He already explained it to me, my lady. The gentleman had stated that after Lucifer's rebellion there was a war that took place in both Heaven and Earth, one so devastating and destructive it caused this planet to essentially be a destroyed battleground. Once all was settled, the realms were split and the supernatural became that which was unseen, while the natural was renewed, and man was created and so forth."

"You say well, Hank," Nathaniel said, "and so it was long ago. Now, the enemy has come before his time to bring about his final confrontation with On High in a way outside the ordained events."

"And if he does?" Billie asked.

"All will come to an end and, by proxy, God will be overpowered in having what is written altered. This has been Lucifer's aim since the beginning: to usurp the throne. We mustn't let that happen."

The ground shook beneath them. Billie lost her footing on the wide tree branch and would have nearly fallen off if Nathaniel hadn't grabbed her and kept her and Hank's feet firmly planted.

Trees snapped and fell over, rocks crumbled off the edge of the lake and tumbled to the water below. The undead across the way rocked on their feet and collapsed. The lake before them began to boil, its putrid steam a foul-smelling mix of rotten fish and sulfur.

"It's time," Nathaniel said.

2
THE ARRIVAL

THE LAKE BUBBLED, the gray of its waters growing darker with each passing moment. The bubbles on its surface grew larger until some were as a big as a basketball. The heat coming off the water reminded Billie of the intensity of a sauna.

With a roar of waves, the water shot upward in a wide and high spout, its apex towering over her and the others by what had to be around ten stories. She and Hank took cover while Nathaniel remained still.

Atop the enormous tower of water burst forth a blast of white light, its presence crackling against the air like electricity. As the water slowly began to descend, so did the mysterious light with it until its brilliance sat upon the water, its violent bubbles of its boil beginning to subside. Amidst the light, the form of a man appeared, average height, average weight. Soon, the light began to dim, leaving the man standing on the water.

The undead on the shore watched him, but did not go near the water to get him.

The man wore black dress pants and shoes, a deep purple collared shirt, his hair—at least from the back—blond and neatly cropped.

Billie tried to inch forward to get a better look, but the moment her foot moved, a harsh tingle rushed to her core as a well of fear and unease burst forth inside her. She found herself anxious and breathing rapidly within seconds.

"Remain there, Billie," Nathaniel said. "You, too, Hank. Neither of you want to be near his presence."

"Oh, you don't need to tell me twice, your angelness," Hank said.

That's what that rush of pronounced discomfort was, Billie thought. She shuddered.

The man on the lake walked across the water; in front of her, Billie saw Nathaniel shake his head slowly from side-to-side.

Is he afraid, too? she wondered.

Nathaniel turned and joined her and Hank.

"That was some waterworks," Hank said. "Disney-quality, if you ask me."

Billie didn't comment; Nathaniel didn't acknowledge him.

"Lucifer has arrived," the angel said.

Talk about stating the obvious, Billie thought.

Nathaniel gave her a look that said he knew what she had thought, but it didn't seem to bother him.

Billie looked past him. Across the lake, the moans of the dead filled the air as they greeted their master. They welcomed him as if they knew him, or at the very least recognized him.

"Does he know you're here?" Billie asked Nathaniel.

"No. My presence has been well hidden. So far as he is aware, his arrival has gone unnoticed. He is no doubt basking in what he sees as a success. I, for one, cannot wait to take my sword to him."

"He's a bad seed," Hank said. "True thing. Even the way he showed up is a complete mockery of God."

"You're a smart man, Hank," Nathaniel said.

Hank's face went flat. "You got that straight."

Billie quickly raised and lowered her eyebrows: *Yeah, right.* To Nathaniel: "I don't want to be up here anymore. I don't want to be in this forest at all anymore either. Can you get us out of here?"

"I can, but that is not what we are called to do at this time."

"So, what are we" —she made quotation marks with her fingers— "'called' to do?"

"Surveillance."

"Spy stuff," Hank said as if he was helping.

Though she knew the guy couldn't help it, he was getting on her nerves.

On the other side of the lake, Lucifer had disappeared amongst the throng of the dead and was out of sight.

"Can he see us?" Billie asked.

"No. He is not omniscient," Nathaniel said.

"Does he know we're here? Um, Hank and me?"

"You have been concealed as well for the time being."

"Time being? Great. Just great. So at some point whatever's hiding us is going to be gone and he's going to come after us." She threw her hands in the air. Her words were choked with tears. "Nice. Go from watching my friend die to almost getting killed to seeing the devil come and knowing he'll come after me eventually." Her heart ached as she thought of August. Though she had known him for only a short time, he had been a mentor and a friend. Her mind drifted over to Des and what happened when they arrived back on the Richardson Building's rooftop in the helicopter. Des, having been left behind prior to their leaving and entering the past, had come to greet them. Instead, he had somehow gone from human to shape-shifting zombie and tried to kill them. August shot him to save Joe's life, but Des . . . the one on the rooftop wasn't the one she'd known. He had been her friend when the undead rose. Together they exchanged info and ideas on how to survive. He'd been human.

Returning from that bizarre Storm of Skulls had created a new timeline where the undead—which turned out to be possessed souls, living and deceased—had not only developed the supernatural ability to shape shift, but some were also enormous and as tall as some buildings.

Billie shed a tear and wiped it from her eyes; she felt a hand on her shoulder. She turned. "Nathaniel, I—"

But it wasn't Nathaniel.

It was Hank. "It's going to be okay. Nathaniel said as much. You got to trust him. He's an angel, you know."

"I know, but I think I've been through more than you have. No offense."

"None taken."

"I just want to go home, you know?" Except she knew there wasn't a home to return to. The Haven—the last reasonably safe place in Winnipeg—must be crawling with the undead by now. Besides, it wasn't *her* Haven. That one was lost when the timeline shifted.

Billie looked past Hank down the length of the large branch holding them above the ground, hoping to see the angel.

He was gone.

After keeping out a sharp eye for anyone—undead or otherwise—coming near the large pine tree, Joe was relieved when Tracy opened her eyes, stretched and groaned. He knew it was ill-advised to let someone fall asleep after a head injury, but he kept on the alert for any sign she'd stop breathing or suddenly went still. Sleep healed the body. A fact of life.

"What time is it?" Tracy asked.

"Not sure. Close to dark, though. How's your head?"

"Feels like I just ran into a brick wall, but I'll manage."

"How many fingers am I holding up?" Joe held up three.

"Five," she said.

"Um . . ."

"Three." She smirked.

At least she seems in good spirits. "We best get a move on when you're ready. We're not far from a multitude of possible hideouts. Just pick the safest-looking one and let's roll."

Tracy stretched her arms and legs once more before slowly getting to her feet. She briefly swooned once standing, but used the tree trunk for balance.

Out on the lawn, the cool night air made Joe shiver. Tracy felt it, too, he saw, because she hugged herself as she walked.

Without any weapons, he kept on extra alert. All they had on their side was the ability to run, but with Tracy in her condition, he didn't know how far they'd get if it came to it.

The power was out in this area of the city, the details of each household difficult to see without walking up the driveway and taking a closer look. Joe quickly made up a mental checklist as to help speed up the process: houses with broken windows were not to be neared, neither ones with open doors; if the front looked okay, the back was approached with extreme caution, with the hope the back doors and-or windows were intact like the front's; the house couldn't be beside another with broken windows, whether just the one side or both; and the simplest one—if one of the creatures could be heard near or within the house, they would automatically move on until the sound ceased.

"It's cold," Tracy said. "Feels like the temperature suddenly dropped five degrees."

"Don't know how that's possible considering the gray clouds have kept the weather in check since this all started. No heat. No rain or snow."

"You don't feel it?"

"No, but I've also trained myself to ignore small things like that."

"It's a shame," she said. "I was trained to notice every single detail, whether internal or external. To survive, you must be prepared for all eventualities and be aware of what's going on around you."

"To each his own."

"*Her* own."

He smirked then tapped her on the arm. "How about this one?" He pointed to a bungalow up on the right. Though he'd have to get closer to be sure, the front windows and doors seemed to be intact.

"Let's hope so," she said.

"Stay behind me." He led the way and verified his find by examining the entrances at the front. A wooden fence ran against the house off to the side, bordering the backyard beyond. Joe went up to the gate, Tracy right behind him. He undid the latch and let themselves in. He listened for any sound of the creatures, but heard nothing. Slowly, he and Tracy entered the yard and began to check over the house the moment a window came into view. There were two on the side along with a door to an attached garage, three windows on the back, and one on the furthest side. All seemed to be fine.

Joe approached the garage door and silently gripped the doorknob. With a gentle turn, he eased the knob over until it stopped moving, then, standing off to the side and ready to use the door as a shield if needed be, he opened it.

He listened for movement. Nothing. He slowly peered around the door to look into the garage. The single-car garage was dark and it was difficult to see anything at all.

"I don't like this," Tracy said.

"Me neither, but it has to be done."

Joe moved into the doorframe and whistled. "Hello?"

No sound came from within.

"I think it's all clear," he said.

"Think? You *think*? No good, Joe. You and I both know not to take guesses."

"Stop it. I haven't made any final decisions. Was just telling you what I found."

"Well, then make a decision because we can't stay out here."

"Okay, let me think." He put his hands on his hips. It was too dangerous to chance it with this house without knowing what precisely was in the garage. Even if an undead had been in there but was killed and laid there truly deceased, there might be others in the area, or if—

A soft scraping sound came from below his field of vision. It sounded again, and when he looked down, a rotting hand was reaching for his ankle.

Joe jumped back, knocking into Tracy. She stumbled but regained her footing.

"Let's go," she said.

Joe stood there, watching as the creature pulled itself out of the shadows of the garage and across the doorframe toward them. When it pulled itself out, Joe saw its legs had been severed at the hips, dry and crusty strands of muscle and sinew dragging behind it. The creature opened its mouth as if to wheeze or hiss, but nothing came out.

"Let's go!" Tracy shouted.

Joe slowly shook his head. "Not yet." He glanced around the yard, looking for something he could use as a weapon and put an end to this thing on the ground. He did a quick jog around the back of the house, but came up empty. Then it hit him. He went up to the leafless oak tree, jumped up and yanked down on a branch that was about as thick as a D battery and as long as a baseball bat. After a couple jump-and-pulls, the branch snapped, the dry wood making a nice jagged break on one side of its shaft.

Joe adjusted his grip on the branch and moved quickly toward the zombie. The thing still kept crawling along the ground, every so often reaching out with its dead hand as if it thought it could grab him from that far away. Joe went right up to it, stomped on its hand, pinning it to the ground. The next instant, he drove the branch like a stake through the creature's head. The zombie's face slammed into the ground as gray brain and thick, black blood bubbled out of its skull. The creature stirred so he yanked out the stick then stabbed down beside the wound he just made, creating a new one which broke the rotting skull enough to completely crack off the side of it. Its brain slid out, as did tar-like blood and a few maggots.

"Okay," he said, standing, "we can go now."

3
FROM HIDDEN PLACES

NATHANIEL HADN'T RETURNED in over an hour. If the gray clouds hadn't continuously blanketed the sky, it would be near dark soon and time to pack it in. She didn't want to stay here any longer, not with the devil somewhere across the lake. Billie was getting tired and stretched wide and big, letting go a long and loud yawn.

"Sure, let them hear you," Hank said.

"Sorry," she said and blinked the yawn-tears from her eyes. "I don't want to stay up here much longer. Do you know why Nathaniel left?"

He shook his head. "I don't know a lot of things, but I do know that everything happens for a reason, and I don't mean that in a vague 'oh, it's all part of a master plan, but I'm not going to say who's behind it' way or whatever."

Billie was surprised at how lucid Hank was at the moment. She didn't know what was wrong with him, but this was the first time he was talking like an average person versus someone who was limited in their understanding of the world and had a hard time figuring things out. She just hoped he wasn't in his "character" mode again.

"Do you know the reason for this?" she asked.

"Haven't a clue."

"You know, I've been part of this whole zombie thing from the beginning."

"Haven't we all."

"I mean, aside from the Rain not harming me—and I still don't know why that was—and trying to maintain a network of survivors for close to a year before hitting the road, I've really been in the thick of getting all involved with this weird, undead, supernatural stuff. I've lost friends, have almost been killed and eaten so many times I've lost count, have seen things that there's zero explanation for" —she flashed back to the Storm of Skulls and the weird event in the past at a bank and Nathaniel's first appearance, at first as an old man who had got a safety deposit box out to reset an old pocket watch, his seeing her, the craziness after— "I'm hoping it's all going to end soon. I'm tired of feeling lost and always on the run."

Hank just sat on the large branch, his legs hanging over the edge, hands in his lap, and didn't say anything.

"It's clear you met Nathaniel before," she said. "Wanna tell me about it?" At least the story would help pass the time.

Hank didn't respond.

"Hank?"

"Hm?"

"Want to tell me how you met Nathaniel?"

He looked at her as if he didn't know what she was talking about.

"You met him before, right?"

"Uh, yeah, but . . . can't remember right now." He scratched his head and looked up into the trees.

She'd lost him and he was back to his old self again, it seemed.

Across the lake, the moans of the dead rose in volume. Billie got on her hands and knees and crept closer to the edge of the wide branch to get a closer look. The zombies shuffled in all directions, some going back into the forest, others sliding down the rocks and falling to the lake in heavy splashes.

She kept an eye out for—*I don't want to use his name. Too creepy. I'll call him "Bad Man."* It was difficult to discern anyone specifically out of the crowd of the dead beyond. The most she could do was just sit tight and watch.

Hank came up behind her. "Them things are on the move."

"Wonder where they're going?"

"Maybe back where they came or some such?"

"Maybe."

The two stayed on the branch and watched the movement below. The foul stench of the dead grew worse, their movement stirring up the funk and casting it on the air. Billie pinched her nose. Hank didn't. A few minutes later, the gray water moved on their side of the lake and undead men and women began to slowly walk out, their raggedy clothes drenched and clinging to their bodies like cloth to skeletons. Some were able to smoothly transition up the shore onto land whereas others needed to climb the large rocks that separated the slanted forest floor from the lake. Dry branches snapped and dead leaves crunched beneath the creatures' feet as they shuffled below them.

"Don't make a sound," Billie whispered.

"I won't," Hank said at normal volume.

Her heart skipped a beat. She hoped the undead below hadn't heard him.

Below, the creatures marched in rank, their presence and stride seeming to emit an ambience of purpose and not just random shambling.

Perhaps Bad Man's visit changed everything? she thought. Even calling the devil "Bad Man" didn't help make his presence any less surreal. It was one thing to imagine this creepy guy in a red unitard stalking around in some invisible way, causing mischief—it was another to actually *see* him and have every preconceived notion as to who he was cast aside like refuse.

"Don't dwell on him, don't dwell on him, don't dwell on him," Billie whispered to herself. The evil one's very image was disturbing, sickening and spirit-crushing, yet she found herself slipping into a moderate trance when his image—that beautiful white light when he first emerged—went before her mind's eye. Something about him appealed to something within her . . . she just didn't know what.

"Billie?" Hank said, still not seeming to understand the concept of keeping one's voice down.

"Shhh," she said.

"I've called you four times. Where were you? You were there, but not there, you know?"

"Keep your voice down!" she said, quickly slapping a hand to her lips when her own voice rose way above where she meant it.

The grunts and groans of the dead grew louder, the steady shuffling footfalls of the creatures falling more and more in unison the longer they passed beneath them on the forest floor.

"Do you think they can see us?" Hank said.

Billie clenched her fist and sent a hard shot to his chest, shushing him.

The dead marched on, then one of the creatures with a broken neck that had no choice but to keep its head lolled back caught sight of them. The undead man with stringy hair and strange black boils on his skin stopped, the other creatures coming up behind him, bumping into him then stopping themselves. They all stood around, seemingly clueless as to what was happening until a few more of the undead looked up in Billie and Hank's direction.

"Don't. Move," she whispered.

Hank scratched his nose.

She rolled her eyes.

Some of the zombies below started to move again and her heart rose with relief, then began wildly thumping when a half dozen of the creatures started to move in the direction of the base of the tree. More

19

followed suit and soon a pack of at least thirty of them were hording around the bottom of the tree, dead fingers scraping and clawing against the bark, moans of hunger and need growing louder and louder.

Billie got to her feet; so did Hank.

"What do we do?" he asked.

"I don't know, shoot your gun!"

Hank blew off a couple of shots, taking out two of the creatures below before having to reload.

The undead horde beneath them crowded in upon itself and the group pushing in from the edges began to claw and climb their way on top of their brethren, gaining height. Some were reaching up and swiping at the air as if they could already grab Billie and pull her down.

"They're coming! They're coming!" Hank said.

His panic was enough to send her own over the edge and she had to restrain herself from feeding him to the undead below.

Okay, stay cool, she told herself. She glanced up and down the length of the tree branch. There weren't any options in terms of escape and climbing the tree itself to get to higher ground would be impossible given the trunk's girth and the height of the other branches above their heads.

The undead continued to climb. The sharp snaps of finger bones breaking as they forced their hands into the cracks in the trunk and its bark sent shrills up and down her spine. Some of the creatures' fingers completely ripped off when they tried to support their weight by them. Others were able to hang on, the muscles and skin along their fingers stretching like elastic bands but still remaining intact.

Other undead climbed on top of those hanging as if their comrades were rope ladders; soon a handful made it to the branch where Hank and Billie stood with rubbery legs.

Reloaded, Hank raised the shotgun. "Come on, you rascals, I ain't afraid of you."

"Shut up!" Billie searched up and down the branch.

"It's not nice to talk—"

She grabbed him by the collar of his shirt and dragged him down the length of the branch, away from the trunk and the undead that climbed up it. The ones that made it onto the branch began fumbling their way down its length toward them. One tripped over its own feet and fell off without a sound. The remainder kept coming, seeming to understand the idea of keeping single-file so they could keep going.

Billie pulled as hard as she could against Hank's shirt until, it seemed, he finally understood to follow her.

"Don't think we should be runnin' this way none," he said and blasted off another round. It tagged the zombie in the gut, sending it back a step but it kept its balance.

"Don't have a choice."

"There's nothing ahead of us."

"I know!"

The massive branch began to taper thinner and thinner, culminating at the end in a fan-like series of smaller branches and dead leaves, all tangled and meshed together in a large clump.

Billie stopped short before a weave of branches. Hank took another shot and stumbled up behind her and bumped into her. Appearing panic-stricken, the shot went wild.

Swallowing a dry lump in her throat, she tried to catch her breath. The undead kept coming up along the branch, each of their steps adding to the weight toward the end, the branch starting to dip lower a few inches at a time.

"I don't think we're going to make it," she said. "Help!" It was directed at Nathaniel or Michael or any other of their kind who'd care enough to swoop in and rescue them.

Only the deathly groans and moans of the undead returned her cry.

The zombies clamored closer, limp fingers outstretched from raggedy-clothed arms, mouths already opening and closing, preparing to feast.

The branch dipped lower. The ground was a solid three stories below, rock covered with dry dirt and dead leaves.

Her stomach twisted at the momentary idea of shoving Hank toward them, thinking maybe they'd grab onto him, start eating, and get themselves so off-balance they'd tumble over the sides of the branch and hit the ground. It might also be enough to draw the others off the trunk and swarm Hank's body like vultures to a carcass.

As much as she hated to admit it, it *was* tempting, but only because of its purpose for survival. One look at Hank changed all that, his face set with determination yet carrying an air of innocence. He had this very subtle smile, a confidence that everything would be okay.

"I'm sorry," she said quietly.

He didn't seem to hear her as he went about reloading the gun.

"I'm scared," she said, the words tumbling out.

"You'll be okay," he said. He sounded normal again.

Maybe he got his faculties back? she thought.

"I've seen squirrels bigger and badder than these guys."

Maybe not.

Billie inched back, her heels dipping into the curves and grooves between the interwoven branches.

Hank backed up, too, and bumped into her. She was going to tell him to be careful but bit her tongue as penance for her terrible thought moments before.

The undead advanced without care.

The branch began to crack and snap beneath her feet—no, not right beneath her feet, but some ten or so feet ahead where the branch began to taper off.

Another of the dead fell off. The rest kept coming, two walking, two others crawling along the branch on their hands and knees.

"Are you okay?" Hank asked. He shot the nearest undead. It went flying off the branch.

She didn't answer.

"I said, are you okay, Billie?"

"No. I think we're going to die."

The undead were a mere four or five feet from them.

Hank looked at her, his lips quickly opening and closing as if saying, "Yeah but, yeah but . . ." He shot another off the branch. With no time to reload, he swung the shotgun at one of the creature's heads. It connected, sending it off the branch. The impact putting him off balance, he dropped the gun when he shot his arms out to steady himself.

"I'm sorry, Hank." She tried to sound cheery for his benefit. She wasn't sure if he truly understood the concept of death. "It was nice meeting you."

The last zombie was three feet away.

"It was nice meeting you, too," he said. "I like you, Billie."

"Um . . . I like you, too, Hank."

Two feet.

"I'll say hi to Jesus for you," he said.

"Wha—"

One foot.

Hank smiled then turned and hugged the undead man in front of him. He tipped over the side, the zombie falling with him. They tumbled to the ground. Billie yelped then put a hand to her mouth as her breath caught in her throat.

Below, Hank lay on the dirt, his legs bent beside him like chicken wings, blood pooling around his head, the undead that had been with him in the tree climbing on top of him and beginning to tear and chew on his flesh.

Through teary-eyed vision, she wondered if sacrificing himself had really happened or if she had *actually* pushed him, had gone through with her sick idea of using him to save her own skin.

Heart aching and pounding in quick, sharp thuds, she slowly moved forward on the branch, hands out beside her for balance, heading for a more stable spot.

Below, the moans of the dead grew in volume. Others from further up by the tree trunk slowly turned and shuffled toward their kin.

Forcing herself to keep her eyes forward, Billie maintained her balance, doing her best to stay quiet and hoping the undead were so preoccupied with . . . Hank . . . she'd be forgotten.

"I'm sorry, Hank," she said, tears rolling down her cheek. "I didn't mean to push you." *Did I? Did he push himself? Am I a . . . killer?* "Was it me or him?"

The branch snapped.

It took a while, but finally Joe and Tracy found a house that fit their criteria. They broke in by squeezing their way through an unlocked kitchen window. It was convenient but it was welcomed.

They kept back-to-back as they toured the house, each room approached with caution and the expectation that something might jump out at them and try to eat them. Only the faint light coming in from outside lit their path.

"Don't have a match or anything, do you?" he asked.

"No," Tracy said. "Why?"

"Make it easier to see. Make a torch or something."

The two headed toward the basement, each step cautious. Joe was confident in his partner, though. If something were to happen, not only would he lay it on the line for her, he knew she'd also lay it all down for him as well. It was almost like he was backing up himself, in a way.

The stairs creaked, and when they got to the basement door, he stopped short when he noticed the knob was loose in its place, the door cracked around the knob's edges.

"What?" Tracy asked, clearly noticing his hesitation.

"I don't know," he said. "Door's cracked."

"Could it have been like that before?"

"Maybe. I know it seems like a small thing, but you and I both know that small things can quickly become big things."

"Tell me about it."

Joe gently tested the knob. It turned over, loose and quick. He put a hand behind him, guarding her. He felt her hand touch his arm as he did, dwelt on it a quick second, then took a step back and pushed the basement door open. The basement was dark except for off in the far corner where a faint bit of gray light came in through the tiny basement window, turning everything into various shades of dark gray.

Joe sniffed the air. Musty, but he couldn't detect anything that might be rotten.

"Ready?" he said.

"Always."

They went down the four steps leading to the cement basement floor.

Both stepped quietly, and Joe didn't need to ask to know she had her ears perked as much as he had his. No grunts, no groans, no deathly wheezing.

So far so good, he thought. To the side were the furnace, the side-by-side washing machine and dryer, and the metal pantry shelf. It was hard to see everything that was on it, but what looked like torn-up toilet paper and paper towels littered the shelves, probably from mice.

The basement was filled with stacks of records, books, cassette tapes, reams of fabric and an entire row of sewing machines that were side-by-side on two eight-foot-long gray, plastic-topped craft tables.

"Busy people," Tracy said.

"Indeed. Scan the room again, just in case, then we can finally get some rest."

"Sounds good to me."

Joe was relieved and even a little surprised that, thus far, nothing had happened to them and all had been more or less smooth sailing. Ever since leaving the Haven, it'd been one life-threatening situation after another, most of which were barely escaped from. Was Someone looking out for them? Pure luck? Was there even such a thing as luck?

"Some of these records are really old," Tracy said.

"Same with some of these books."

"Didn't you say you used to be a writer?"

"Comic books, yeah, but I still read novels, too. Can't write good comics without reading good novels. Just the way it is."

"Must've been fun."

"Used to be," he said, thinking back to that simpler time, the one before zombies, before death, before even meeting April, the one girl he'd ever fallen in love with, so quickly, so easily. Her beautiful face—black hair, gray eyes, cute demeanor and such utterly soft lips—and the way she looked when he found her the day of the gray rain, when the world transformed and the dead began to rise. Her blood-covered mouth, an old woman's trachea hanging between her teeth like a stringy turkey neck. Every time he thought of it, his heart broke anew, and the crushing defeat of his spirit when he recalled what it was like to accidentally break her skull with a rolling pin swung full force.

"Joe?" Tracey said.

"Yeah."

"You're crying."

He blinked his eyes. She was right. A couple tears leaked down his cheeks.

"Sorry," he said, embarrassed.

She simply looked at him, eyes glazed over in compassion. Tracy understood his pain. She'd gone through something similar with a boy named Josh. He had been the one for her and all had been set for a happy ending until the day of the Rain and the world transformed, died.

The two had finished most of the basement, the last place to check in, and around the washer and dryer. Joe knew nothing would be there, unless some undead creature was lying about with no legs and no mouth, the hunger for human flesh the only thing to keep it company. Still, had to be done. Safety first.

Joe stood by the washer, Tracy the dryer. Together, they opened the lids, ready for something to pop out. Nothing.

"I guess we're in the clear," Tracy said, sounding relieved. Joe knew she needed a break just as bad as he did.

He nodded. "Let's head upstairs and catch some shut-eye. We'll get a fresh start tomorrow." They left the washer and dryer lids up.

"Food?"

Joe checked the pantry. Aside from the torn bits of toilet paper and paper towel, there wasn't much save for a can of chickpeas, a box of crackers with tiny holes around its bottom—probably from rodents chewing on the cardboard—and a fresh pack of No Name saran wrap.

He grabbed the can and handed it to her. "Maybe there's a can opener in the kitchen."

"There's a freezer over there under all those books."

"'Kay." He went to the freezer and began to take down some of the books and placed them on the floor.

Behind them, a loud metallic *bang* of a gunshot made them both duck, legs and arms already positioned for defense. Tracy stood by the dryer, its lid down.

"Sorry. I got dizzy. Must've bumped it," she said.

Heart racing, he said, "It happens."

Releasing a sigh of relief, he moved closer to Tracy to help her, but stopped short when the books on top of the freezer began to shake as something pushed the freezer lid up from the inside.

4
TAKING CHANCES

"Move!" Joe said, shoving Tracy toward the basement steps.

The freezer lid lifted then thunked down, lifted then thunked down, the books on top of it jumping and jostling with each thump. Some fell over, others spilled to the floor, lightening the weight on top of the lid.

Tracy was already halfway up the steps, Joe at the bottom. He backed up into her, nudging her closer to the stairway's top.

The freezer lid jumped and thudded again, this time the height of its opening having doubled. Hands appeared between the lid and the rim. It was too dark to make out the exact details or their color, but it was most definitely one of the creatures and not somebody using the freezer for protection, even if someone else secured it by putting the books on top. The putrid funk of deceased flesh instantly filled the air like a punch to the face; Joe immediately gagged. How long that creature had been pent up in there, he didn't know, and could only guess the sudden sound of the dryer lid slamming down set it off. Either that, or the monster had smelled them even from inside the freezer. So much for whoever's idea of locking the creature in there.

Joe pushed back into Tracy, forcing her all the way up the stairs. Once at the top, he pushed her through the doorframe.

"Find something to protect yourself with," he said, quickly shut the door and locked it from the inside.

Tracy banged against the door. "Don't you dare, Joe. I'm not leaving you alone in their with that thing. Get out of there!"

"Go find a knife or something!"

"Joe!"

"Discussion over." He ignored her pleas for him to come out of the basement and get away from the monster.

The basement reminded him of another one, the one with Blue and his gang, those men that had tormented the girl in the ragged, pale yellow dress, using her to tease one of the creatures. He killed the men, and the zombie in an effort to save the girl. He was too late. She had been bit, so he had to kill her, too.

The zombie in front of him snarled and made its way forward in the dark, its sliding footsteps indicating at least one ankle was broken. The creature hissed. Joe stepped forward, hands up, ready.

Tracy yelled through the door in the background.

Grimacing and ignoring the terrible smell, he stomped toward the creature and swung out, punching it in the head. The zombie stumbled back, then growled and lunged forward, grabbing him around the neck. Joe grabbed onto either side of the undead's forearms and kicked straight out, nailing the creature in the chest, forcing it back. Its scraggly, decaying arms slipped between Joe's hands and it tumbled backward. Not wasting time, Joe kept moving toward it, minding his own footing to ensure the thing didn't lash out and try and take him down at the knees. Reaching forward, he gripped the zombie at the back of the head by the hair, pulled it up, all the while jerking the thing's head to the side as it tried to lean forward and snap at him with rotten teeth. Punching the creature in the throat, then ramming the palm of his hand up against the underside of the zombie's jaw, forcing its mouth closed, Joe threw the creature at the freezer. The monster slammed into the few remaining books on top of it, scattering them. With a hard kick, Joe took the creature's knees out from under it, causing it to collapse. As it turned around, mouth open again, he punched it in the forehead, slamming its skull back against the freezer. Quickly, Joe opened the freezer's heavy lid, grabbed the zombie by the back of the head again, and put it face down over the freezer's edge. He jerked the heavy lid down as hard as he could, crushing the creature's skull in between the lid and the freezer's rim. Bone cracked, followed by the wet squish of compressed flesh. He raised the lid and brought it down as hard and as fast as he could again, mashing the creature's head to a pulp until the thing's body fell, its rotten skull having been cut off around the mouth. The top of its head thudded as it dropped inside the freezer.

Sweating, careful not to breathe too deep lest he throw up, Joe opened the lid, picked up the zombie's body, and tossed it in the freezer. He slammed the lid shut, hands shaking, legs rubbery. His eyes ached from fatigue.

Tracy still pounded against the door, screaming for his safety.

Billie hung on with all she had. The branch had snapped and swung down like a pendulum. She clung to it like a rope in gym class, the dead below feasting on Hank's body.

Have to stay focused, she thought, though already her hands were beginning to slip against the rough bark. She could only imagine the splinters that would ravage her palms if she slid all the way down its length and onto the mound of the undead below.

The loud munches of the walking dead were enough to give her an extra boost of strength to hang on as tightly as she could. She squeezed her eyes shut, doing so somehow making her feel stronger and making it easier to hang on.

"Pleasedon'tseeme, pleasedon'tseeme, pleasedon'tseeme," she whispered, mouth pushed into her arm. Heart racing a mile a minute, sweat bursting out all over her body, she hoped and prayed she'd somehow get out of this.

The groans and wheezes grew louder below, so much so she opened her eyes. Zombies gazed up at her, milky-white eyes fixed on her, mouths agape, their bodies swaying back and forth. Others remained focused on Hank, his body nothing more now than red mush mixed with some fabric and bones.

"I'm dead," Billie said. She lifted her legs and set them around the branch as well, hoping she could muster the strength to inch her way up. She tried, but she quickly lost purchase and slid down a foot or two, her fingernails tearing against the bark, the inside of her forearms scraping along its rough surface. The interior of her thighs burned from the friction of her rapid descent.

Eyes wide, overwhelmed by the sudden onslaught of pain, she could only just hang on and nothing more.

"No," she said, trying to catch her breath, "must try. For Hank. For me. For Joe. For Des." She grit her teeth. "For August." She screamed behind tightly-pressed lips as she attempted to climb the branch again; the raw skin of her forearms lit up in fiery pain every time she moved them along the bark. She made it up a couple of feet, getting back to where she'd been before she slipped. She clung hard to the branch.

Hard.

Harder.

Wood snapped beneath her.

The undead had latched on to the bottom of the large branch, clawing and pulling on the fan-like clump of smaller twigs and branches, trying to climb up. Each jolt of their weight against the branch wreaked havoc on her arms. Blood leaked down her skin, pooling in her armpits and dripping down her sides. Arms numb, it was hard to tell if she was even holding on anymore. She actually had to look at her arms to make sure.

The branch shook. Billie slipped a few inches, her arms getting torn up even more. Screaming from the pain, the terrifying thought of becoming zombie food setting her heart into an all-out gallop, she looked around, checking for any last-second options.

"Hold on!" she shrieked at herself.

But she couldn't. She slid down the branch, the flesh on her arms tearing to ribbons, the zombies below quickly getting closer.

Some fifteen or twenty feet from the ground, Billie let go, rolling her body in the air as hard as she could to the side, and landed on her right shoulder and hip some ten yards from the hungry undead.

The right side of her body numb, she tried to get to her feet, only to collapse.

"No! Get up!" Her words floated away from her then echoed in her ears loud and clear.

Had they been her words? Hank's? August's? Nathaniel's?

What words?

Darkness rimmed her vision.

"Noooo . . ." she groaned, eyeing the undead as they made their way toward her.

Billie dragged herself along the ground, arms stinging and bleeding. She came up near a large bush that had long since lost its leaves. Reaching out, she grabbed its stems and slowly pulled herself up. Her left leg worked—barely—her right was useless.

Hobbling, she pushed her way into the forest, not looking back or wasting any more precious seconds on the undead.

She slowly moved around trees and in between skeletal bushes, hoping to find some sort of haven.

But there was nothing.

Just dead trees, bushes, shrubs and rocks.

Rocks. The ground beneath her had changed to rock. She was outside the forest, along the lake.

The zombies got closer and broke through the bushes.

Barely able to walk, Billie screamed at them, raw and visceral. Her primal shrieks didn't faze them and they kept moving forward.

Backing up, running out of room, she bordered the edge of the rocks and the gray waters below.

"I'm tired," she said, the words trickling out. The hard realization hit her that despite any hope she once had even just moments ago, it was all gone. This war, these creatures, angels, demons and everything in between—no more.

"I'm sorry," she whispered, maybe to Joe, or to Nathaniel, or even herself.

The undead reached for her.

Billie backed up and pushed herself off the edge of the rock into the gray water below.

ONE YEAR AGO...

Bethrez entered Vingros's chamber not worried he would chew him out for putting an end to Holgrack's commandership. If anything, Vingros would be glad the sniveling worm was out of the way as, though he'd never admit it, Bethrez knew Vingros had regretted the decision of promoting Holgrack to commander after Holgrack had returned empty-handed from a recent battle, without the influence on even a single soul.

Vingros liked the dark, Bethrez knew, and only on occasion permitted himself the luxury of a dimly-lit torch to light the otherwise gloomy den.

"I can hear you breathing," Vingros said, his voice coming from where Bethrez knew the large demon kept his throne.

"The portal is ready albeit there is one problem before testing."

"Don't tell me, it's in the wrong location."

"Yes, how did you—"

"You idiot! I know what's going on in my circle and am apprised of news before all else, save the master himself."

"Yes, my lord, but I thought it best to come to you to let you know that we are ready except that one detail otherwise we await the master's command to open the portal. Is he aware of—" Bethrez thought better of the comment and kept his mouth shut.

"I will send others to move the portal—"

"I wish it were that simple, but the portal is larger than the room it's constructed in, thus cannot leave without being dismantled."

"Oh, Bethrez, you disappoint me. Do you not remember that as master of the Fourth Circle I am able to bend the very depths of the earth to my whim?"

"No, my lord," he lied. Fact of the matter was, ever since being tasked with creating the portal, the work had taken up most of Bethrez's time, and if not all his time, then his thoughts, pushing out all else.

"The portal shall remain where it is, but I will use the rocks and stones to move it to its rightful location. I ask you, once there, will it be ready?"

Bethrez grinned. "It will be ready, however, I request to be present upon first usage, namely, the first one through. If it fails like before, then I will be shot back here. If it succeeds, the doors to the Earth will open and we will all go through."

"The master will not tolerate another failed experiment. You have had over six hundred years to get it right."

Bethrez wished to explain that to enable his fellow demons access to the Earth en masse and in the manner of which mass possession was possible, was not an easy feat as safeguards from the battle long ago had been put in place to prevent such a thing. It *took over two centuries alone to thoroughly study each and every safeguard and realm-lock before even an attempt at a means to disarm them was possible. Construction on a single prototype portal took anywhere between eighty to one hundred and thirteen years. Yet Vingros wasn't interested in such things, he knew. He was also aware their master was on a clock himself, one that couldn't be outrun unless such a device was constructed.*

"Depart now, Bethrez. I will call when I have need of you."

"Thank you," Bethrez said with a bow then left the cave.

5
HANG UPS

TRACY SLAPPED JOE in the face, sending a hot sting across his cheek.

"You're unbelievable," she said. She was stunned he'd lock her out of the basement, and what for? So he could play hero and take out a rotter all by himself? Yeah, that's real impressive, not to mention stupid and dangerous. She knew he'd killed many undead creatures on his own before, but what she didn't get was why he'd suddenly cut her out and take one on with her right there. It'd be one thing if she couldn't handle herself, or had been severely hurt, or even had simply not been present—but when she stood right there beside him when the creature emerged? What gives?

"What's your problem?" he said.

"What's yours? Why did you lock me out of the basement?"

"I . . . didn't want you to get hurt."

"Don't feed me that crap," she said. "We might not be best friends, but I know you well enough to know there was another reason."

"Honestly, there wasn't. I saw the thing, you were by the door, I pushed you out in case the worst happened."

She threw up her arms and shook her hands by her head, frustrated. "Are you listening to yourself? *You're* the one who backed me up the stairs by the door. *You're* the one who thought that somehow the worst would happen when we were together versus the worst happening when you handled that on your own. And without a gun!"

"I knew what I was doing."

"That doesn't matter. You willingly went head first into death and shut me out. What's going on, Joe? Did something else happen? Is it me? Seriously, what's going on?"

He looked at her, eyes empty of emotion or concern, just . . . lost.

Is he over the edge? Did it finally happen and just came out of nowhere? she thought. *I understand his pain and his battle against the undead. I get all that, probably better than anyone else he's ever met. Just don't get how he could suddenly snap. Thought there'd be a progression, if that was going to happen. Thought there'd be signs.*

She loudly exhaled and shook her head. "I-I don't know what to say. Just think it was a stupid move on your part."

REDEMPTION OF THE DEAD

"Think what you want. The thing is . . ." He didn't finish.

"What?"

He simply folded his arms.

"No, no, come on. Don't start to say something then cut yourself off. Give me a break. I hated that before the world fell apart and I hate it now. Spit it out!"

He turned around and headed toward the kitchen. "Going to go look for something to eat. Sorry, Tracy."

She gritted her teeth and stared after him with squinted eyes. "Stupid idiot."

"Heard that," he said from the other room.

"I don't care," she shouted.

The house went quiet. She ran her hands over her hair, smoothing it back. Quietly, she said, "Maybe you should ask yourself why *you're* so upset." But she already knew the answer.

It was so simple, so obvious.

She'd grown to care for him.

There was nothing food-wise in the kitchen. The water was off. Even after checking the master valve, nothing was running into the house. Joe swallowed back his thirst and sat alone on the bed in what seemed to have been a teenager's bedroom. KISS posters dominated the walls. Clearly whoever had lived here was a fan. He browsed the CD rack and there were a dozen of their albums, their edges covered in dust.

Tracy was right: it had been a bonehead move to try and take on the zombie by himself, especially since he was unarmed. He was thankful he was still alive, though there was a brief moment while taking on the creature that he thought it might be for the best if the thing killed him. Finally, then, he'd be free of this world, the heartache, this disgusting reality of undead monsters and supernatural forces.

Except when you hit the other side, he thought, *then you'll be spending eternity with the supernatural anyway. You've seen enough to know that.* He just hoped he'd make it to the right side when his time came.

Misplaced affection had been the real culprit. His love for April, her untimely death, undeath, then death again—Joe knew full well he'd never get over her. Not completely. At best, he'd remain as he was: used to a life without her, the pain of the past always present and hanging over the future. But this world, the one he was in, the one he and Billie and August emerged in after the Storm of Skulls—it wasn't theirs. April could still be alive here. If so, he'd have to find her. There was no choice.

But Tracy . . . he thought. The girl was growing on him. He saw so much of himself in her that it was surreal he even found her, never mind actually got to spend lots of time with her. She understood him, he knew, his mission, his pain. She was on a similar quest of her own, an undead world a twisted salve to a pulsating wound.

He'd pushed her out of the basement for the same reason he immediately tore off into the gray rain the day it first fell: to ensure the girl he cared about was safe. Something had come over him the moment he saw that creature emerge from the freezer, an instinct to protect her overriding any thought for his own safety.

"She would have been fine standing right there with me," he said to himself. "She could take you down if needed and would probably have no trouble doing so." He touched his cheek where she slapped him. His skin was still sensitive.

Joe just wasn't sure if he was substituting Tracy for April, and the feelings he had for his beloved were being projected onto someone who *might* be able to take her place.

"You can't treat her like that, though," he told himself. "She can't be a surrogate. She deserves better than that. Deserves someone who cares for her just for her, no strings attached." He sighed. "Can't believe I'm even thinking about this stuff when there're more important things to worry about."

The thing was, he knew he'd remain restless until he knew for certain April was deceased in this reality.

It'd be the only way I might be able to move on, he thought, but knew it was very unlikely. *As if you're going to find her, though.*

The real problem at the moment was Tracy, and he wasn't sure if he should come clean with her and tell her what was going on inside himself.

After searching the kitchen herself for something to eat and coming up empty, Tracy paced the living room floor, the can of chickpeas in one hand, a clenched fist in the other.

You're stupid if you think you can stay mad at him. You need each other because

REDEMPTION OF THE DEAD

you both know what it's like to go it alone in this Hell-on-Earth. "But it's *his* fault!" She clamped a hand to her mouth; she hadn't meant to speak so loudly. There was no stirring upstairs so Joe probably hadn't heard her.

She'd just been so relieved he was okay after the fact. He'd been in worse, she knew, but somehow at that moment, it was like his life was in serious jeopardy and the thought of him not making it out alive . . .

"You can't do this," she whispered quietly. "It's stupid and dumb. It's one thing to let him in as a partner against the undead, another to even consider going beyond that." The thing of it was, she knew a part of her was hoping he'd fill the hole in her heart left by Josh. In a world like this, one where loneliness presided, emotional walls were built, death was carried out as easily as breathing—it began to wear on a person. It began to wear on *her*.

I'm not going to get all mushy-gushy with him. If anything, I'm lonely, there's needs, I'm sick of nothing but rot and decay. Don't use him as your glimmer of sunshine. It's not fair to you and it's not fair to him. "Besides," she said, "he's got issues of his own and is too busy having a pity party over another girl." *You're doing the same thing to yourself so don't even go there.* "Oh, but to go there . . ."

She looked at the can of chickpeas. Man, how she hated those things. Mushy and gritty, like damp dirt, but they were healthy and if this was all there was for her and Joe, then that was the way it was.

"Got to get it to him, though, which means I got to get up there." She grunted. "Why couldn't *he* have been the one holding the can?"

Joe sat with his back to the door, legs drawn up, forearms resting on his knees. His thumbs were getting sore from all the twiddling. He ran a hand over his head. It'd been so long since he last shaved it, the hair was coming in pretty good, thick and bristly. He didn't want it to grow back. To let it come in like he used to, he'd look like the old Joe—Joseph—the person he'd been before the Rain. To see that in the mirror every day—no, no way.

He got up from the door. *Maybe there's a razor or scissors or something in one of the medicine cabinets. I need a shave anyway.* He yawned and opened the door. Tracy stood a few feet from it, staring at the can of chickpeas. She seemed startled by his sudden emergence.

The two looked at each other.

Guess this one might be up to you, he thought. *Don't string her along. Get back to surviving. No time for this other nonsense.* "Um . . ." he said and ran his head over his head, once again hating the hair growing on top.

Tracy faced him, arms at her sides. She raised her eyebrows, obviously signaling he was the one that had to speak first.

But if that's true, what was she doing up here to begin with? He slowly exhaled. "Okay, fine. Look, I'm sorry." *There. That wasn't so bad.*

"And?"

And? Okay, maybe it is *that bad?* "I shouldn't have left you out of it. It's hard to explain why. Can you just trust me that I had my reasons, but now realize it was a dumb choice and just move on?"

"I don't know," she said. "Are you going to do it again?"

"Are *you?*"

"What?"

"Sorry. What I meant was, yeah, I won't do it again if it can be helped."

Her eyes bore into him. "What do you mean?"

"What?"

"If it can be helped?"

"I mean that if it's okay for you and I to take on the undead together, then we will."

A puzzled look came over her face.

"Okay, start over. If there's a situation where we're separated and we have to fight alone, we'll fight alone, otherwise we'll fight together. Cool?"

She seemed to consider his words and began rolling the can of chickpeas back and forth between her palms. "Okay, deal, but for a guy who's supposed to be a writer, you suck at words."

"Gee, thanks."

Tracy smiled. That sweet smile.

No, not sweet. Stupid! He reached forward and grabbed the can of chickpeas from her hand. "Come on, let's get this over with. I hate these just as much as you do."

"How did you—"

Joe didn't bother to answer and hated himself for having hinted at how similar they were.

6
YOU CAN T DIE IN HELL

HEAD BARELY ABOVE the water, Billie tried to swim using her one good arm and leg. The right side of her body had gone numb from the fall and she wouldn't be surprised if the trauma from the impact had not only broken the bones on that side, but damaged the nerves so badly that, right now, she couldn't feel a thing. She hoped the cool water would help some, but more so, she hoped the gray water wouldn't affect her. It hadn't a year ago when the gray rain fell, so most likely she was safe, but still, she couldn't help but worry. Plus she'd lost her glasses when she jumped in.

They were broken anyway, she thought.

Billie was a decent ways from the rock she jumped off. Many of the zombies followed her in, but vanished beneath the water's gray surface and never came up again.

Thank goodness they can't swim, she thought. The swimming was slow-going. She went under every time she tried to speed up. She also ended up starting to go in a circle since all the effort was done with one side of her body.

Every time her leg moved beneath the surface, she felt the trepidation an undead person would grab her foot from below and drag her down to the lake's floor. Every time she moved her hand, she could almost feel cold, decaying fingers wrap around her own and tug her beneath the surface. The only thought that kept her going was the idea the water was very deep and even if some of the undead were standing at the bottom and reaching for her, there'd be no way they could touch her.

She had to get someplace safe, that was priority one. Forcing her head above the water, Billie scanned the shoreline. Dead trees and bushes lined it like a stained-glass painting but without the color. The rocks along the edge were huge, their tops so high above water level there was no way she'd be able to climb out.

There's a break in the rock line somewhere, though. The undead had crawled out and there's no way the entire lake is bordered by a wall of rock. There's got to be another one. Her head went under the water; she furiously kicked her leg and moved her arm, bringing herself up to the surface. The water stank, a mix of turpentine and strong male body odor.

"So tired," she said. Even being in the water as she was, lying back only added to her sleepiness; she had to focus on staying awake

"I need help," she breathed, and went under again. This time her body went vertical beneath the surface; gravity took over and pulled her down. Thankfully, there was still air in her lungs so she wasn't completely dead weight. She wiggled her body, kicked her leg and flailed her arm, trying to get the water beneath her and her head above the surface. She was even able to get her other arm and leg moving, though just barely.

Don't want to drown. Not like this. She could only imagine how painful it was to choke on lake water, deal with being unable to breathe until she passed out then finally died. And in this water, she thought she had a pretty good chance of coming back from the dead as well.

God, help me, she thought.

Billie kicked and fought against the water, slowly gaining ascent inch by desperate inch. Lungs beginning to hurt, she told herself to clamp down and just keep swimming. Finally, she broke the surface, took a big gulp of air, then quickly went down again. She kicked and squirmed and came up once more. Laying prone immediately, she briefly dipped below the surface before her face was enough above the water she could breathe comfortably.

Glancing around, she saw she was further out from shore than she originally thought. Desperate to get to dry land, she angled herself so her head was pointed toward the shore and slowly began to swim toward the rock. She'd find a way back onto land. She had to.

She didn't know what time it was, but judging by how fatigued she was on top of all her injuries, she guessed it was close to midnight if not past. Yawning, she kept kicking.

Billie went under again. This time she dipped forward, going vertical before tipping forward completely so she was face down. Panicking, she screamed and let out most of the air in her lungs in the process.

No, no, no! She instinctively screamed again, deflating her lungs even more. Her eyes went wide at the realization. *Okay, calm down. Calm down. Think. Which way is up?* She paused, got her bearings, and began to lean back, thinking she'd go vertical again and would be able to kick to the surface. Adrenaline beginning to pump through her limbs—*all* of them— she scrambled against the water and tried to head to the surface. Despite how hard she swam or how hard she kicked, the surface never came. She stopped, lungs burning for air, and tread under the water. Looking up, she couldn't make heads or tails which way the surface was in the gray murk. No starlight or moonlight thanks to the ever-present brown and gray-clouded sky.

Her only guide was gravity, and right now, it was winning.

Billie's lungs pounded for air, her heart thumping so hard in her chest it felt like it was going to break free and fall out. Black fuzziness overcame her vision and a low buzzing filled her ears. Detachment began to set in and for a split second she thought she was comfortably at home, about to fall asleep. The weightlessness brought her back to where she really was and she took in a lungful of lake water. She tried to cough, choke it out, but it was useless. All she did was force the last tiny bit of air out of her lungs, making her body breathe in another gulp of water in reaction.

Immediately, she started crying, understanding what she had done and that she was about to die.

Sinking, heartbeat slowing, Billie thought she'd soon go into a state of complete relaxation, like she once heard somewhere of drowning being like that: lose air, get sleepy then peacefully pass out before dying. Instead, even with her eyes closed, darkness drew in, black, pure. The sensation of her body disappeared for a moment before returning full swing, each movement, each part of her, utterly sensitive to the water—then there was no water.

Billie opened her eyes, a sudden gust of wind rushing up her body as she fell into total darkness. Her heart didn't race. She didn't feel a pulse, but she did feel her stomach going up into her chest as she fell further and faster into the black abyss. Fear gripped her and every nerve in her chest and gut trembled, sending quakes of terror through her body. The solemn realization she was dead rose within her. She began to shake and kick against the air as if she could somehow fight it and ascend back to the lake, to the world . . . above.

In a flood of emotion and knowledge she understood what was happening. She glanced up as if to confirm only to see a small halo of brilliant light far in the distance, growing tinier and tinier the further she fell until the light was gone and there was only darkness.

Screaming, she cried out. "Help! Help me!"

No one came to her rescue. There was no one here.

Shaking, she hit the ground, the impact sending a shockwave of pain through her body. Her muscles cramped, her bones felt like the marrow had been replaced with fire. Shrieking, she sat up and the pain suddenly left her.

Gasping, Billie choked on the dry air around her, like the hot air of a sauna. The stone ground she sat on was uncomfortably warm and the longer she sat on it, the hotter it got until sweat broke out across her body. She went to touch her skin, to see if there was any damage, but there wasn't any. Her skin was dry, too, no moisture on it despite feeling otherwise. Breathing growing irregular, she got to her feet and was dismayed her right leg and arm were still unusable. They didn't hurt like before, but she couldn't get them to move no matter how hard she tried.

"Hello?" she called into the darkness. "What is this place? Where am I?"

A haunting presence grew behind her and her body locked as fear took over.

"You're in Hell," the presence said, its voice low, airy and scratchy. "You are in Hell, Billie."

Screaming, she tried to run away, at best managing a swift limp, dragging her bad leg as she scrambled to get away along the hot ground. With darkness all around and not knowing which way was what nor what might be around her, she instinctively moved with trepidation, slowing herself even more despite not wanting to. Something was behind her. She didn't hear anything, but knew for certain the thing that just spoke to her was right at her heels.

"Come back here!" it shouted, its voice carrying on the darkness like an echo in a cave.

Was that it? Was she in a cave? Maybe she *was* alive and—she didn't know—went through some underwater tunnel only to surface in a cave?

But she knew it wasn't true. It wasn't a thought or an emotion, but a deep, raw *knowledge* down in her soul. She *was* dead and she was in Hell.

Why Hell? She was a good person. Sure, she made mistakes like everyone else, but she didn't kill anyone, didn't rob a bank. The only killing she ever did was swat mosquitoes and shoot zombies with a nail gun.

"You deserve to be here," the presence said.

Its words traveled deep within her, echoed throughout her being. It was true. She *did* deserve to be here.

Ahead, a faint orange glow rose in the distance. The closer she got, the more its sound became clear. Despite being at least a half kilometer away, most likely more, she heard the harsh roar of the flames and even began to feel the heat emanating off them, compounding the pronounced heat already on the air around her.

"Run, Billie, run," the voice said.

Her one good leg picked up speed. Strangely, she wasn't out of breath like she thought she'd be, but yet she was frustrated at not being able to breathe against the searing hot air that had grown in temperature since her arrival.

"Run."

Shrieking, she kept going, not wanting to turn around and not wanting to run into the fire up ahead.

Scaly creatures began to materialize against the orange glow, their bodies bony silhouettes against the haunting light.

Billie didn't need to be up close to know what they were. She first saw them the day they went to the past.

Demons.

They were the ones behind the rise of the undead. They were the forces truly at work.

Panicking, she turned left, trying to avoid both the creature behind and the creatures in front.

"Help!" she shrieked. "Help me!" The thing behind her kept chasing her; it also seemed to be keeping its distance, maintaining its authority by grunting and growling, causing her to be too afraid to turn around and look. "Is anyone else here?"

"You are alone, Billie. Alone with us. We will kill you slowly over and over."

Overwhelmed by fear, her legs gave out beneath her and she fell to the hot stone ground. She reached out along the stone and tried to pull herself along its surface. It was impossible. Her skin couldn't rest against the stone for any length of time before burning.

Quivering and crying, Billie tried to stand, but her feet wouldn't get under her.

"I won't look back, I won't look back," she said.

"Look back, Billie. Look back. LOOK AT ME!"

She had to listen. The thing would destroy her if she didn't.

"Help . . ." she groaned.

Her eyes settled on someone in the distance. A man. He looked . . . familiar. The presence that had followed her was still there, but didn't come upon her. In the distance, back near the flames, the demons were still headed in her direction.

But that man. He was so . . . he wore a trench coat. His head was shaved.

"No," she said. "No. He can't . . . not . . . JOE!" *He's dead, too? He's here?* "Joe, it's me, Billie. Can you hear me? I can't move, Joe. Help!"

"No one can hear you," the evil voice said.

"Shut up!" The words came out before she had time to think them over.

"Don't talk to me like that!" the voice said.

A split second later, she felt like she'd been whipped with a chain. Hot lashes laced across her skin. Wounds burning, she put out a trembling hand to see how bad it was. She was shocked there was no blood, and her skin . . . her skin was dry, brittle. Dead.

Joe was in the darkness, some of the creatures coming toward him as a hurricane of others flew all around and ascended at rapid speed.

"Joe!"

"QUIET!" the voice boomed.

Another hot lash of chain sliced across her skin. Billie shrieked, cried, screamed for Joe. The hot chain struck her again. She bit her lip against the agony. Why wasn't he responding? Why couldn't he see her if she could see him?

Billie called out to him, told him to look out. He didn't acknowledge her.

The creatures pounced on Joe.

The chain sliced her legs and back. Hot pain rolled up and down her body. The creatures near the fire drew closer.

A blinding white light up ahead lit up the darkness as it streaked from somewhere high above and cut through the black abyss like lightning through a stormy sky. The light materialized beside Joe, all the while fending off the creatures. The thing's movements were so quick and precise, the creatures didn't stand a chance. A moment later, the strange being grabbed Joe and the two streaked upward, the remaining demons following suit.

The being's light faded against the dark, Joe gone with it.

"Joe . . ." she said, her voice a whisper.

"Quiet." Another strike and it felt like the chain had ripped right through her body clean to the other side.

Wailing in pain, Billie rolled on the ground, begging to die. "Kill me. Kill me like you said. I can't take it anymore. I just . . . can't."

"As you wish."

A blast of violent electricity rocked her to the core, every muscle fibre lighting up in sheer agony. Her head went woozy and burning pain became her only consciousness. The hot stone ground beneath her burned and seared her flesh, crisping her skin and starting her aflame.

Shaking, shrieking, wailing, she waited to die, her stomach forming spasming knots when she understood that she *wasn't* going to die, but instead would stay in this state forever.

In Hell.

7
SLEEP

It was hard to admit, but Joe was thankful he'd made amends with Tracy. The resolution even helped keep the chickpeas down and mute the unpleasant aftertaste. He lay on the couch in the living room, using a pillow from upstairs. He kept the pillowcase off just in case it was contaminated with something. Tracy was upstairs in the KISS bedroom, sleeping on the bed, no sheets, just a pillow without the pillowcase, same as him. He had suggested she sleep in the master bedroom, but she said she'd feel weird sleeping in someone else's bed like that. He understood and would've done the same himself. Despite there being another bedroom upstairs, he opted for the couch to give her some space and privacy. They each also took a separate bathroom for the same reason, the water being out and all.

As Joe lay there in the dark, he was overcome with a sense of awe, thinking how much his life had changed over the past year, how prior to the Rain there was no concept of what was going on. Life was supposed to just continue: him writing comics, keeping busy, watching TV, regular stuff. Not anymore and never again.

He rolled onto his side and hoped Tracy was sleeping well. He knew he needed some shut-eye, too, as they'd be heading out tomorrow. If he woke up early enough, he'd go to April's apartment building and see if she was still alive.

Tracy eyed the stucco on the ceiling, its bumps and shadows playing with her imagination and making odd shapes, faces and animals. It'd been thoughtful of Joe to let her have some privacy. She just hoped the gesture wouldn't go to waste and she'd actually get some sleep.

They had decided that, aside from the incident in the basement, the house was secure. They were too tired to move on so would sleep until completely rested, then scour the house for possible supplies before heading out. Joe said he even saw a set of keys in the landing closet, but didn't see a vehicle in the garage. There was still hope for transportation, though, as the keys could belong to one of the cars on the street, the owners having parked there instead.

First order of business would be to get back to the Hub, and hopefully get there without running into any trouble. It'd be nice to be there again. It was there things made sense, the mission was clear, and Tracy felt at home. Out here, she was adrift without an anchor, able to go on her own for a while before needing to lock back in to something permanent.

"Okay, enough. Go to sleep," she told herself and closed her eyes. *Good night, Joe.*

8
BETWEEN WORLDS

BILLIE'S SOUL CRIED for reprieve, her body thrashing in agony as flame engulfed her head-to-toe. She couldn't scream, her vocal chords having been burnt away, her mouth swollen shut, her skin melted . . . and yet she would not die, only stayed in a perpetual state of torment.

The demons loomed over her, their pale gray eyes floating on the flames around her body. They cackled and howled, a profound sense they were celebrating victory not just over her here, but also over her life on the Earth as if they'd had some say in it.

Please . . . please, make it stop, she shrieked inside her mind, her own inner scream mysteriously deafening to her own ears.

The fire upon her grew hotter and she regretted even having been alive never mind regretted being here and, she began to understand, being here by her own choice, by her own crimes against a Perfect Law.

Body lurching and jolting, she didn't know how much more she could take, each agonizing second that passed a deadly reminder she'd have to take it, because there was no escape.

Demons cackled.

Fire roared.

Her screams filled her head.

"ENOUGH!"

Brilliant white light cut through the flames surrounding her, confiscating her vision, the hot core of lightning all that she could see.

Who's that? Who's there? The pain left her, the sudden bliss of reprieve immediately filling her with joy and gratitude, so much so she began to sob. Blinded by the light, she couldn't see what was going on, but could hear the demons shrieking and the swishes of something sharp and hard cutting through the air.

The sounds of evil soon subsided, and an instant later, powerful hands took her in close to a warm body, strong arms wrapping around her. A rush of wind blew past her from her head down to her toes and she knew she was flying.

"Billie," a voice said, tender, familiar, as she was set down on her feet.

She hadn't been flying, but this person had. "Nathaniel?"

The white light faded and the angel stood before her. His golden robe was covered with elaborate folds, a gold belt around his waist. His silver shield was on his back, his silver blade in its sheath on his belt. They were surrounded by golden light, warm, loving.

"What . . . who . . . did you . . ." She didn't know what she was trying to ask but knew it had something to do with what just happened.

"You are in between worlds. I saw you in the depths when I came for Joe. I'm sorry for leaving you, but I had to bring him to the surface first."

"Is he . . . is he dead?" *Oh, please, no.*

"No," Nathaniel said. "He had fallen through the earth that day at the bank."

"Fallen? What . . ."

"It will all make sense soon."

She glanced at her feet and to her surprise she saw she wasn't standing on anything despite the sensation she was. Below and all around was golden light, with streaks of yellow, orange and white beams dancing around them like electricity between conductors. "Am I dead?"

Nathaniel's expression grew soft as did his voice. "Yes."

"Was I really in—"

Sorrow filled his face. "Yes."

"Why?"

"Because you didn't take the Atonement provided."

She didn't understand.

"Christ died for you, Billie, but you never believed that. You never decided to give Him your sin in exchange for forgiveness. That was why you knew you deserved to be there. You knew you had broken the Law."

"You're right," she said. "I didn't." Tears formed and leaked out of the corners of her eyes. *Tears.* She'd been told what to do to avoid damnation, but she hadn't acted on it. Stunned, she touched her cheeks, felt the moisture of her tears and realized she was back to her old self. She was even using her bad arm to reach and touch her face. Overwhelmed with gratitude, she said, "Thank you."

"Don't thank me."

She smiled gently and glanced up. "Thank You."

Nathaniel smiled, too, proud.

"Is it too late for me?" she asked.

"No."

"I thought once you died, that was it. You'd be wherever you wound up forever?"

"And this is true, but you didn't fully comprehend the Message so

REDEMPTION OF THE DEAD

you were spared. You were also shown what happened to Joe, how the demons saw him, how they followed us back to the surface and understood that the timeline had changed."

"That pocket watch you saw," he said, "is God's timer. It was left in my trust, my task to ensure its safety and come in every week to reset it."

"Why? Timer for what?" she asked.

The angel's face grew stern. "The Apocalypse."

"The—you don't mean . . .?"

"Yes, I do. The watch is perfectly timed with the intended true End Time, meant to be reset every seven days until I receive word I am to leave it be. Once the clock runs out, the Apocalypse begins, its seal on the doorway to Hell is lifted. The demons never knew where I hid it and try as they might over the years, I had always managed to evade them and come here to complete that which was commanded of me. Everything changed that day of the Storm, and I was tracked there, further, was interfered with."

"Not by them," Billie said. "You said it was my fault because I caused you to miss the reset time."

"And you were used by them to distract me. You see, where you were and where you and I are in the golden light, we are outside of Time, eternal places where all occurrences are measured and encapsulated in a single moment instead of second by second, minute by minute."

"So you mean those demons can enter Time from the outside whenever they want, go into whatever Time they want?"

"No. What occurs on Earth occurs and is over, lost to history. However, they are permitted to enter in the present as part of man's free will, choices and temptations, items for another discussion. In the end, they found a new way to enter by means of a portal of their own design. There have been rumors over the centuries of these plans, but they have never come to fruition. The portal stirs up the Storm of Skulls and, it seems, projects a peculiar side effect: time travel to the past. You and your friends were caught in it. Because you were out of your own Time, that was why you couldn't interact with anyone in the past, except that which was supernatural—me, them. I saw the helicopter outside and came in with the aim to finish my business with the watch first. Only then, after I saw you, and missed the reset time, did I realize what had happened and the distraction that had altered the course of future history. The seal—the watch—would have drawn them back, disabling the mass attack, but it needed to be activated right away, which it wasn't and all had changed. There were events after you left, which you have yet to discover, that prohibited this."

"Okay, enough. My head hurts. I'll just take your word for it."

"This was why one group of demons had to tell another, instead of they themselves emerging in a point of Time where they already were."

"I need a Tylenol."

Nathaniel touched her head with his fingertips. A flood of warmth filled her forehead.

"Thanks," she said, and also realized her eyesight had been restored despite not having her glasses.

"You're welcome, and I'm sorry if I confused you. I guess this sort of thing is natural to me so it's hard to explain."

"And why doesn't God step in and fix these things?"

"What do you think He's doing right now with you and me?"

ONE YEAR AGO . . .

The fiery lake roared as countless souls screamed from within, all pleading for a second chance and for mercy, but judgment was set and this was to be their eternal home, to be tormented day and night forever for transgressing the laws of Almighty God.

Vingros sneered at the souls that dared approach the edge of the fiery pit and tried to climb out. Each one that did, he kicked back down, sending them tumbling to the depths of burning and pain.

When he reached the two stone pillars that stood six feet apart at the lip of the lake, he spread his arms and placed two enormous hands against the serpents' fangs etched on the rock. The ground rumbled and a six-foot-wide stone bridge rose out of the depths of fire and spanned across to the center of the lake. As he crossed it, he sneered and growled at the sea of human faces—now no more than skulls—as they peered up at him from out of the flame before a fireball would come and swiftly engulf them and drown them in fire again.

The enormous throne of rocks and worms stood in the middle of the lake upon a small island, big enough for a ring of guard demons to surround it and cast down any who would dare to leave the fiery pit and approach, and a small platform on which to kneel at the throne's feet. Vingros found his place and got on his knees.

"Greetings, Master," Vingros said. "I have great news."

The throne was clouded over in thick gray smoke, the one within concealed. It was said that when he did emerge, very rarely did he show his true form but instead remained as he was on the day he was cast from Heaven—white, golden and beautiful.

The devil's voice came from within the smoke, low and powerful. "Yes, Vingros, what is it?"

"Bethrez has advised his portal is complete. I have overseen its movement to its proper location, and I have been assured that aside from one final inspection, it should operate as promised."

"It must, for time is running short. Do you have a precise timeline or are you merely here to dangle this before me in a foolish attempt to gain leverage or favor?"

"No, Master, not at all. Based on my understanding, the word can now go out to gather the troops from all seven circles in whichever arrangement you wish. The portal will accommodate them all, I'm told."

"Excellent, and so I shall bring it to pass. Go your way, Vingros. Next we meet will be at the portal."

"Very good, Master." *Vingros stood, bowed, then turned and went back down the long rocky bridge across the lake. Once back on the main land, he touched the fangs on each of the pillars and the bridge sunk below the flames.*

Elation took him as he went to summon his messenger to take the news to the other circles. They would assemble en masse while Bethrez checked the portal one last time. From there, finally, the Earth would be theirs and their army would outnumber Heaven's.

9
LONERS

JOE AWOKE WITH a crick in his neck, his head against the armrest.

"What . . .?" he said and started feeling around for his pillow. He looked over the side of the couch and saw it had somehow gotten out from under him during the night and wound up on the floor.

Groaning, he reached over, picked it up, and put it under his head. As he began to relax, the soothing release of discomfort on his neck began to take over.

He sighed and whispered, "Awesome."

He guessed he had probably been asleep for five or six hours. It was enough. Even before the world went crazy, he struggled with getting a full night's rest.

Rolling his legs over the side of the couch, he sat up, took a moment to fully wake up, then hit the bathroom before double checking the kitchen for any food. Like last night, there was nothing.

It was an invitation for trouble, but this thing with April had to be settled. It was getting to the point he'd be of no use to Tracy or even himself if he kept going through life with one eye looking back over his shoulder.

Quietly, he went to the bedroom where she slept and gently opened the door so as not to wake her. She lay there in the bed on top of the mattress, her body twisted like an S, mouth open, eyes closed with seeming effort—exhausted.

"Sorry," he whispered. "You're going to hate me after this, but I got to go do something. Hope you read my note and do what it says. Hope you'll understand, which I think you will." He closed the door. "I hope." Walking down the stairs, he added, "Good bye, Tracy."

Joe took the car keys from the landing closet and went out into the street, eyes peeled for the undead. He stood there pushing the unlock button on the keychain, listening intently for the *ka-chunk* of a door unlocking. He couldn't hear anything no matter which way he faced or how high he held the keychain. The last resort was to try the panic button, something he didn't want to do, but right now didn't have a choice. He pressed it a couple of times to no result, but on the third the loud blare of a horn honking shook him and he fumbled with the

53

keychain, turning it off. The flashing red lights of the car had been a few driveways over. Who knew why it was there. Careful any undead might have heard the noise and had come looking, he went to the dark gray SUV and used the key on the door. Once inside, he started the vehicle and was relieved to see a half tank of gas.

After driving it over to the house, he went inside. Tracy was still sleeping. He wrote her a note, left the keys beside the piece of paper, then raided the kitchen drawers for cooking knives. He found two paring knives, a steak knife, a cleaver and a large meat tenderizer mallet. He left the cleaver and mallet by the note, and wove the remaining three knives through his belt, like needles through cloth, keeping them secure and within easy reach.

Joe went out the door alone, facing the world of the undead like he had been in the beginning.

Laying on her side, huddled up with her legs tucked by her chest, Tracy shivered and reached for the blanket. Finding none, she drifted off to sleep again only to come to some time later, still cold. She opened her eyes, checked the bed over, upset there was no quilt or cover or—

There's not supposed to be, she realized, coming back to the land of the waking.

She stretched, yawned and closed her eyes a few moments before the chill became too much and she had to get out of bed to get some blood pumping. After using the bathroom, she went down to the living room to see if Joe was up. He wasn't on the couch.

"Joe?" she said, loud enough he should hear her even a couple of rooms away. "Hey, Joe?" Nothing but silence.

Tracy checked the house, top floor to bottom, every room, even the basement and near the freezer. Joe wasn't in the house. She went to the garage, thinking maybe he wanted some air but didn't want to go all the way outside. The garage was empty, too. Rubbing her arms to keep warm as she walked, she looked out the windows to see if he was outside. He wasn't, but she saw an SUV in the driveway.

"Come on," she said. "Are you serious?"

She moved through the house and went back in the kitchen, noticed the note on the table.

"Oh no, he didn't." She went over to it and pulled it out from under the cleaver.

Tracy,

Sorry for running out, but have to look into something. To be honest, I was too scared to tell you. I know you'll be super mad at me for this, but it has to be done. I'll explain if I see you again. Stay here. I left a couple weapons. I also found the SUV those keys belonged to, so the vehicle's in the driveway, half a tank of gas.

She picked up the keys, then went back to the note.

About our fight, I'm still sorry even though I know I'm causing another one by doing the same thing that started the first.

You'll be safe in this house. Don't try looking for me. Just stay here, keep making sure the doors and windows are secure, stay out of sight. For food . . . I'll leave that to you. If you can tough it a day or two without it, I'll bring something with me when I come back.

Hope you're not too mad, and if it's any consolation, I will miss you.

Joe

"Oh no, I'm not mad," she said, "I'm *furious!*" How dare he do exactly what he said he wouldn't? What could possibly be so important he not only decided not to include her in this little walkabout of his, but didn't even tell her what it was about?

"I swear, once I get my hands you, I'll tear you to pieces." She crumpled up the note. "Hope the undead get you first."

Her heart ached. She didn't mean it.

Why did you do it? I don't want you to get hurt. "I never want you to get hurt."

Tracy sat at the kitchen table for over twenty minutes, lost in disbelief at his abandonment. Someone of his skill and experience should know how stupid a move it was.

There was no way she was going to stay put for a day or two while he sorted out whatever it was he needed to deal with.

"But I don't want to go out there, either," she said. She wasn't scared, but after having Joe by her side for a while now, going it alone didn't feel natural anymore.

She supposed, though, that that's the way it had to be: always alone.

No one to trust. No one to help.
Only herself.

***

Joe kept to the side of the road, dodging in and around cars both parked and crashed. Some of the undead were completely oblivious to his presence. A couple of others saw him, but their stride was so slow he easily outran them. Only thus far one had attacked him, a blonde with half her hair torn out, ripped lips and an absent nose. Joe had taken the paring knife and jabbed it in her eye, hitting the brain, making short work of her.

His stomach sat in unease as he traveled toward April's apartment, upset at how easily and callously he was able to take down the undead, often forgetting they were once humans with lives, dreams, families, hopes.

It took nearly four hours to get there, to April's street back in the city. The dust from the other day still hung in the air and Joe was finally able to see from what: a building that had been torn down by one of the giant undead. Sadly, the giant creatures were still out there, their heavy footfalls shaking the ground every time they took a step. Once in a while they'd let out a foul call, harsh and primal, like a yelping injured bear.

Legs sore and thirsty as all get out, Joe finally turned onto Broadway. April's place wasn't far from here and, thanks to the throng of jammed cars long-since abandoned and the rubble, Broadway was the perfect avenue to worm his way through, concealed from any undead soul looking for him.

Each car he passed told a different story, their crunched shells and chipped paint statements of violent accidents by panicked drivers. Blood spatter decorated many of the windshields, the majority of them cracked or even missing huge chunks of glass. Flat tires, open gas tanks from syphoning thieves, absent doors and broken mirrors all told of the day chaos ruled the street. Most of the vehicles were stained gray from the Rain. Others weren't as bad, probably having been in a garage then used right after the fact once it was noted people weren't people anymore and many had become the walking dead.

A child's backpack sat beside a red-blotched-gray Toyota, the Barbie backpack propped up against the rear passenger door of the four-door vehicle as a lonely memorial to a little girl lost. Halfway down the street, on the hood of one of the cars was a diaper bag with a bloody infant car seat on one side, a red-stained change mat on the other.

The torn limbs and rotting flesh littering the ground gave Joe comfort in that if those chunks of decomposing meat-on-bone were lying there untouched, then most likely the undead had moved on from this area. Either that, or this open feast of leftover body parts had yet to be discovered.

You'd think they would have found it by now, though, he thought.

He kept on, staying out of sight. A dozen or so undead stumbled up and down the dead lawn outside the Legislative Building, most with their eyes to the ground as if scouring for lost change.

In the distance, a giant zombie bellowed. Joe hoped they couldn't see him moving in and around the crashed vehicles from their vantage point.

As he crossed the street by the Art Gallery, he stopped by a lamppost with a flyer taped to it. Most of the paper was covered in gray streaks from the rain, but he was still able to make out the image of Spider-Man fighting the Lizard, the flyer from over a year back stating an exhibit at the Art Gallery showcasing comic art from the likes of John Romita Jr., Jim Lee and a few others. It immediately took him back to his comic book days and his heart yearned for that simpler time. It was almost fitting he saw this nostalgic flyer on his way to April's. He had been at what he thought was the height of his career when he met her. Made sense he'd be at the lowest point of his life as he made his way to her place on a quest to say goodbye, if the worst had happened.

A U-Haul trailer was on its side over to the left, the truck pulling it still upright, the hitch twisted as the trailer hung on despite falling over. From around the back of the trailer, a handful of zombies emerged.

The dead silence of the house weighed upon Tracy as she sat on the couch in the living room, the one where Joe slept. She'd done as she was told, but was hating every minute of it.

"This sucks," she said, and groaned. "I'm so bored."

She knew Joe was right about staying here, but she also knew that just sitting around wasn't going to cut it. There was no radio, no TV, no Internet, not even any toys to occupy her mind.

Don't try looking for me, the note had said, but, she decided, that's exactly what she was going to do.

Just need a plan, she thought. *He could be going anywhere and it's been hours since he left. Based on average foot speed, he could be anywhere within a fifteen-to-twenty kilometer radius.*

It was going to be harder than she thought. She had to narrow it down. What would Joe need to take care of that would be so pressing he'd leave her here and head off on his own?

"Is he just going out there to blow off some steam, kill some zombies? But he also said he'd be back in a day or two. That'd be a crazy amount of steam if it takes him that long to chill out. His family is dead and so is his ex-girlfriend, or that girl that really did a number on him. Not sure about his other friends, though it didn't sound like he really had many." Talking it out helped paint a clearer picture of what needed to be done. "He also said that his world was different than mine, that this one isn't the one he remembered. Maybe he's off to confirm that's the case?" The muscles in her face relaxed. "Maybe he's off to see if he can find himself, an actual *himself,* a Joe that lives in this world?" *Doubt it. Never seen anyone look like him at the Hub. Never encountered a look-alike on the streets.* "Unless the Joe of this world lives somewhere else. He didn't say there was a Hub in his world either, so who knows what the differences could be?"

Her heart sank at the prospect it was a lost cause. She could guess all she wanted and pursue a dozen avenues, but specifically nailing down his whereabouts would be impossible.

"Crap," she said, and struck the cushion beside her. "You're an idiot, Joe, you know that?"

She lied back on the couch, put her hands behind her head, one knee up, the other leg folded across it, and considered just staying put.

"Who am I kidding?" she said. "I know exactly what I'm going to do."

The undead moved swiftly, all six of them having all their body parts from what Joe could see. They were all male, all seeming to be a similar age, too. Quickly, Joe jumped up onto the hood of a van, then got on its roof. The undead crowded in around it, arms up, palms slapping the van's sides, trying to reach him. One of the dead began to crawl up the hood.

Okay, dumb idea, he thought. He must be more tired than he realized because he actually thought he'd be safe up here off street level.

Two of the other zombies followed their companion's example and started to climb the van, too. The moment the first reached onto the roof and started to hoist itself up, Joe kicked it in the head, sending it toppling over the side and onto the pavement. The next was immediately behind it, face in a twist, lips snarling, mouth wide with rotten teeth. In one fluid motion, Joe took the steak knife from his belt, shoved it deep into the zombie's mouth at an angle, delivering the blade upward through the roof of the mouth and into the creature's brain. He yanked the blade free. The zombie fell over. Joe jumped down onto the hood, did the same to the third just as the first started climbing back up onto the hood again. Joe kicked it down once more as the others started to horde in. Back on the van's roof, Joe waited for the three to get their balance, then let the first come forward. The two behind tried to climb onto the roof at the same time, crowded each other, and one fell off.

On the roof, an undead man in a ratty purple T-shirt reached out. Joe took the knife to its neck and sliced across, severing the flesh and trachea in one powerful sweep. He twisted the blade over in his hand and came back across the neck, this time taking the flesh all the way to the back against the vertebrae. With a hard kick to the thing's head, he knocked its skull from its body.

Three down. Three to go.

The next undead was already upon him, came in low, and grabbed Joe's legs out from under him. Joe hit the roof, a jolt of pain striking his shoulder blades from the impact. He also felt a pronounced pain in his lower back, but it faded. He hoped he hadn't put anything out. He kicked at the zombie, who started climbing up his body, teeth snapping, eyes wide with a feral need for human flesh. The moment the zombie's head was close enough, Joe drove the steak knife into the thing's temple, wedged it in, and the creature stopped moving. Unable to get his knife out and not wanting to waste any time, he kicked the dead man off him and rolled off the roof, landing on his feet beside the van.

Both the remaining two creatures had been on the van and they quickly stepped off and came toward him. Joe grabbed the first by the arm, spun him around and threw him into his bloodthirsty comrade. He took both paring knives from his belt, one in each hand, and got ready for them to come forward again. The first did and he plunged the blade deep into the creature's gut, then ripped the knife across its belly, its rotten flesh easily giving way to the blade. Its guts spilled out, slopping around the zombie's feet. It slipped on them and fell, giving Joe enough time to move away and drive both paring knives into the eyes of the other. He swiftly withdrew the blades, then slammed them back in the eye sockets for good measure. The creature dropped.

The last undead tried to get up, its feet still slipping on its own intestines like someone trying to stand on freshly-cleaned ice. Joe came in from behind it, rammed one paring knife into the base of its skull, skewing the blade upward to the brain, and came in with the other from the side via the zombie's ear, just in case. The creature's legs slipped out from under it; it fell and didn't move.

Wiping the sweat from his forehead, Joe looked at the bodies and found the one that still had the steak knife in it. He went over to it, reached down, and put a boot on the side of the gutmuncher's head while pulling the blade out at the same time. It came free after a violent jerk.

All three blades were coated in the dead's slimy black blood and Joe didn't want to replace them in his belt until he had a chance to clean them off. He assumed he'd find something sooner or later so, blades in hand, he continued his trek down the street in search of April's apartment.

10
GRASSY HILLS, EVIL BEASTS

"Okay, I'm a little weirded out," Billie said.

Nathaniel had opened a portal between realms and brought her back into the world she left after drowning in the lake. She had asked him if she was returning as a ghost.

"No, no, of course not," he said. "I'd never see you become that which we fight against. You are going back risen from the dead, complete and whole. I have a special job for you and you must complete it." He handed her a bracelet. It was a simple gold band with a clear stone in the center.

"When it lights white, you know you are near. The moment you are, you will retrieve."

She assented and now he brought her here to the top of a huge hill overlooking many others, all covered in dead, dry grass. The sky above was still gray and brown out here in the countryside.

Billie turned to talk to the angel, but he wasn't there.

"Hello?" she called into the air. "You can't just drop someone off in the middle of nowhere and expect them to do a job especially since you said what I should do involves people." No reply, not that she expected one. "I thought angels were supposed to be nice."

She proceeded down the hill, admiring the beauty despite all the dry, yellow grass and the various shrubs which looked more like masses of twisted coat hangers than vegetation. After the ravages of Hell, it was strangely beautiful. Had life gone on normally, maybe one day she'd wind up in a place like this—far away, secluded, a chance to breathe and just take in the Earth as God made it before Man screwed it up.

Keeping a sharp eye out for any creatures, she was relieved that, so far as she could tell, she was out here alone. Not a single soul dotted the landscape. The only thing that gave her a sense of direction right now was a cottage way in the distance, the only structure out here that was a place to go to. She headed that way, keeping an eye on the bracelet for the stone to glow white. What she was supposed to find with it, she didn't know. The angel didn't say.

The air was stale and the freshness one would expect to experience out here was nowhere to be found, yet to breathe the air of the Earth . . .

As she walked, she thought about where she just was and even though it was over and now locked in her memory, the mere thought of the agony of those flames still caused her to tense up and be sick to her stomach with regret. She couldn't believe that such an awful place could exist and that people went there. Couldn't believe the evil creatures that lived there had found a way to infiltrate the land of the living and violate human beings by possessing them, their body no more than a shell-like vehicle to be driven around, used and abused.

Even here on these fields, the spiritual side to all this really bothered her and it was certainly not what she had expected nor hoped for even when the world died and the dead began to rise. But it was reality now and she had to resolve to just accept it and move on.

She rounded a hill and found a path of worn grass mixed with a little bit of dirt. The ground was extremely dry, no rain having come down since a year ago Nothing but death.

A low moan rose on the air, coming from beside her. She stopped in her tracks, and slowly turned her head to the side, seeing nothing but a hill that rose several feet above her head.

That didn't sound human either, she thought. *Not "dead human," anyway. To low, full.*

Cautiously, she slowly walked forward, keeping one eye on the cottage far ahead, the other on the hill next to her, anxious for something to come at her.

"Why'd you leave me out here, Nathaniel?" she sang quietly through gritted teeth.

After around twenty more paces, the low moan returned, a long one drawn out followed by a series of short ones, some loud, some quieter. It didn't sound like they all came from the same source.

Billie picked up her pace. *Great. Now there's a whole shwack of them after me and I'm completely unarmed.*

She kept moving, checking over her shoulder, listening as the moans grew louder, closer. The foul stench of rot and carcass hit her hard; she had to pinch her nose and breathe through a palm over her mouth to block out the smell.

The hill beside her began to taper off, its crest getting lower until it matched her height then her waist then knees before leveling off.

The moans continued.

Billie turned.

A herd of cattle—at least twenty-five of them, if not more—was slowly moving toward her as a group. Each cow had clouded, milky-

REDEMPTION OF THE DEAD

white eyes, all fixed on her. She noticed their normally brown and black hides were drawn taut across their frames like cracked leather, the hair rubbed off in large random patches. A few of them were missing a limb or two. One didn't have hind legs and was dragging itself along the grass.

The low moans rose in volume the closer they neared, as if plainly telling her they saw her and she'd be their next meal.

Billie knew the Rain had affected all things living, but to see such enormous beasts like this coming toward her really hammered home the foul deathly taint that was on all that lived. Seemed everything good this world once had to offer had completely fallen by the wayside.

Those eyes . . . she'd only seen cows in pictures, never up close like this. They didn't look like that in magazines; they were gentle, even cuddly. Those white eyes stared at her with malice behind their gaze. She imagined the demons within the beasts, each of their sinewy frames wearing the cow like a bad suit.

The cows bellowed a deathly moan, and started stomping toward her. Billie tore off down the path; the sound of hooves on dirt and grass rose up behind her, growing louder and louder. She sprinted as hard as she could, not knowing where she could go to escape these things. She had precious few seconds if escape was even possible. They'd gain on her in no time, four legs to two, even if those four were undead.

Digging deep and summoning as much leg power as she could, she bolted down the path, not daring to look over her shoulder at the herd coming after her.

The yelps of panic bubbled out involuntarily and soon she was shrieking as she ran. She never was like this even when the dead first rose, but she was broken and couldn't take any more. Nothing mattered but instinct and survival.

The undead hooves clomped hard and quick along the ground, each fifteen-hundred-pound beast gaining ground with each passing second. Soon their moans were so close Billie's innards began to vibrate. Her legs fatiguing, she pushed herself harder, her only hope being Nathaniel wouldn't just drop her off simply to die and go back to that terrible place.

A loud buckshot cracked through the air; the sound of dead weight thundered behind her. A wild series of thuds and moans followed right after, presumably some of the cattle tripping over the fallen one.

The fallen one? Who did that? she wondered. Too terrified to look back, she hoped that whatever just happened would happen again. It did; several gunshots rang out, the blasts heavy and powerful. Thuds and trampling hooves filled the air. Billie dared herself to take a sneak peek

63

over her shoulder, but couldn't bring herself to do it. The path in front of her was the most stable so she chose to follow it instead of veering off to the side and onto the rolling hills.

More gunshots, probably upwards of ten having been executed since she first heard them.

"Thanks! Thanks! Thanks!" she screamed, hoping whoever was out there would hear her. It was all she could do.

Low, deep moans came in loud along with a wheezing snort. This time Billie *did* look over her shoulder and saw a mid-sized undead cow with sloppy patches of rotten flesh over its body chasing her, just mere feet away.

Screaming, she ran fast then felt something harder than rock slam up into her backside, knocking her up and off her feet. She flew face forward into the dirt and grass, skidding her arms, knees and chin. Immediately a harsh pinch gripped her Achilles through her shoe.

She crawled on her belly, trying to get some distance, but was instead pulled back by her foot. "No!"

She rolled over, the cow's muzzle twisted to the ground with her foot. The beast jerked its head up, trying to get her foot back to the way it was, lifting her legs off the ground in the process before they fell back down in a hard bump. Billie used her other foot and kicked at the thing's head. Stomping against its skull was like stomping hard on a cement floor.

A couple more gunshots took down two more cattle in the herd beyond. The remainder were still heading toward her.

"This one, this one, this one," she screamed, pointing at the cow that had her ankle in its mouth. Its powerful jaws squeezing down, she felt her ankle pop out of place. Yelping from the pain, she kicked against the thing's head with her other foot nonstop until after a thunder crack, the cow's head exploded in bone, brain and black blood. She kicked free the foot that'd been in its mouth, did a reverse crabwalk and got back to her feet, only to trip when the foot that the cow had injured gave out from under her in a sharp spike of pain. Either her ankle was broken or it was indeed out of place.

Doesn't matter, keep going. She got back onto her good foot and hobbled and hopped down the path. The last of those things would be on her in a hot minute—a hot *second*—if a miracle didn't happen soon.

More shots rang out. More thuds. More scrambling hooves.

A shadow figure swooped in from the side, grabbed her in its arms, and picked her clean off her feet as it ran. Now upside down over the figure's shoulder, it took Billie a second to realize that whoever this was was huge, wore jeans, and smelled smoky like from a wood-burning stove.

"Hey, slow down," she said, bouncing up and down against their shoulder, her gut taking the punishment. "You're hurting me."

"Better me than them," he said. There was an accent to his voice. Polish? Deutsch? It was hard to tell, but definitely European, *thick* European. "My brother got the rifle. You come with me. He take care of the beasts."

At least you speak English, she thought. Maybe Nathaniel *did* know what he was doing?

After a few minutes, the man slowed his gait, eventually stopped and put her down. He towered over her—he must have been nearly seven feet tall!—the width of his chest and shoulders was wide enough three of her would be able to lay across his torso. He wore a gray and beige plaid shirt, had blond hair and a scruffy golden beard. His eyes were green and despite the danger of what just happened, Billie just stared at them. So green.

"You okay, yah?" he said. His voice was smoother now, less choppy and whispery than when he was running.

"Yes," she said. A sharp pain in her ankle told her otherwise. "I mean, no. No. My foot . . . ankle . . . the cow bit me."

"Come here, yah?"

Before she could reply, he knelt down in front of her, and pulled her close so hard she fell against him. He lifted her sore foot.

"You have shoe that's ripped," he said. "Did it bite?"

Billie winced from him handling it. "I don't know, maybe. It bit, but I don't know if it bit through. Didn't feel any teeth, but I've never been bitten by a cow before so I don't know."

The man tugged the shoe off and felt up and down her ankle, squeezing it in parts. Each time he applied pressure it sent a deep shockwave of ache through her foot and calf. A sudden, violent inner pop rocked her leg and she collapsed into his arms.

"There, better," he said.

She pushed herself off him. She still couldn't put any pressure on her foot without it hurting and feeling weak, but it did feel like something inside had realigned itself. "Thanks."

"We go this way," he said and pointed toward a small hill that, she saw, hit the path she'd originally been on on the other side.

A couple more shots rang out.

"That's it," he said.

"What's it?"

"All dead, the cows. Twenty-two shots, twenty-two cows."

"Oookay." She followed him over the hill and back onto the path on the other side. That cottage was close, and it took only a few moments more to understand this was where they were going. She pointed to it. "You live there?" He didn't seem to have heard her. "I said, do you live there?"

"We do."

Hard footfalls closed in behind them. Billie turned around with a start and saw a smaller, thinner version of the man she was with. He had the same face, same hair, same beard, but was only slightly taller than she was and had a bony, farmer-strong kind of build. He also wore jeans and flannel, his a plaid of baby-blue and dirty gray.

He spoke to the larger man in a language she guessed as German. The big man replied in the same, the two never breaking stride ahead of her during the exchange. She jogged to catch up. The men stopped talking.

Oh please, she thought, *don't be those people who show off by talking in a different language and look at you as if you're stupid because you don't understand them.* "Um . . ." she started, but couldn't think of anything to say.

The three walked in silence, each passing minute making her feel more and more like an outsider. After a few minutes more, they reached the cottage. It was quaint, but very old, probably eighty-plus years. Most of it was made with stone, the rock streaked with gray from the day the Rain fell. The roof was gray as well, with patches of brown shingle showing through. Obviously the roof hadn't been up kept over the years. The windows were filthy and she couldn't see inside. The door was made of thick wooden boards, with age cracks running through it. It was dark brown and not as gray-stained as the rest of the place. She assumed the door being partly inset in the frame protected it from some of the Rain.

"We go in," the big man said.

Billie waited for him to enter then followed behind the shorter one. When she came in, she felt like she was in a museum. It was one room with a wooden table in the middle, a kitchenette from the sixties off to the side with a wood-burning stove, fridge and a faded pink countertop. It looked terrible. A stone fireplace against a wood-paneled wall was off to the other side, closer to the door. A coat rack was beside the door and not much else aside from a wooden chair and a few iron pans hanging on the wall. There was something cozy about this place, though, something homey.

There was a door against the back wall.

"You eat first, yes?" the big man said to her.

"Hm?" she said and stopped scanning the room.

"You eat first."

"Actually, I'm starving. Sure. And—" He raised his eyebrows. "Thank you for helping me."

The big man smiled at the other.

The shorter one said, "He's happy."

"Happy?"

"Yes. Before, he told me he thought you were very pretty."

A flush of warmth came over her and she was mad at herself for suddenly going all girly from the compliment, but it was amazing to hear after so much sadness and tragedy and depression. All she could do was smile.

"I cook for you," the big man said.

The smaller man grinned. "Just let him have his way. He treat you nice. Don't worry, you safe."

She hoped he was telling the truth. Being in a cottage in the middle of nowhere with two strange men wasn't any girl's idea of safe.

The big man seated her at the table and told her to, "Wait while I make you specialty."

You mean I get to have real food and not just scroungings of leftovers and canned beans? She couldn't help but be excited.

The two men went to work, the big one doing the cooking, the other leaning against the counter, arms crossed. They exchanged words, once again leaving Billie alone to her English thoughts and musings.

Tired, she rested her head in her hand. She didn't mean to fall asleep.

11
THE WINDOW

COMING UP ON April's apartment building instantly took Joe back to the day of the Rain and him running out into the storm to see if she was all right. The building before him looked more or less the same as the one from his world—filthy brick streaked with gray, broken windows, blood scraped along the sidewalk.

Holding the knives—he hadn't yet found something to wipe them on—he went toward the door, ears open to any sound that would indicate he wasn't alone. He checked the apartment registry inside the door for her name. The glass over the listings had been smashed, most of the tiny white plastic letters scattered on the floor.

"Doesn't matter," he said quietly and started heading up the stairs to the top floor where April's suite was.

The hallways and stairwell were quiet, the silence amplifying his footfalls on the linoleum steps. Once at the top floor, he scanned the hallway, remembering the little girl who originally pointed him to April's suite in the other world, the girl who ended up getting devoured right after by her own father.

"Sorry I couldn't save you," he whispered. The man he'd been the day of the Rain was a far cry from the man he was now. Himself—Joseph—died after April did. The man of tenderness who loved words and poetry, comics and cereal, no longer existed. The days of hoping for love and a future . . . no more.

The door to April's suite was closed. The handle looked untainted, which he took as a good sign. He didn't expect her to actually be in there if she was alive, but he hoped he'd find something within that might lead him to her whereabouts.

He put all three knives in one hand and carefully gripped the handle in the other. The knob turned a quarter inch then stopped. He turned it the other way. Same thing.

Locked.

Heart sinking, he knew there was no way he'd kick this door down. Apartment doors were thick, heavy, and locked in place so severely that it'd take a bear to barrel through. The deadbolt alone was unbreakable never mind any other locks that might be in place inside the door. In the other world, the door had been unlocked and he had kicked it open.

"Options, options, options," he said to himself, the words slurred together. "All right, here we go."

He went to the suite next door, checked the handle. It was locked as well. He hit the suite at the end of the hallway and was relieved to find the door open. He went in and checked the place over for any creatures. Books and open movie and videogame cases covered the living room floor, the TV gone, the unit that held it tipped over onto the ground. The kitchen was an equal disaster; same with the bedroom and bathroom. The place had obviously been looted at one point.

Joe went back to the kitchen, found a dish towel, and wiped down the knives. After replacing them in the slits in his belt, he sat the kitchen table back on its legs and opened the window above it. The window was about three feet by two, big enough to fit him, but also dangerous because he was three stories up and there wasn't a ledge to climb out on. Joe hoisted himself on to the sill, turned around so his back faced the outside, and drew his legs up so all his weight was on the sill's edge. Carefully, he gripped between the bricks around the window and used them as small handholds while he slowly got himself onto his feet, his toes still hanging inside the kitchen on the sill.

He glanced at the ground below. "This is dumb." If he fell, he'd break his legs for sure, and that was *if* he even landed on his feet. He didn't want to think about what would happen if he landed on anything else. The window to the next suite was a far reach from where he was, but the windows themselves linking the bedrooms to the kitchens were possible to climb along if he was careful.

He reached slowly, straining his fingers to grab around the corner that led to the next sill—the bedroom window—then slowly did the same with his foot. Only the tip of his toes touched the sill he was aiming for.

Maybe it'd be better if I went back in, went down and tried this from outside? He quickly scanned how the windows were situated and the height going from one to another would be impossible to scale. *You're crazy for doing this for a girl.* He drew himself back to the kitchen sill and regained his balance. *You're also the guy who vowed to do anything for her if needed. This falls into the category of "anything," if that was ever true.* There was only one way to have a chance of doing this if he was going to go for it.

Taking a deep breath, he went to the edge of the sill again and reached for the other one. Fingers barely touching around the brick, same with the tip of his toes, he knew the next move he'd make would determine if he lived or died. *Don't fight it. Use the adrenaline. Keep your hips in, don't think about the ground or where you actually are.* Inhaling and exhaling three breaths in rapid succession, he took the leap. The second his reaching foot set more of its weight on the sill, he immediately hopped it over down its length and leaned the same way, keeping himself more or less in balance. He made it, heart racing. His fingers ached from gripping in between the bricks so hard. There was no going back now. He had to do this two more times before he'd hit April's bedroom window. From there he could kick in the glass and climb in.

He didn't know how long he stood there on the sill, gathering himself and psyching himself up for the next leap, but once he did, the second jump came easier than the first. His legs were shaking so badly from the rush he didn't know if they had the strength to do it one more time and keep him stable.

The seconds slowly ticked by; Joe steadied his breathing, imagining he was somewhere else, like a sidewalk where balance wasn't an issue. He tried not to think about his fingertips and how numb they were along with the sharp pain in his wrists from holding on so tight.

"Take it easy," he breathed. "Just slooooow down. Relax." Heart racing, he decided the best course of action was to just do it, live in the moment of the leap, and get it done. He was at that place that any more dawdling and he'd have to give up and climb in the window in front of him.

"Okay, go," he told himself and reached for the brick bordering what should be April's bedroom window. He took hold and reached out with his foot. Once he found purchase, he took a deep breath and leaped sideways. Gravity took over as his hand slid down the brick, scraping it. He caught the edge of the sill where his foot should have landed and hung there with one hand, yelling from the surprise. His right hand was so tight up against the corner of the sill that he couldn't squeeze his other hand beside it. His only choice was to reach up and cross his arms in an X, his left hand over his right and grab the sill that way. From there, he brought his right hand out from under his left and worked it beside it. Hanging there, ready to let go, he tried to do a pull-up against the sill, maybe get his elbow on it and hold his weight that way. He couldn't gain more than six inches when he tried. The sill was too narrow to accommodate his elbow, forearm, and his shoulder that would inevitably lean forward against the glass.

He imagined letting go, the spike of pain rushing up his legs and into his hips when his feet hit the ground, the loud snap of bones cracking as they shattered from the impact and he collapsed.

"Can't go out like this," he said. If he broke his legs, both of them, he'd probably pass out from the pain and lay there helpless as zombie food.

He needed to break the glass, but needed leverage to make the impact count. "Yeah," he said, thinking of a way. He cautiously reached for his belt and pulled out the steak knife. He worked his hand past the handle and up to an inch or so from the end of the blade, then and flipped the blade over, dull edge on the inside. He brought his palm onto the sill, giving his other hand a rest of taking all the weight.

Like a hammer, he told himself.

He drew his hand back enough so there was enough space between the butt of the knife and the window, and then rapped it on the glass. The outside of the blade cut his finger as he did and terror ran through because those were the same blades he used on the undead. If the blade wasn't completely clean, their blood would make its way into the cut and he'd be done for.

"Worry about that later," he said, still freaked out over it.

Joe used the knife to rap on the glass again, this time striking hard. He was mindful to keep hitting the same spot. "Come on!" He struck the glass again and he heard it crack. One more blow and it shattered, creating a hole about the size of a fist. Joe quickly used the knife handle to bang out the surrounding glass as much as he could, then threw the knife through the hole so he could fully use his hand again.

He shuffled down the sill so he was better in line with the hole and hugged his body as close to the wall as possible even so far as leaning *into* the wall to make his weight work for him not against him.

"Just pull," he growled through gritted teeth. Fierce pain took over the tendons in his wrists as he hoisted himself up, the window's remaining glass coming into view. The right side had the hole, the left not. He leaned forward with his right shoulder and kept pulling. He got himself up to about his ribs, his hands stuck so tight against him he couldn't adjust them to fall onto his forearms then try to climb in. If he eased himself back down so he was hanging again, he knew he wouldn't have enough strength to pull himself up one more time.

With a shout, Joe bashed his head against the glass, at first hearing nothing but the slam and its reverberation inside his skull. Three more strikes and the glass broke. He pushed himself forward, toppling into the window, the glass cutting along his chest. He crashed upside down on his arms as he came in over the edge. He lay there, catching his breath, inverted body shaking.

"Never again," he said, blood flowing into his eyes. He screamed, not caring if anyone living or dead heard him.

12
ESCAPE FROM CHINATOWN

Tracy took the SUV, heading back into the city the way she and Joe had tried after escaping the overturned truck. The dust was still on the air, but at least she could somewhat see through it and try and navigate around the crashed cars and auto pile-ups. Each time she had to ride up onto the curb and drive down the sidewalk was a geeky thrill.

The undead she had passed on the way down Main turned to face her but didn't pursue.

Tracy turned on the radio and tried the dials. Didn't hurt to check. At least it showed she hadn't given up hope. Up ahead, closing in around Higgins, the rubble on the street was piled high, most of the buildings in the immediate vicinity torn down by the giants. Parked in front of a hill of brick, cement, steel and bodies, she felt the vibrations of the giants' footfalls as they roamed up and down the streets.

Dead end. Which was fine. The Hub was over to the left anyway beneath the Disraeli Overpass.

Armed with the cleaver and mallet, she left the SUV and kept out of sight as she headed toward the bridge. A lone zombie stood swaying by a bus stop. When it saw her, it started to move toward her. Tracy picked up her pace and marched toward the creature head-on, cocked the mallet, then brought it across the zombie's head, busting the skull. The creature fell; immediately she came down on it hard and struck the head again for good measure before continuing on.

She didn't have to get to the Hub to see what happened: it was destroyed, reams of debris and concrete all around as if the Hub had exploded.

"Can't be . . ." she said. The Hub was the most secure place in the city and had gone undetected by the monsters for so long. "I was just here." She hadn't been away for terribly long, and to come back to see it destroyed so quickly sucked the hope out of her. When did it happen? Were there any survivors?

Furious and heartbroken, she kept her mallet and cleaver at the ready and ran to the ruins to see if anyone was there that needed her help. Once at the edge, her heart sank when she saw that most of the place was caved in, chunks of stone, cement, rebar, and debris blocking off the tunnels that led to where people stayed. Tracy slid down the rocks and cement and walked around the bottom of the hole like it was an empty pool. The ground was packed hard. She went where it would branch off to the living quarters and took the mallet, trying to use it as a shovel to see if some of the packed debris would give way. It was like digging in a gravel pit with baseball-sized stones.

"Hello?" she yelled against where she dug. "Anyone trapped? Can you hear me?"

Silence. Blasted silence.

She hammered against the ground a few more times then got up, cursed, and headed back the way she came. As she climbed out, she looked off to the side and saw a crowd of the monsters not far away and there was another crowd not far from them.

"Better get going," she said quietly and headed back to the SUV.

If the Hub was anything, it was good at strategic planning. There was an underground safe house reinforced to withstand immense pressure and weight, enough to not collapse under the giants. The safe house was meant for only one thing: refuge in case the Hub was overrun. If there were any survivors from the undead invasion of the Hub, they would be there. The problem was, with the road blocked, she'd have to head there on foot.

Cleaver and mallet in hand, Tracy quickly checked the SUV. Seeing it was how she left it, she made her way over the hill of rubble. Standing at its peak in a cloud of dust, her heart sank when she saw a sea of the dead wandering in a group on the other side where she needed to go.

Going headlong into them would be suicide. She checked the perimeter, but with the dust so thick it was difficult to tell if there were any of the monsters along the sides. Weapons ready, she walked along the top of the rubble, staying more on the side of the SUV than that of the dead, and headed to its end, which, it turned out, had wound its way into Chinatown.

Chinatown had been one of her favorite places in the city before it all went to hell. The food, the architecture, the strong sense of detachment from the West even though she was only a few blocks away from Main. Now the district was in shambles, with buildings crushed, others with holes in the walls, bloody body parts littering the ground, vehicles overturned—even a fire hydrant had been knocked over, the water long run dry.

She went down the hill and made it to street level. The dust wasn't as bad here, but she still had to strain to see and the dirt still coated her tongue and dried out her mouth.

Booming footfalls shook the ground beneath her feet. There had to be a giant close by, but she couldn't see where. Despite their enormous size, they had a way of coming out of nowhere just like their small counterparts.

Stay near the cars, the walls, and they won't see you and just take you as part of the scenery. It was an old trick, one of the first she learned when out on the street and hunting the undead. One had to draw their attention to really captivate them. After that, their flesh-hungry instinct took over. They could smell, that'd been proven, too, but it seemed their sense of smell wasn't as keen as once believed. They could be distracted and avoided if a person knew what to do.

And Tracy knew what to do. She was trained for this. Being with Joe, though, had softened her edge a little. She hadn't intentionally allowed it, but like rocks crashing into each other beneath a current, her own jagged edges were beginning to round smooth.

Groans of nearby zombies alerted her to a batch of them on her right. She went for cover behind a bus bench. Remaining perfectly still, she let them pass, then stood once they were a good ways down the street.

She kept to the side of one of the buildings, then rounded into an alley, wanting the advantage of its fire escapes if she was suddenly chased down.

Another trick.

She picked up a garbage can lid off the ground and decided to use it as a shield despite how ridiculous she felt doing so. It didn't matter. She had to use what she could find. A dumpster was off to the side of the alley. She approached it, cleaver ready, shield on guard, and peered over its edge. The repugnant smell of garbage that had been rotting in there for a year made her eyes water. She checked inside and saw the remains of a boy, his body ripped to pieces, arms, legs and head missing. Inside, there was nothing of use. Just packed black garbage bags, pizza boxes—in Chinatown, no less—and other trash. Nothing that could be used as a weapon.

Grimacing, she hefted the cleaver in her hand and resolved it'd have to be her best friend for the time being.

Tracy neared the mouth of the alley. Something dark dropped from the fire escape above her, landing at her feet.

A body.

An undead body that began to move and get to its feet. So much for the fire escape trick. She swung the cleaver down on its head before it could fully right itself, splitting its skull and sending gobs of bloody brain matter into the air.

She kept on, making it to the edge of Chinatown. Giants shook the ground. The top of one's head could be seen a few streets over. The thing moaned and grunted airy sounds as it moved.

A group of zombies stumbled out of the large broken window of a storefront ahead. They set their eyes on her, as if they had smelled her from within the building. She started to run in between the cars, hoping to lose them. More zombies joined their ranks as if someone had just rang the supper bell and it was time for everyone to gather. It wasn't long before they started to close in on her.

Tracy swiped the cleaver side-to-side, forcing its strong blade into every rotting skull she could see. Losing herself in the combat, she struck one zombie with the metal edge of the garbage can lid while driving the cleaver into the neck of another and severing its head. Using her skilled and swift movement, she lopped the head off another, kicked the one in front of her, backhanded the one behind her with the garbage lid, and ducked in between a car, squatting beside one of the doors to buy herself a few seconds.

The undead rounded the car from both sides. Heart racing, Tracy stood, opened the rear passenger door of the vehicle, then quickly crawled across the seats before shoving open the door on the other side. Bad plan. She was greeted by a crowd of the undead. Not wasting any time, she turned back into the vehicle, ignored the zombies that were crawling their way through the car, and climbed over the seat to the front and planted her foot on the edge of the broken front passenger window, using it as a step to get her on top of the vehicle. She slid down the windshield, hit the ground with a roll, and bolted from the horde.

She needed distance. The zombies liked to crowd and create a ceiling with their rotting fingers and hands, trapping a person in.

Tracy weaved in and around the cars. The few straggling zombies she passed tried to reach out for her, their efforts feeble. One came right in front of her and was quickly dealt with by a cleaver to its face.

She looked at the large, bloody blade. *I'm actually starting to like this thing.* Different than a gun, but simple to use as though it was an extension of herself, a sharp deadly hand instead of one made of flesh and bone.

In the parking lot of the Walker Theatre, she thought about going inside to get away, but didn't want to risk there being more undead within and inadvertently trapping herself.

The horde was further down the street, but would soon be upon her if she didn't keep moving. The ground shaking more and more fiercely beneath her feet from the nearing giants, she tried her best not to trip and only went down once before quickly regaining her footing and running onward.

There was an alley just around the corner by the building up ahead. She went for it, cleaver ready to come down on anything that entered her path. She rounded the corner and entered the alleyway. A handful of zombies were at the opposite end. A giant zombie appeared over the roofline of a building across the street, coming her way. Whether it actually saw her or not, she wasn't sure, but didn't want to risk it.

The objective: eliminate threats.

Method: kill the small ones first, then mind the big one.

Tracy charged headlong into the four zombies at the end of the alley, taking two down straight away by cutting through their rotten throats with ease. The third grabbed her makeshift shield, yanked it from her hand then came in to grab her. She backhanded it across the jaw the same time the fourth reached for her. She brought the cleaver down and sliced off one of its hands. Back to the third, she brought the cleaver up under its jaw in a powerful uppercut and sliced off its decaying face, taking some of the jawbone with it. Blood and brain gushed out the front of its face as the creature fell to its knees before toppling over onto its side. The fourth zombie took hold of her with its good hand. She took the cleaver to the wrist like she had the other one and severed it. With a kick, she knocked the creature away, then lunged at it full force and brought the cleaver down on top of its skull, ending it. The creature dropped.

Tracy removed the cleaver from its head, the blade dripping with syrupy black blood.

"Gross," she said, looking at the pale gray undead hand still clinging to her wrist. She pulled the body part off and tossed it on the ground.

The foul stench of rot suddenly overwhelmed the area. Tracy turned around to see the enormous zombie—female, with the sagging body of a sixty-year-old—looming over her.

She had no choice but to run back the way she came. The giant zombie chased her with massive strides, gaining on her in seconds. It reached down and took a swipe at her. She jumped and rolled to the side.

Shoving the mistake aside, she dodged again when the giant zombie reached down.

There'd be no way she could take the monster down by herself, and if she emerged out of the other side of the alley, she'd run into the horde that she'd originally escaped. It'd be all over.

"Thinkthinkthink," she said. She glanced up and backward at the enormous creature chasing her. It bent down, its hand crashing into her back, sending her flying forward across the pavement. She dropped the cleaver out of instinct so she could use her hands to guard herself when she landed face first and skidded along the pavement on her forearms.

Getting to her feet as fast as possible, and choosing to ignore the fire of severely-scraped forearms, she ran. She was thankful the creature had thrown her as it bought her some distance. It wouldn't last long, however, so she'd have to gamble. She ran out of the alley and sharply turned left, hugging up against where the building met the sidewalk. The giant zombie rounded the corner. The smaller ones were about a block away. She dared not go any further lest they see her and come after her. The giant zombie reached down, curling its fingers around her. Before it could clamp them shut, she hoisted herself over one of its fingers, landed on the other side, then sprinted back into the alley, aiming straight for the dumpster. The second she reached it, she climbed up and over and slammed the lid down on herself in a thundering metallic boom.

Sitting in the rot in the dark, Tracy hoped that her sudden change in movement was enough to let her slip from the giant's vision while it had to maneuver to change its course.

The dumpster shook with each thundering footfall of the undead giant beyond its walls. The monster bellowed a ghastly moan, clearly furious at its prey. She hoped it didn't know where she was. The terrible smell in the dumpster was so thick she could scarcely breathe even with her face in her hands covering her mouth and nose. She shuddered to think what kinds of bacteria were living in this dumpster just looking for a new warm and wet place to procreate and build an empire.

The dumpster rocked and shook so bad she thought maybe the monster had picked it up and was shaking it like a rattle, the thundering booms enough to throw her in a disorienting loop.

She didn't know how much time passed until the booming footsteps began to fade and the dumpster finally stopped rocking. Wanting to sigh in relief, she threw up in her hands instead, the smell too much. She couldn't breathe. Scrambling to her feet, she pushed against the lid, fell back down thanks to the soft garbage bags giving way beneath her shoes, then got herself up and gasped for air. She yacked over the edge of the dumpster, decorating the pavement with mushy, partly-digested chickpeas.

"Never again," she said through spit-gobbed lips. "No way, no how."

ONE YEAR AGO...

"It is magnificent," Bethrez said.

"That may be," said Vingros, "but does it work?"

"I have done all that I can. All seems to be in order."

"How do you turn it on?"

"Oh," Bethrez said, "only the master shall do that."

"And I shall." Lucifer emerged from the legions of demons, his white-glowing form partially hidden behind a veil of thick, gray smoke.

All went to their knees at the sound of his voice, Vingros and Bethrez among them.

"Rise," he said to them as he walked past.

The host of others remained on their knees, while Vingros and Bethrez stood and joined their master at the portal.

"All is ready, Master," Vingros said.

"And Nathaniel?"

"His whereabouts are accounted for."

Lucifer inspected the portal. "At last we will learn his secret and gain control of the course of history." He motioned for the two demons to come closer. To Bethrez, he said, "Turn it on."

Bethrez bowed. "As you wish."

Vingros remained at Lucifer's side as his master stood before his congregation and raised his hands. All demons before him got to their scaly feet. Some were more reptilian than others. Many had long bulbous spider-like bodies covered in dark green and black scales, with long, thin muscular arms and legs. Black leather wings with lead-like spikes at their tips draped over their shoulders like capes.

"The time has come, finally come," the devil said. "This is the gateway to our freedom and absolute power. It should have been mine since the beginning and now, because of your loyalty, it will be at last. Enter through the gate and we will be as we should have been: omnipresent over the race of men, the cherished people of the One we fight. In a moment, you will all be transformed and will hover over the Earth to capture it as we had before in Eden, and which we lost at Calvary. No longer will we be denied our claim to what is rightfully ours. We were all there on that day we were sent here. Now today will be a new day where we shall decide our destiny, even more so, the destiny of His inheritance."

Vingros heard the hum as the portal was activated. He glanced over his shoulder and watched as Bethrez took a step back and admired his handiwork. The outer edges of the portal glowed a ghostly red, the crimson light growing brighter the closer it got to the center of the portal itself. Inside, brilliant orange and yellow spider webs of *crackling light burst forth, highlighting the smoky vortex they would soon all enter.*

Lucifer raised his hands even higher and the host before him raised theirs. "Today we show Heaven how powerful we really are. Come now, my followers, and continue with me as you did at the first. Let us prove our exile was not in vain, and let's once and for all conquer the Earth in the name of all spirits, in the name of utter power, in the name of Hell!"

The demons roared and all spread their bat-like wings as they rose off the rocky ground and flew toward the portal. Vingros came by Bethrez's side and nudged him away as the demon seemed too lost in his achievement to acknowledge the swarm of his brethren flying toward him. Bethrez's request to enter first was denied. Time for testing was over, he was told. It was time for action.

Crowd upon crowd of the demons entered the portal, disappearing into the vortex.

"They will enter," Bethrez said, "and as they rise to the heights of the heavens, they will transform into death-giving water and fall upon the inhabitants of the Earth. Many will succumb quickly. Others, over time. Those who have died before will rise and become one with us. Once complete, a reminder will remain over the Earth of our presence in the form of gray clouds, brown sky. No longer will the colors of creation remain and no longer the memory of the One who made it."

"Will you enter as well?" Vingros asked. "It will be a chance to aid in the greatest cause since Time began."

"I have aided. This is my creation, my method. It might not be my power that runs it, but it is mine."

"And never forget that it is my power that operates it," Lucifer said, coming up beside him.

"Of course not, Master, of course not."

The three watched as legions of demons transferred from the realm of Hell into the realm of the Earth.

It was beautiful.

It was glorious.

"Yes," Lucifer said, "finally. Glory."

13
ROCK BOTTOM HEARTACHE

No MATTER HOW many times Joe wiped the blood from his face with his sleeves, he couldn't stop his eyes from watering, their instinctive ability to flush out debris constantly on the go.

He checked his arms and hands, pulled out the bits of glass from his skin. Most of the cuts were superficial, but there was one chunk of glass that got into his forearm pretty deep and he had to wipe his fingers of the other hand several times against his pants because the blood made the glass so slippery. He yanked it out, a high spurt of blood following right after. It kept gushing so he stuck his fingers in the hole in his shirt around the wound, stretched the fabric until it tore, then ripped off the lower part of his sleeve. He wound it around and just above the wound like a tourniquet, hoping it'd be enough to stop the blood flow until he could properly clean it.

Joe got to his feet, his hands and wrists aching anew. The window sill and the wall beneath it looked like they belonged in a slaughter house rather than in an apartment, smeared blood streaking from the sill almost all the way down to the floor. Steps slow, Joe looked over the bedroom and was relieved to see no signs of looting. The bed wasn't made, but that was as far as it went in terms of mess.

Maybe she had locked up before leaving and anyone who came didn't want to fuss with the door and went after easier targets? he thought.

The room's walls were bare, the bed a queen, covered in a white quilt with matching sheets, the pillowcase white with a plethora of mini pink roses on it. Beside it was a playpen. The dresser was a light gray with a mirror attachment on top, enough to see oneself from the waist up. Despite all the rot and decay outside, the room actually smelled nice, but didn't carry the Strawberry-Vanilla smell April had, not that he expected the scent to linger an entire year. Still, to breathe in that soothing scent after so long . . .

There was a bookshelf with some James Patterson and Danielle Steel. Actually, Joe noticed, the entire shelf was full of bestsellers, every name recognizable. Were readers really that susceptible to sticking with brand name authors and ignoring everything else, missing out on so much quality literature by those whose names didn't end with "King," or

REDEMPTION OF THE DEAD

"Grisham," or "Rowling"?

Doesn't matter. The book industry is as dead in this place as the undead roaming outside. He suppressed his old self once more and went out into the hallway. At the other end was the kitchen and front room. Behind him was the bathroom. He went in it and looked beneath the sink for a towel, ignoring the mirror above it, not wanting to analyze the grisly visage he caught a glimpse of in the mirror in the bedroom. Taking a towel, he covered his face and patted away the blood, doing the same over his body through his shirt. He double upped the towel and pressed it to his forearm. As he went down the hallway, he picked a few more bits of glass out of his skin and emerged in the front room.

This wasn't the living room he remembered when he went and found April the day of the Rain. Not that he trusted his memory to capture every vivid detail as everything happened so fast, but the brown microfiber couch and chair seemed out of character for her, same with the large plasma TV mounted on the wall. Joe looked over the walls and saw pictures.

None of them had April. They showed a black family: two young parents and a cute little girl with tightly-wound braided pigtails.

This was the wrong suite.

No, can't be, he thought. He revisited his trek up the stairs in his head, the walk down the hallway, the ransacked suite at the end, the windows. "This *is* the right one. Has to be."

Joe went to the door, unlocked it and checked the hallway. He *had* climbed into the right suite. This *was* the right floor.

He was in the *right* place.

And April was not here. Was never here.

The harsh realization that she might never have existed in this reality made him tremble inside and sent his heart rate through the roof.

He went searching for a phonebook, found it.

"Maybe . . . no, wait, I don't know her last name, she never gave it. I never asked," he said. *Didn't think hanging around with her would be so brief. Thought there was time for that kind of thing.* "So much for that idea."

How different is this place? Would the timeline change at that point in the past at the bank, or is something else happening or happened that I don't know about?

April.

With a growl, Joe threw the phonebook across the room. Its thick, heavy spine hit the wall, cracking the drywall. He didn't care.

"What a waste of time," he said. "Shoot!"

His eyes watered up, this time not from the blood.

Joe left April's apartment, spirit broken. Not only was she not here, he now had to make his trek back to Tracy and face her wrath.

Maybe I shouldn't even bother, he thought. *She's probably better without me anyway.* He sniffled. *As if that's true. You need her as much as she needs you to survive.* He chose to stop thinking about her for the time being and instead wracked his brain, trying to think of any other possible way to track down April. Without phones or Internet, he was pretty much out of options as to a starting point.

"You got to let this go, man," he said. "It's going to kill you in the end." *You're already dead inside so what does it matter?* But he knew that wasn't true. Not anymore. Someone else had begun to wake him—the *real* him—and she was no doubt fuming mad over him leaving. "Don't turn her into a substitute April. You'd be the opposite of what you were supposed to be if you do that."

Still clutching the towel to his forearm and dabbing his cuts whenever too much blood leaked out, Joe continued down the street, heading back the way he came. With every step came a fresh curse against himself on how stupid he was for being so hung up on April, so much so he was willing to potentially sacrifice others for his own peace of mind and heart.

You've lost so much. April, my family, myself, Des . . . Billie's out there somewhere. August, too. Oh man, almost forgot about her. Hope she's alive. Now you risk losing Tracy, too. Maybe loss was his lot in life? He was still kicking despite the intense moments of despair when he wanted to just kill himself and finally be at peace. Now, he wasn't so sure peace would even be possible if he *did* kill himself. After meeting the angel and seeing those demonic creatures, he knew there was a life beyond this one. He only hoped over there the dead hadn't taken over. *As if they're worse than the demons you saw.*

Joe avoided the undead when he saw them, stopping to hide when needed, getting in behind or under things when required as well. It was a long walk back to Tracy, however, long enough for him to think of a good excuse for leaving other than, "Oh, I had to go look up this girl I knew, the one I told you about. Had to make sure she was . . . dead . . . before I could try and get on with my life." *Pathetic.*

Joe got himself onto Main and made his way toward the dust in the

REDEMPTION OF THE DEAD

distance. He double checked his knives to make sure they were still weaved into his belt and were in position for easy access if he needed them. "Not *if* I need them, but *when*."

And he was right, because a whole pack of zombies emerged from a side street and were headed his way.

Welcome to my pity party, Tracy thought. All the emotions she'd kept suppressed over the year since the dead rose started to come out right after she climbed out of the dumpster. It was like her whole body decided to release the madness and turmoil within . . . and drag her down in the process.

The safe house was beneath the Millennium Library. The enormous building had gone down when one of the giants fell into it yet the main floor remained mostly intact. The debris and structure that fell on top of it ended up covering the main floor in a semi dome, concealing it from the outside. During some of the scouting missions, members of the Hub had discovered what happened and suggested it be a backup location should something happen to the main one. Over the course of several months, when people could be spared, crews went over with materials, slowly wedged supports and beams in there along with other construction supplies and, following a similar construction of the Hub, eventually created a substructure out of the library's first floor beneath the demolished building. Soon survival supplies were moved in along with defense equipment and general items for human needs that were rounded up after much scavenging.

Like the Hub, there was a special locking system in place to get in. It was different than the Hub's and Tracy verified she had her "key." She did: a mini screwdriver.

What if Joe returns to the house early and I'm not there? She stopped walking. *Maybe I should go back? No, I'm furious at him and I'm going to stay furious until he hears about it.*

She didn't want to give him a second thought, wanted to focus on the task at hand, but she couldn't help but let her mind drift over to being concerned about his safety.

"Don't go down that path," she told herself slowly, and she dismissed the notion that she already had. "Enough. Stay focused."

The city looked different because of all the damage and chaos, but if she had her bearings right—and she rarely didn't—the safe house should be a couple of streets over. No problem, but only if she could avoid detection of the zombies milling around not far in front of her.

14
THE COTTAGE

THE MEAL HAD been amazing. Billie could still taste it on her lips after the big man—whose name turned out to be Sven, his brother Bastian—made her a German breakfast of a few sausage links, bread rolls and artificial egg whites. He had even made her coffee!

Despite being in a strange place, she could go for another nap after such a great meal.

The men sat with her at the table, Sven at the head of it, Bastian across from her. No one spoke and she was beginning to understand that these two boys only spoke when they had something to say and didn't just talk for the sake of talking to fill the silence like her and most of her friends used to.

Taking a sip of coffee, she loved how rich and flavorful it was, unlike back home where all she knew was instant coffee from a jar.

Sven would look at her, then look away, wait a few minutes then do it again. It got to the point where Billie blurted, "What?"

Sven averted his gaze, clearly embarrassed. She knew he thought she was pretty, but come on, it was starting to get creepy. Besides, he looked to be at least ten years older than her. Not that she was paying attention to that.

"Sorry for my brother," Bastian said. "We've had a bit of a hard time here, like you."

"Oh, I'm not from here," Billie said.

"We know."

"Huh?"

"You talk funny."

"I talk funny, right," she said with a grin.

"But listen, yah? We have something for you. You see, we know of why you're here."

Her heart stopped. Did she just hear him right? "Um, you do?"

A knock came from behind the door off the kitchen. A second later, a woman emerged, with black hair sharply cropped at the chin, pale skin, and very simple features. She seemed Russian or French, but when she spoke and greeted Sven and Bastian, she had a strictly British accent. Billie thought the plain gray dress the woman wore and the white sneakers, though an odd combination, was actually kind of cool.

The woman closed the door behind her, but before it shut all the way, Billie caught a glimpse into the room beyond, which looked way too big for such a small cottage. The intriguing part was the row of computer monitors and panels of switches and lights. Had she not known any better, she'd believe she was in a different room of a spaceship, one made to look like a cozy home on Earth to help her feel at ease.

That's not what's happening, is it? An alien invasion on top of a zombie apocalypse?

The woman didn't sit down, but instead walked up to her. She held out her hand for a handshake. "My name is Isabel."

She took the woman's hand. "Billie."

To Bastian, the woman said, "Is she ready?"

"No. Not yet. We haven't had chance to talk. You were supposed to wait until we get you."

Back to Billie, Isabel said, "Well, doesn't matter. She's here now."

Billie stood and waved her hands in front of her. "Wait, wait, wait . . . who are you and what do mean by 'expecting me'?"

"This is Bastian, Isabel and I'm Sven," the man said.

"I meant who are you guys specifically and how do you know me?"

"The man in white said you would come," Isabel said. "He said you were to show us where to go."

Billie remembered Nathaniel's new mission for her was one of recruitment as well as recovery. He had said, "It's time to rally our forces as the Earth has almost completely fallen to Evil. Little time is left. I want you to gather those to join us at the Last Battle as they have tools that will help us." She just didn't know that those "tools" and people would be somewhere overseas.

"You must also find the Divine Fragments," he'd said and handed her the bracelet. "When the stone is white, wait."

When she asked fragments of what, she had already been dropped off on the hill outside.

"Come," Isabel said and led Billie to the room at the back, where Sven opened the door for them.

Billie had been mistaken about the size of the room. It *did* fit with the overall size of the cottage as through the crack in the door what she had seen were actually a series of large mirrors that sat at an angle, reflecting the goings on at the level below. It was there at the bottom of a very narrow, winding staircase the computer monitors and panels were, along with an expanse of cubicles along the sides of the wall, the area down the middle loaded with long tables covered in scraps of metal, rubber tubing, lengths of two-by-fours, tools, welding equipment and some items she didn't recognize, but looked to be some sort of series of vats with a greenish bubbling liquid inside.

"This is special place," Sven said, coming up beside her.

"Amazing," Billie said. She hadn't seen this much tech since her last trip to Best Buy over a year ago. And even then, Best Buy only had modern items, not ones that looked like a cross of Star Trek meets Steampunk. "What is this place?"

"Special," Sven said again.

"Don't mind him, okay," Bastian said, "he just nervous."

Normally she would find a guy who was into her getting all goofy around her as annoying, but Sven was big, handsome, strong and . . . big. She could get into that.

"All we know is you were to come here and take us somewhere else," Isabel said. "That's all the old man in the white coat told me when he rescued me several months back. He mentioned this place, but I didn't arrive here until later. At first, I didn't believe him of course, just some old coot with a story, but after he dematerialized into thin air, I thought maybe there was something to his statement, then when the boys saw you, a girl matching the description he gave me, we had to get you in here safe before assessing our next move."

"And what is your next move?" Billie said.

Isabel led her down an aisle between a row of cubicles and the long tables in the middle with all the gear on it. "Rebellion. All you see here are preparations for warfare, bits of tech we've cobbled together from the old world while also adding twists of our own, resources being limited. It might look impressive, but understand dozens of people lost their lives finding it for us. Many of our people lost theirs just trying to get to the people that found these old computers, machines and odds and ends."

"How are you powering them?"

"Solar panel on the roof. You wouldn't have seen it as it's on the south side. We've also been able to us a generator in conjunction with it as the solar radiation filtering through the gray and brown clouds is minimal. Every bit helps, we figured."

Billie and Isabel passed two eight-foot tables completely covered in an array of pistols, machine guns, rifles, grenades and even what looked like a small bazooka. Billie looked over her shoulder back at Sven, who gave her a warm smile.

"Most of our weaponry until now we've kept simple, saving all we can artillery-wise. Knives, machetes, spears, compound bow and arrows—saving bullets is one of the rules around here."

"Well, you did a good job," Billie said.

"We work hard," Bastian said.

"So I see." They came to the end of the room. Given its length, Billie knew they were far past the cottage above, a good twenty yards away. She gestured to the area they just passed. "And all this has gone unnoticed?"

Sven and Bastian cast their eyes to their feet.

"What?" Billie said.

"Sadly, no. There were problems. All of us working here are from all over the world, each with their own story on how they got here, who they lost, why they won't give up. Others couldn't accept times have changed and tried functioning like they had in the old world, making alliances that were out of sync with our aim to create a stronghold for the sake of safety. Deals were being made, people found out and ratted out. Led to a major fight both down here and up on the hills. There were so many of us when this all started, over four thousand coming and going, gathering, helping—now we're down to just ninety-four. *Ninety-four.* That's self-inflicted casualties and ones from the monsters. When we came to our senses and things began to settle, we swore to work even harder, not just to help ourselves, but to help others once we felt ready. That was going to be the plan: head out of here in about six months' time and work our way through the cities, checking for survivors, gather more to our ranks. We figured that if we were organized enough, we could create our own military and perhaps succeed where that of the old world failed."

Putting her hands on her hips, Billie took in a slow, deep breath, held it a moment, then breathed out slowly. "Seems to me the plan was seen as a good one by those looking on," she said, referring to the angelic forces she'd become acquainted with, "but your timetable and theirs were on different schedules."

"Whose?" Sven asked.

"Angels," Billie said squarely.

Sven arched an eyebrow. So did Bastian and Isabel, each looking at her like she was crazy.

"The man in the white coat, you didn't think he was human, did you? You said he disappeared right in front of you." She knew she was no better, though, because when she first saw Nathaniel in his elderly man form, she thought he was just an old guy with an unusual dress code. It was only when he spoke to her despite her being invisible to everyone else did she realize he was something different.

Isabel smugly smiled and wobbled her head with pride. "I knew it."

REDEMPTION OF THE DEAD

As if.

"Yah, me too," Sven said, clearly lying. He jabbed his elbow into Bastian's ribs.

"Me too, yah," Bastian said.

"Whatever, guys," Billie said. She took a moment, got her head together, then got down to business. "'Kay, I was told to recruit those who would stand with us against the dead. Why me or for what purpose, I don't know. In the end, I was sent here—"

"How?" Isabel asked.

"Let me finish. I was sent here to get you guys. Fine. Here we are." She furrowed her brow. "Actually, where are we?"

"Austria," Sven said.

Of course. Austria. "Okay then," she said. "It's clear that you guys, at least for now, are weapons people. This whole place is loaded with things we can use." Turning to Isabel, she asked, "How much arms do you think you have?"

"Oh, I don't know, enough to thoroughly equip probably a thousand men."

"Serious?"

"Yes. What you see here are our experiments. There's a chamber beyond where we store our completed work."

"Your completed work?"

"Would you like to see?"

It was getting a little too hard to swallow, yet it made sense there'd be factions out there working on ways to take the Earth back from the dead. "Okay."

Isabel went to what looked like a regular garage door in the corner. Sven lifted it open for her, and the four of them went into another large room beyond, this one as big as the room they were just in, however the walls, floor and ceiling were made of cement. Lining the walls were rows of arms, ammo, defense shields and helmets. A couple of cars that were outfitted for combat were in the middle, but the biggest surprise of all lay beyond the vehicles.

"You got to be kidding me," Billie said slowly, walking ahead of the group and heading right for the row of over a dozen armored humanoid transports. They looked like robots outfitted with wheels along their legs. The actual form was very boxy with a domed hood at the top for the head. Billie thumbed toward them and called back to the others. "You call this 'cobbled together?' Man, you actually built these things?"

"Over time," Isabel said.

89

"They test ride very good," Sven said.

"Ride?" Billie said.

"Ride," said Bastian.

"You can actually go in them?"

Isabel came up beside her and ran a hand over one of the armored humanoid's hull. "This is our D-K-Fourteen-P-Two-X." She cleared her throat. "Our Dead Killer Fourteen—as it took fourteen separate designs to make it work—Phase Two—second edition of the fourteenth model for more stable use—Exoskeleton."

Billie's legs went rubbery. "A mech? Are you serious?" She knew what mechs were, but those were the things of science fiction and Japanese animation not science fact.

"It was the only suitable design for hand-to-hand combat. Not meant for strict one-on-one battles, but for entering a horde of the undead and being able to keep the upper hand the whole while."

"You've tested it?"

"Just on the cattle."

"Is amazing, no?" Bastian said.

Sven came up beside Billie and looked at her. "Special."

She blushed without meaning to. "You have twelve of them?"

"Thirty-six," Isabel said, "the other two dozen are off-site in two secure locations for safekeeping."

Billie rounded the front of the DK-14-P2-X. It was almost triple her height, probably around thirteen or fourteen feet tall. The computer geek inside her was itching to climb into it and see how it worked. She'd feel awkward asking, though, so she didn't say anything. "How long until you can get everything up and running?"

"Three hours."

"For just the DKs or everything?"

"Just the DKs. About six for everything else. We have procedures in place for assembling an army if required."

Billie nodded. "I was told to recruit so that's what I'm doing." She went right up to Isabel. Sven followed behind like a puppy dog, Bastian beside his brother. "Assemble everyone, then. Do you have GPS or some sort of navigating system?"

"GPS went down when the satellites were stopped being up kept, but we do have navigating procedures for long distances. Where are we going?"

"Winnipeg," she said.

"Where?"

"I'll show you," Billie said.

15
THE SAFE HOUSE

Tracy had been able to take down three of the dead. Those ones were of the extremely slow-moving variety and were harmless unless they got their rotten fingers on someone. Two others had gone down with the cleaver. She lost the mallet when she meant to bash another one's skull and instead missed when the creature unexpectedly moved in the opposite direction. It had been knocked from her hand by another before she had a chance to try again.

Now she was moving as fast as she could down the adjacent street, able to outrun some of them, others hot on her tail. Her hand was pressed to her side, her shirt damp with blood. As she'd observed before, many of the undead were getting more and more aggressive, even more capable and were transitioning from slow-moving, incompetent flesh-eaters to feral killing machines.

Tracy couldn't lead them to the safe house, but she also didn't want to spend the better part of the day trying to outrun and hide from them. They had to be taken down except there were too many of them.

She turned and jumped in behind a taxi that had gone and rammed itself up over the curb, and waited a moment to see if she'd lost them. Their ever-nearing footfalls said otherwise. Back on her feet, she maneuvered in between the traffic-filled street, using the cars like a hedge maze to slow down the dead. At the end of the street, she ran into a parking lot which had been an old construction site, one that appeared to have been in the process of repaving the lot and setting up short concrete walls as dividers between certain areas.

She saw a shovel on the ground by the cement mixer. She picked it up along with a bucket of dried cement beside it. The bucket weighed at least fifty pounds and she was thankful she was able to lift it albeit with a heft of effort.

As the dead started to come out of the maze of cars, she swallowed the dry lump in her throat and approached them head-on. She knew she wouldn't take them all down, but if she could remove some of the threat, perhaps the others would get the idea and move on, or at the very least become a small enough group for her to finally evade.

The moment the first zombie neared, Tracy dropped the shovel, grabbed the bucket of cement by both hands, and spun around in a circle, gaining momentum. She whipped the bucket across the zombie's head, splattering its skull. As the creature fell, she went to do the same thing to the next one, but the momentum from her original spin made her fumble and she ended up lobbing the bucket at the undead woman instead. The creature held out its arms as if to catch it. The bucket slipped between its arms and landed on its toes. The monster merely stumbled around it and came forward.

Tracy lunged for the shovel, picked it up, then brought it back around like a baseball bat to the female zombie's head, the shovel's rusty metal scoop slicing through the creature's skull like a pickax into tightly-packed earth. She pulled the shovel free and brought it down on the next approaching zombie, this one an elderly woman, short, with half her face rotted away. Knocking the woman's skull from her body like a ball off a tee was easy work. Right after, Tracy jabbed the shovel into the rotting guts of a nearing undead Asian man. She tore through his stomach in one fluid motion, his guts spilling out at his feet in slops of black goo and intestines that looked more like rotten lasagna. He kept moving forward and she brought the shovel back the opposite way and smacked him in the head, knocking him down.

About to turn and run out of there, she was intercepted by a hillbilly of a zombie with three teeth, a long beard that was ripped out from its jaw in places, and overalls without a shirt underneath. The thing flopped its arms over the shovel's shaft, the force enough to cause her to drop it. She pushed Huckleberry-dead to the side, pulled out the cleaver, and brought it across the back of the hillbilly's head. She got the blade a good ways through, but it wasn't enough to kill it. The creature turned around, grabbing her in the process, mouth open and coming in for the kill. She jerked the cleaver free from its skull, got it over its mouth, saving herself from getting bit, and pushed herself away. She immediately lunged back, bringing down the cleaver on its head, splitting it like a coconut.

She hit one and kicked another, shoved two small ones at the same time into the two behind them, causing them to trip over each other and fall.

Having thinned the ranks some, Tracy took the cleaver to the heads of two more before sprinting away, once again using the crushed vehicles on the street as a means of confusion to any that pursued her.

After a couple of blocks, the stitch in her side forced her to stop running. She took a few deep breaths then moved at a brisk walk.

Finally, she was on the right heading to the library. Mouth dry, she couldn't wait to see if there was something there to drink. Cautious of the undead that might have followed, she remained off the street and hid in a partly-buried bus shelter until she felt the coast was clear and she could emerge and get to her final destination.

The secret lever leading into the safe house was inside a telephone booth that had been partly crushed in the rubble the day the Millennium Library fell. The booth itself sat on an angle against the heap of ruin, most of it above the surface of the debris, its bottom portion hidden beneath slabs of concrete. Tracy pulled out her "key," the small flathead screwdriver given at the Hub. She put it in the middle screw that kept the phone unit itself in place against the rear inside wall of the phone booth. The screw she turned was actually an extension of a key, which unlocked the phone unit as a whole, allowing it to swing open on small hinges. Though Tracy thought the whole *Mission Impossible* aspect of this a bit excessive, she understood the reason for the secrecy: security, randomly hidden. She pulled a small lever inside the phone unit and there was a loud click; the lower half of the rear phone booth wall swung open. She closed the phone unit, crouched, and stepped into the back of the phone booth. Once in, she closed the small door behind her, counted three steps forward, two to the left, all the while keeping one hand along the rough cement wall of the narrow corridor she found herself on. Navigating in the dark wasn't easy for anyone, hence the step count. At the end of the narrow corridor, about ten feet from where she first entered, was another door. She felt for the handle, found it, then opened the door.

The dim lighting was easy on the eyes as she stepped down a short set of stairs to what used to be the library's first floor. If the lights were on, somebody had to be home.

The room had been partitioned into strategy centres, living quarters, kitchen, bathroom facilities, a large workshop, and a chapel. The partition walls were made of wood, unpainted so the colors and types varied, each running floor to ceiling. If anyone was here, they'd be in one of these sections.

Tracy went down the center aisle. "Hello?"

The closer she neared the first partition, the louder the voices behind came. When she peered in, she saw two men in ratty T-shirts and jeans looking at a map that was spread out on a table, small pebbles and stones of different colors placed purposefully along the map's grids. The men saw her, but didn't give her a nod. She wasn't sure if they recognized her or not.

Doesn't matter, she thought, and went further in. She checked the various divided areas, some empty, others with folks chatting, some exercising, others resting. Toward the end was the aroma of what smelled like veggie soup.

She followed her nose to the end then stopped walking when she sensed someone behind her. Dean Brandt, one of the original planners of the safe house and on its team of architects. He was also the unofficial head honcho. He looked much older since she last saw him, the stress of the recent days having turned most of his hair gray. He was unshaven, scruffy, and looked like he hadn't been out of the safe house for months. His dirty collared shirt and brown slacks made him look even worse than he probably intended, not that looks mattered these days.

"About time you showed up," he said, his sixty-or-so-year-old voice sounding uncharacteristically young against his old and haggard appearance.

"Other things came up." She stepped closer to him.

He embraced her and she wasn't sure if it was for the right reasons. Either way, she didn't like being touched. He let go. "You obviously know what happened."

"I saw."

Dean put his fingers to his lips. "Oh my. I hope you didn't get hurt."

"Wasn't there when it happened."

"Good. Not many made it, at least from what we can ascertain. I came here immediately after I escaped. Others followed. So few compared to what we had."

"I can see that," she said, remembering how many people were actually down here with them.

"A handful of other survivors that managed to stay alive elsewhere in the city and the suburbs followed a couple of Hub survivors in here, which is fine, just mentioning. One couple had been with us. Saw their young daughter eaten alive, completely devoured by a whole crowd of the monsters. They lasted with us for just a few short hours before completely losing it. They started to yell and thrash and destroy things around here so we had to throw them out. I don't think they made it on the outside, though. Sorry. Don't know why I'm telling you all this."

"It's okay," she said. "Got to tell someone. Hard to keep in." She coughed. "You didn't take in a young man, short, short hair, unshaven, wearing black, did you?" Joe didn't know where the safe house was, but she thought she'd check anyway in case someone of their party brought him down here from the outside.

"No one that fits that description, no. Friend of yours?"

"His name is Joe and we've been together for the past bit." *Wait.* "Not together-together, I mean, on the run together, watching each other's backs and stuff."

"I see." He looked at her as if she was holding something back, which she was, but it wasn't his business anyway.

"One of the reasons I came here is for arms," she said. "How are we in that department?"

"We have some old stock and a small new one. We salvaged what we could from the old site, but didn't come up with much. Most of it was buried and it's too dangerous to go excavate now. What do you need?"

"Ideally a .9mm, probably two, enough ammo to last me a couple of days, and any walkie-talkies, if you have, so I can keep in touch with the safe house."

"Got the former, I think, but not the latter. Communications in general have been shaky, and had even started to get so prior to the attack on the Hub. Safety first, networking later, and all that."

"Take me to the armory," she said.

"I'll take you to my quarters," he said.

She looked at him crossly.

"It's where the guns are."

"Oh."

16
TWO ROADS

At first it had been tempting to walk to that pack of rotters, hold out his hands and let them take him, but Joe decided not to let his emotions get the best of him and instead swiftly dealt with the undead threat that had come near him.

Now, tired of walking in the dusty air and heading back to the house he shared with Tracy, he tried to think of excuse after excuse as to his leaving again only to come up short every time.

There really is just one choice in all this, he thought. *I got to tell her the truth. She's got to understand or it'll at the very least make sense to her.*

The trek into the city was supposed to have lasted a full day, even two, but instead the round trip would take him about nine hours.

Joe pulled the steak knife from his belt and was near the area of their overturned truck. He wanted to see if he could find the X-09 nearby as Tracy had lost it during the tumble. Keeping his eyes peeled for any walking dead, he adjusted his course and it didn't take long until he was beside the vehicle and checked it over top to bottom. He couldn't see the gun anywhere even after brushing through the debris surrounding the truck.

Did she have it and accidentally dropped it elsewhere? He hoped not because that meant the gun could be anywhere, with *anyone*. He rounded the vehicle again, scanning back and forth beside it for the weapon, double checking.

It wasn't there.

"What, did the zombies take it?" he said with a smirk. Maybe this was a good thing? Maybe it was a sign that it was time to move on, and since the X-09 had been so much a part of himself, it was the first thing that had to go.

Thinking about the gun made him think back to Billie and August, even Des, and how, despite their differences, everything seemed to click with them and they got along. He was happy that their camaraderie wasn't based simply in them all being survivors and having no choice but to work together. There was a chemistry there, each with a role to fill: him with the gun and deadly aim, Billie the brains and attitude, Des comedic relief, and August a father figure and spiritual guide.

REDEMPTION OF THE DEAD

He couldn't wait to see August and Billie again. It'd almost be like old times except for Des being gone.

Feet getting sore, the injury to his side pulsing and stinging, Joe looked forward to getting back and putting his feet up—after talking to Tracy, of course. He hoped she was taking it easy, relaxing on the couch, keeping an eye out through the window for any undead that might be going through the neighborhood. Maybe she even searched out another house or two and found some food. His stomach growled. He couldn't remember the last time he had a proper meal and his half of the can of chickpeas had run its course. He noticed the lack of food having an effect on his energy, and though he felt fine from the neck down, he was tired from the neck up, fatigue hanging over his eyes, his brain given to bouts of fuzziness.

"Sooo thirsty . . . ." *Just go home and relax.* He shook his head. "I mean, just go back to the house and relax. Get a new game plan going. It'll work out." He stopped walking, turned in a circle, checking for zombies, then, seeing none, faced the direction he was going. He was at the corner of Main and the Chief Peguis Trail, the bridge that would take him over to Henderson and right into the Haven. Standing there shouldn't have been as big a deal as it was, but the first thing that came to mind was the image of a forked road.

"Robert Frost," he said. Maybe the old Joseph was closer to the surface than he thought? But if he went down Chief Peguis Trail, he'd definitely be back deep in the undead world he spent so much time fighting.

Him, Billie and Des had left the Haven because the zombies were coming in from downtown and infiltrating the area they had pretty much left alone save for a pocket of them here or there. Joe hadn't checked out the Haven in this world so wasn't sure if it was undergoing the same transition, though judging by the number of undead downtown, maybe the switching of locations hadn't taken place?

"Not going to risk it," he said, ashamed he wouldn't start up the crusade again. *At least not without a gun.* He glanced in the direction of the truck and felt the inner nudge to go back and do one more sweep for the X-09. With his head fuzzy, he mistrusted his own memory of his previous effort to find it.

You got to move on, he told himself. He thought back to his looking for the weapon. *It's not there, let it go, and if it is there, then you're not meant to find it. Maybe on the way back, if I come down this way with Tracy. I don't know, we'll see.*

Joe looked down the Trail one last time then headed down Main as planned, body on edge and ready for any attacker that might come his way.

Over an hour later, Joe arrived on the street with the house, having taken down a few gutmunchers along the way. Satisfied none of the creatures were around as he neared the house, he noticed the SUV was gone. Either she was too, or, maybe she brought it into the garage for safety reasons. He jogged to the door and rang the doorbell. He waited. No answer. He rang the bell again. Same thing. He pounded on the door with the side of his fist, the pain in his wrist igniting in the process. The curtains were all drawn so there was no way to look in.

Maybe she's asleep, he thought, which he didn't have a problem with.

He rounded the back and entered the way they had originally through the kitchen window. The house was quiet.

Joe went to the sink to turn on the water. "Right, not working." He noticed his note on the kitchen table and that the mallet and cleaver were gone. "Uh oh." Quickly, he ran from room to room, even the basement, calling Tracy's name. He turned up empty. "She better not have—"

His side stung and he knew he had to take care of it right away. He attended to it immediately, using the distraction to let his subconscious work out where Tracy might have gone. "Maybe for food?" he said as he looked through the medicine cabinet. He found painkillers and popped four in his mouth, chewed them quick to get them working fast, eyes watering from the awful bitter taste. Man, he needed some water to wash the grit down and his thirst was driving him mad. He didn't find any gauze or dressings for wounds, but did find a bottle of peroxide.

Taking it, he wandered through the house, looking for a sewing machine. He didn't find one and couldn't think of where the people who lived here might have kept any darning supplies, if they had any.

"This is going to suck," he said and went down to the workshop in the basement, found a tube of super glue, then headed to the bathroom where he took his shirt off and checked out the wound. Edges ragged, the wound looked like someone had mashed a piece of cherry pie up against his side then added bits of wet cracker just for good measure. Hopefully it wasn't as bad as it looked.

Joe leaned over the tub, opened up the peroxide, then braced himself for a buttload of pain. He poured the peroxide on the wound. What felt like someone taking a whip to his skin stung the area, causing his insides to lock and quiver. He did it a few more times, each splash worse than the last. Side numb, he was able to dab away the excess peroxide with a towel, then got to work pinching the open flaps of skin together after putting a line of super glue between. He didn't know how safe this was, but he had to keep it closed somehow. As always, the super glue proved strong enough to bind anything together. He checked the gash on his forearm and, after cleaning it, glued it shut as well. Holding a towel to his side, Joe left the bathroom and hit the couch in the front room where he stretched out as much as his side would let him, letting himself ooze into the cushions and take a breather.

He still didn't know what to do about Tracy, and could only pray she was okay.

The short nap was needed, and though Joe hadn't been out for long, it was enough to take the edge off and give him the boost he required to get going again. He checked the house once more, thinking maybe Tracy had returned while he was sleeping and let him rest. She wasn't there and the SUV wasn't in the garage.

"I have no idea where she is," he said. *Smart plan would be to stay put, but she took the SUV* and *the weapons. Is she coming back, even? Should I wait until tonight to see if she returns?* "This sucks."

He decided to wait a short while longer, and if she didn't return, he aimed to go to the only place he could think she might have gone.

The Hub.

ONE YEAR AGO...

The demons had left Hell's great chasm except for those who were commanded to remain with the damned and oversee their suffering.

Bethrez shut down the portal and the magnificent vortex of red, orange and yellow light disappeared, leaving the three in darkness, only the ambient glow of the Lake of Fire their illumination.

Bethrez couldn't help himself but ask: "When will you enter, Master, and oversee the completion of this domination?"

"That is for me to know, Bethrez, not you," he replied.

"I'm sorry."

"Now, leave me, for I have matters to attend to." He touched the portal.

Both Bethrez and Vingros bowed and began to back away when the portal suddenly activated and the vortex came back to life. At the same time, a brilliant white light appeared far into the darkness.

"Go see," Lucifer said.

Immediately, Bethrez and Vingros spread their wings and flew through the dark, heading straight for the white light. Glancing over his shoulder at his creation, Bethrez shuddered at the sight of hordes of demons returning after having just left.

What went wrong? *he wondered.*

"Keep your eyes forward, you fool," Vingros told him.

Bethrez faced front again and kept his eyes on the white light. As it came more into view, a jolt ran through him when he saw Nathaniel, the very angel they had come to capture, flying down toward the floor of Hell. In the angel's glowing light, Bethrez saw a crowd of demons harassing a man who did not belong here, for if he did, he would not still wearing his clothes from Earth.

"How did he—" Before he could finish the question, Vingros had his sword drawn and was heading right for Nathaniel.

Somewhere in the distance, Bethrez heard: "Joe, it's me, Billie! Can you hear me? I can't move, Joe. Help!" He turned around midair and went to investigate the source of the sound, a human voice, a female *human voice.*

As was his habit, he looked over his shoulder and Vingros was already too late; the white fiery trail of the angel was already ascending at extreme speed with the man in tow.

The master is going to be furious, if he finds out, *Bethrez thought,* even though he didn't quite know what to make of it himself. Better return instead.

Returning to the portal and hovering above it, he was dismayed to see that the legions of demons had already come back, but what was this? His master was pressing his hands against the portal, seeming to be feeding his energy into it, manipulating its very size and the sheer illumination of power as exhibited by the red glow and orange and yellow spider webs which were now shooting back and forth across the portal's frame as big and as thick as bolts of lightning.

"Return. Return! RETURN!" *Lucifer shouted.* "After him!"

How does he know Nathaniel was just here? *Bethrez wondered.*

Scores of demons about-faced and re-entered the portal. At first Bethrez thought that by meddling with its size, Lucifer had sabotaged it because the demons did not disappear through the vortex the moment they entered, but went through *it, carrying at trail of the power's overflow with them as they sped off into the dark and after the ascending angelic light of their enemy, which was now a mere pinprick against a mat of black.*

Bethrez stopped midair and reconsidered returning to his creation with the prospect of being reamed out by his master for yet another failed attempt at usurping the power of Heaven. And even if he did explain that it was his master's fault for changing the portal, it would still *be his responsibility and he'd quickly become a disembodied spirit, doomed to wander the Earth until ultimately cast to his doom in the Lake of Fire along with the damned of humanity.*

When the last of the demons went through the portal and disappeared into the dark high above, Bethrez mustered his courage and flew down to his master's side. Landing, he was surprised to find his master laughing.

"Amazing," *Lucifer said.* "I knew I could do all things if permitted, and I am permitted!"

"Master?" *Bethrez said.* "What did you do?" *The words slipped out.*

The devil removed his hands from the portal. It went dark, but retained its size.

Lucifer turned to him. "Do not take me for a fool, Bethrez. You will receive this one warning. You fail to remember that I see things differently than all here, for I was created the most beautiful, the most powerful. You are but a shadow to me!"

Bethrez cowered just as Vingros landed beside him.

"And you," *Lucifer said, storming over to Vingros.* "He was here and you let him get away!" *The devil shot his hand out of the clouds surrounding him and grabbed Vingros by the neck and yanked him into the cloud. From within, Vingros shrieked and was silenced. A small wisp of red floated off the devil's gray cloud and dissipated; Bethrez knew it was Vingros's spirit rising to the Earth where he would remain undetected by his kin until the time came for his sentence to be carried out.*

Bethrez kept his eyes to the floor, not daring to look up after what just happened.

The devil went past him not saying a thing. He didn't have to. The message was clear.

17
CRYSTALS

BILLIE, SVEN AND Bastian stood outside the cottage. Billie said she needed to get some fresh air so the two came with her to keep her company and stand guard. However, air wasn't the real reason she wanted to go to the cottage above. Her bracelet had begun to glow white while she was alongside one of the walls in the large room beneath. If what she was looking for was nearby, it had to be accessed from outside unless they blasted a hole in the wall, which she doubted Isabel or the others would go for.

"Can I walk around the cottage?" she asked Sven.

He looked to his brother, then nodded. The three went to the side; a shed stood on the left side of the cottage about four feet from it. Billie kept an eye on her bracelet; the stone in the center glowed white until she moved around the shed and to its furthest side from the cottage.

"What is that?" Sven asked, pointing toward her bracelet.

"I'm not sure," she said. "To be honest, I'm just learning about it myself." He looked at her like he didn't understand. "I'm sorry. I don't make sense. This bracelet" —she held it up— "is supposed to lead me to something. The problem is, I wasn't told what. All I know was I was supposed to follow it when it glowed white."

"Why would someone give you something without saying how it works?"

"Well, it's from that angel and he's big on the whole discover-for-yourself thing."

Sven lifted his gaze and scanned the area.

Billie walked around to the far side of the shed. The light on the bracelet went out. Turning back, it lit up again and she walked between the shed and the cottage, the light remaining all the while. Around the back of the shed and, like before, once at the farthest side, the light went off.

Between the cottage and shed again, she stayed in that area, moving her wrist about, checking to see the utmost range of where whatever-it-was was supposed to be. After a quick step to the right, the stone turned from white to bright gold, light shining out of it like a fluorescent bulb. The bracelet started to vibrate and rich crimson wafts of energy rose

REDEMPTION OF THE DEAD

from the ground and into the bracelet, striking the middle of the stone. A moment longer and the stone's light was extinguished. She tried to move the bracelet around again to get the white light going once more, but it didn't light up. Upon further inspection, she noticed that a portion of the stone had transformed from its clear state to the same deep red of the energy from the ground, its form in that area like a diamond. The rest of the stone remained smooth.

Not knowing what was going on, all Billie could do was say, "Well, I guess that's it."

"You scary, lady," Bastian told her.

Sven didn't say anything.

Billie, Sven and Bastian had been airlifted via chopper to a small village some ways from the cottage. Billie didn't remember the exact time of the flight, but guessed it to be a good two hours. Isabel had mentioned their contacts at a base in a small town—Billie couldn't remember the name—had radioed in and asked for any news. Isabel told them about Billie's arrival and that she would be sent right away. Confused why she was the one being sent from place to place instead of these bases simply coordinating over the airwaves, she wasn't sure, but knew the answer probably lied in recovering the Divine Fragments.

Now, in a small town that was utterly abandoned by both the living and the dead, Billie, Sven and Bastian touched down in the chopper and waved off a pilot named Jacob, who took the chopper back in the air and left the three there so as not to draw attention to them.

They proceeded to a large brick and wooden structure further into the town proper, each small home she passed a reminder of the devastation the undead caused: broken windows, some houses burned to mere ashy skeletons, others with doors open and blood streaked down the front steps, bodies lying in a heap on the porches of others, the smell thick and sour. At the large building, the three climbed the metal staircase, which led to a tall metal door around a story and a half up. There was a window beside the door and the quick image of a short man in behind the glass wearing a navy blue workman's jumpsuit and matching baseball cap. The man opened the slider on the door, said nothing, then opened the door completely.

"Welcome," the short Asian man said. He waved them in.

"No security?" Billie asked Sven over her shoulder.

"They were expecting us and know what we look like."

Right ahead was a balcony railing which overlooked a large single room with crates, tables, wire mesh booths, tools, army personnel and two helicopters near the warehouse entrance.

Billie furrowed her brow. "Whoa, 'kay, *where* are we? Feels like I'm in some kind of Chinese market."

"Japanese," Sven said.

"But we're not anywhere near Japan." She raised an eyebrow. "Are we?"

He shook his head.

"We try to make good on promise," the Asian man said.

"Promise?" Billie asked.

"What's word I'm looking for? Not 'promise' . . . on delivery. We try and make promise good on delivery."

"Delivery of what?" Would've been nice had Nathaniel briefed her more specifically on where she was going and who she'd be talking to. All she knew was she was supposed to recruit and recover.

"We have weapons," the man said.

Sven held out his hand to the man. "What's your name?"

"Akiyo," the man said and gave a deep nod.

"Sven," he said, pointing to himself, then to her, "Billie." He also introduced Bastian.

"Nice to meet you," Akiyo said, taking Billie's hand in his and shaking it quickly as if he'd been excited to meet her this whole time.

Down below, Japanese chatter floated on the air in a block of sound Billie found intriguing and captivating. She always thought that if she were to learn an exotic language, Japanese or Chinese would top that list.

Sven gave her a nudge, shaking her from her thoughts. Akiyo was further down the walkway, heading to a set of stairs in the corner. Billie, Sven, and Bastian followed and went down the metal, cage-like staircase with him.

"Here we make bomb," Akiyo said.

"Pearl Harbor bomb?" Sven asked.

Billie shot her elbow into his ribs. "Not cool," she quietly muttered to him.

Akiyo didn't seem pleased either. "No, not quite. Would never recreate that which caused us so much pain."

"Oh," Sven said.

She was surprised at Sven's ignorance, but let it go. Who knew what

REDEMPTION OF THE DEAD

kind of education the big man had prior to the zombie uprising?

"We make own bomb. Big bomb," Akiyo said.

"Why make new ones? Can't you scavenge from your old country?"

"Headquarters in lockdown. No infiltration. We tried. After Japanese army fell, emergency procedures set in place so enemies could not steal our technology and use it against us once the war with the monsters was over."

"And you know this how?"

"Cousin was part of system. He made it through first wave of defense, but his squadron fell during the second attack. He and a few others survived. Eventually, we connected. Unfortunately, he died on a raid to get supplies from food chain warehouse. He was good man."

"I'm sorry to hear that," Billie said.

"Yah," said Sven.

Akiyo simply nodded then led them through the main level.

As they walked past the work benches and tables, Billie started to feel a surge of hope finally brewing up within her. She was no military expert by any means—even with the fighting she'd had to do since leaving the Haven—but could see by the number of guns and what appeared to be remote explosive devices that there could be a chance to ending the undead's reign forever. *That's if they don't get all supernatural on us.*

"We have men and women ready. All except for four are inexperienced soldiers and have trained from the ground-up for past five months. We have been coordinating with other underground defense hubs to ascertain proper time and place to attack. So far, we face several options of offense, one being to cover ground piece by piece, territory by territory."

"One of the things I've never understood is why the armies and stuff before didn't just fly over everything and bomb the heck out of the dead?"

"Plan overruled," Sven said. "There were defectors, but I heard story that too many bombs would destroy Earth in process. Easy to just say to wipe them out. Different to do it. People cannot live in sky after bombs go off. Not everyone can find bunker either."

"Believe it or not, there *was* an order during the original attacks," Akiyo said, "and for first time in history, nations aligned with each other to combat common threat. But I also heard some countries had secret agenda and feigned allegiance with others. Part way through attacks, as has been going around, people started fighting amongst themselves and it was essentially World War Three, the zombies only *part* of threat instead of whole thing like they were supposed to be."

Billie crossed her arms, snorted. "Leave it to people to be petty even in an international crisis."

As they strode past more tables, she couldn't help but notice some of the younger Asian women eye Sven up and down.

Whatever.

A large cannon was off to one corner, partly covered in a tarp. It stood at least fifteen feet tall, the unit holding it aloft like a telescope some five feet wide.

"What's that?" Billie said, pointing to it.

Akiyo simply smiled. "Secret weapon number four."

Next to another table, Billie asked him, "What are these?"

"An experimental light cannon. It shoots an extremely bright beam that casts wide range and, though we have to test it, we thought it would blind creatures. It's clear that they see. We just don't know if their eyes function same as ours, but since they were once us, there's good chance their ocular function the same and, if not, then at least similar. If things can't suddenly see, they might just stop and stand there."

"Or lash out while freaking out."

"That, too."

She walked with Akiyo a few more paces when out of the corner of her eye she saw the bracelet light up again.

"Didn't know jewellery could glow like that," he said.

Billie glanced over her shoulder to Sven and Bastian and gave them a nod. Akiyo's feet left the ground as Sven hoisted him up and walked with him to the far side of the room.

"Hey, what's going on? Put me down!" Akiyo said.

"Mouth closed, okay?" Sven said.

Bastian hovered over Billie's shoulder. "Another one?"

"Looks that way."

"Why does it do that?"

"Do what?"

"Make those light things come out of the ground."

"I wish I knew." She also hoped that the energy coming from the ground wasn't from Hell.

She paced with the bracelet in between two tables, one covered with scraps of leather, cloth and work boots. The other bore scraps of metal.

Nearly at the end by the table with the scraps, the bracelet glowed gold and, like before, began to vibrate a soothing massage into her wrist. From the ground, royal blue crackles of energy materialized and floated up into the bracelet's stone. Once done, like before the glow ceased and another portion of it had changed to blue crystal.

"I guess part of this is to fill this thing up," Billie said, "whatever this is."

Around an hour later and conveying the information about the upcoming attacks, Billie Sven, and Bastian bid Akiyo good bye.

A biplane waited for them just outside the town, a woman with incredibly pale skin the pilot. Billie did not want to get on that plane, the woman's skin being the main problem. She thought back to May and Del, who had kidnapped her and August and ended up being shape-shifting undead creatures themselves. Perhaps this new woman was part of a revenge plan? The only reason Billie ended up boarding was because Sven put his big arm around her, squeezed her close, and vowed to protect her if anything happened. It didn't take her trepidation away completely, but it helped.

Billie eyed the pale-skinned pilot the whole trip, expecting at any moment for her to suddenly lash out and try and eat them. Instead, it had been a smooth ride straight through to yet another village, this one only about four streets wide, original population probably around two-hundred-fifty, she guessed.

The woman landed the plane on a nearby field and led them to a cozy-looking country home. Like the others, this one had a secret, too. Billie took Sven's hand and went on in.

The country home yielded not just more tech, but a crystal for her stone like the others, this one green. So did the next three locations they visited. All seemed to have been within a couple hours' flight from each other, give or take. Billie had fallen asleep on the flight to their current drop spot. Took Sven a couple hard nudges to get her awake, he said later.

This plane landed on the roof of an enormous skyscraper. Billie guessed it to be around a hundred stories high.

The two were led by an African American man down the stairwell from the top floor all the way to the bottom. The man cited the elevators contained trapped undead hence the aerobic descent.

"We'll take them out when we take the building out," the man said, "but until then, we have the elevator master controls, thus in a position to unleash the creatures should our security be threatened by those we do not wish to enter here, namely looters and loose cannons."

Once at the basement door, the man—who refused to give a name—opened it and took them into a room with supporting columns throughout.

Billie couldn't believe what she saw.

18
MEET UP

JOE HAD TALKED himself into giving Tracy more time and ended up spending the rest of the afternoon, evening and late-night waiting for her. He checked on his wounds, the glue having dried, enabling him to give them another flush with peroxide. He'd have to save what was left in the bottle, however, as it was now almost out.

Starving, he plopped back down on the couch, the ache of fatigue creeping up along the back of his head.

"Come on," he groaned. He closed his eyes and whispered, "I hope you're okay."

Though tired, he knew he wouldn't be able to sleep. Unless he'd spent a day exerting himself, usually he'd just lie in bed and, when finally exhausted, drift off. He wondered if he should wait until morning and if Tracy didn't come back by then, to head out to the Hub to try and find her.

Or maybe you should go now, he thought.

The soup had been filling, the chunks of veggies something Tracy had missed for the longest time. *Thank goodness for canned goods.*

It was the middle of the night—or thereabouts, she figured—and she grabbed a few Zs after eating to regain her strength after not much of a diet the past while. She hoped Joe was faring all right. If his estimated timeline was to be trusted, he should be back at the house starting tomorrow, the day after if he got delayed. Tracy decided the best course of action would be to go with someone back to the house, then her, Joe and the other person could attempt to raid some of the neighboring homes for supplies before returning to the safe house.

The intel at the safe house wasn't as sophisticated as she had hoped, unlike the Hub. She'd never been here before so didn't know its exact workings. She hoped for a similar structure of folks reporting in, giving info on the goings on outside, their ideas, tactical advice, new finds and all the rest.

Tracy took the time to speak to everyone, give them Joe's description, and ask if they'd seen him. None did, though one cited seeing the body of a man with no hair a couple days back, but Joe had been with her at that time so it was someone else.

As if you should have expected this to go smoothly, she told herself.

Feeling like she was stuck and not liking the idea of having to stay put, she resolved to re-arm then head back out onto the streets and make her way to the house she and Joe "borrowed."

After loading up with a couple .9mm pistols and a belt full of clips, she moved up and down the hallway, considering who she would invite to come along with her. However, she already knew who she was going to pick. The man's name was Felix and he had been one of the people who she asked about Joe. Felix stood at around six and a half feet tall and probably weighed some two hundred and fifty pounds, most of it— judging by the curves in his arms and legs—muscle. When Tracy found him, he was lying on a cot against the corner of a room, reading a book.

"Felix?" she said.

He lay the book down on his chest. His brown hair was thick and layered in mats. His face was a mix of mottled skin, scars, and a healed-over broken cheekbone. "How can I help you, Tracy?" he replied with a sigh.

She put up a hand. "Never mind. Maybe this was a bad idea."

Felix simply nodded and set his eyes back on the book.

"Or," she said, "maybe you can actually stop and talk to someone instead of always acting impatient."

He didn't look up from reading. "Don't act like you know me. We've crossed paths maybe twice in our entire lifetimes. Take your attitude somewhere else."

She rolled her eyes. "Fine." Walking away: "Why do I even bother?"

As she made her way out of the safe house, she did her best to keep her head focused on her own safety instead of dwelling on Felix being such an idiot. To a degree, she couldn't blame him. Though he never told her personally, she caught wind he had come from a large family and one day while they all hid in the basement of the house they shared, some undead had gotten into the above level and, as one thing led to another, the zombies had accidentally set the house on fire. Only Felix escaped, the rest of the family, even some young children, had perished in the flames.

"We've all lost someone," Tracy muttered as she emerged back on the street. One gun at the ready, she moved close to the buildings, eyes always on the search for anything rotten and moving.

Getting back onto Main Street, she moved swiftly in between the cars, keeping out of sight even though right now the streets seemed clear. All it'd take was one gutmuncher to see her and she'd soon have several on her tail.

Makes you wonder if it'd be worth finding a motorcycle, she thought. *Could just rev up and weave in between this mess. Be a heck of a lot faster than always moving on foot. Of course, you got to find the key for that motorcycle . . .*

The lack of the undead made the trek easy and she was already at the Redwood Bridge.

Tracy rounded a stalled ice cream truck and was greeted by a handful of undead roaming between the cars in front of her. Trigger finger ready just in case, she went around the cars on the far right and kept out of sight. No sense picking them off unless she wanted to have a whole swarm of them after her.

The zombie traffic thinned out to next to nothing again and she couldn't help but sense something was wrong. Usually, these journeys were more eventful; not that she wanted to blast zombie heads. The undead numbers seemed very small even compared to when she and Joe had been on their way back to the city before the dust storm. She couldn't help but be suspicious something else was going on.

Yeah, what though? she thought. *Some of the creatures showed a few signs of intelligence, but most are as brain dead as a door knob. You can't tell me they're planning something.* Yet there had been all those ones going the opposite way when they drove in.

Tracy passed a Safeway, all the windows along its front smashed from looters, a couple creatures wandering the trashed aisles within, shopping carts strewn around the parking lot. The Extra Foods right next door looked pretty much the same.

By the time she was by the Tim Horton's, she was itching to just be back at the house, locked in and safe, and ready to catch some shut-eye.

Got a while yet, she thought.

A row of zombies came up from the intersecting street in front of her. She counted off ten of them. There might have been a couple others she missed as the group of zombies were all clumped together in a pack of dead men and women as they shuffled down the road.

All it took was the one on the outside to see her and the whole pack turned and moved toward her, their shuffling footsteps picking up speed at the sudden prospect of a kill.

Tracy raised the gun, but didn't fire. She instead quickly sidestepped to the far left, her eyes always on the target. The zombies moved as one, tracking her movement. She was nearly past them now and almost in a position to make a break for it. In between two cars, she aimed the gun over the roof of one, moving backward, getting distance, when something hard wrapped around her ankle. She looked down to see an undead creature sticking out from beneath a car. Tracy immediately popped a bullet into its head, shook her foot free, then took off around the front of the vehicle.

The zombie horde she'd been tracking had changed position and were much closer to her than expected.

Tracy fired off several rounds, pegging a couple of the creatures, while taking the time to move away. They followed after her. Her gunshots had drawn out others as the street started to fill with the undead. It was like every street running off Main had their own cache of the walking dead and suddenly decided to offload right into her path.

Tracy ran up the end of a Buick and got onto its roof. Taking careful aim, she sent bullet after bullet into the crowd of oncoming zombies. Each shot had to hit paydirt. She hoped that by killing some of them, the others would get the message and move on, but that never happened. They were single-minded killing machines.

Firing off round after round, she frowned when the clip was empty. She reloaded and continued her assault. Many of the undead dropped, while others stepped around or over their kin to get closer to her.

A handful of the creatures were too close for comfort, so she ran down the front of the vehicle, hit the street and ran about a block before getting up onto the cab of an old pickup. Employing the same strategy, she blew the heads off the dead as they got closer. She had to thin them out before she could attempt to outrun them. All it would take was for one to get in her path and grab her. The horde would come in, overpower her in an instant, and take her down.

Loud gunshots came from the direction of downtown and Tracy watched in amazement as numerous zombies in the horde fell down.

She kept up her own efforts, thankful to whoever was helping her. Was it Joe?

He must've found a gun, then, or even found his old one, she thought.

The gunshots rang on, zombies hitting the pavement one after another.

Low *thunks* brought her attention to the front of the pickup. A couple of creatures were climbing up the hood. She took aim and took them out.

Finally, after several minutes of shooting, the undead crowd began to thin enough she felt it safe to get off the truck, run and get some distance.

"Thanks!" she called.

"You're welcome," said a familiar voice from behind.

Tracy turned around. She hadn't heard him approach against all the gunfire.

It was Felix.

"Surprised to see you here," she said, "but thanks."

He simply nodded and the two ran down the street, finally able to get some distance from the undead that stumbled after them.

The gunshots had been far away, but they were close enough to tell Joe he had to be careful. The real question was who was firing. Not many people made it a habit to go out and about and kill zombies.

The pain in his side still sharp and pronounced, he kept moving. The cut on his forearm didn't hurt all that bad.

The smart choice would've been to stay at the house, he thought, but the idea Tracy was out here alone bugged him and he had to make sure she was okay. *If you find her.*

The gunshots had died down about five minutes back. Joe glanced at the McDonald's on his left and suddenly got a craving for a burger. Despite what anyone might say, McDonald's was still one of his favorites. No one made a juicy quarter pounder like they did.

It didn't take long to see where the gunshots came from as Tracy appeared a few sidewalk lengths away, walking with a huge guy he didn't recognize.

Is he why she came downtown? He sighed.

They finally met up.

"It's about freakin' time," Tracy said.

"For what?" Joe said.

"Didn't know where you were."

"Had to take care of something."

"Yeah? Like what?"

Joe glanced at the big guy, then said, "I'll tell you later."

She arched an eyebrow. "Nice cuts."

"Thanks for noticing."

"From your little excursion?"

"I said, I'll tell you later." Joe stuck out his hand toward the big guy. "Name's Joe, Joe Bailey."

The man wrapped his enormous paw around Joe's hand, swallowing it whole. "Felix."

Joe waited to see if the guy would give a last name, but he didn't. "Okay, then," he said and tugged his hand away. To Tracy: "Where were you?"

"Looking for you. Didn't really work out, the way I originally planned. Doesn't matter. Here you are."

"Indeed."

Tracy shifted awkwardly on her feet. "How's the house?"

What? "Um . . . fine." *Is she making chitchat because Felix is here? Time to take control.* "Listen, what's the plan? Should we go back to the house or find somewhere else? The place was empty of supplies anyway."

"Felix and I came from the safe house."

"The what . . . ?"

"Like the Hub, but smaller. They have food there."

"What about the Hub?"

"Destroyed."

"Oh, Tracy, I'm so sorry."

"Me, too."

"So this safe house . . ."

"Only close place we can go."

"Then let's do it."

Tracy headed down the sidewalk, moving back toward downtown. Joe jogged up to her. Felix took up the rear.

"What was the undead situation on your way over?" Joe asked.

"Ran into a patch of them, but Felix and I took care of it."

Joe sighed. "Well, I'm glad you're safe."

"Me, too."

"Sorry for running out on you."

"I'll bet."

"What does that mean?"

"It means you let your own demons get the best of you, that's what it means. I'm not stupid, Joe. You had some things to work out, fine. Next time . . ."

"What?"

She huffed past him. "Don't do it alone."

Joe stopped walking, Felix nearly bumping into him from behind. Tracy was right. His days of going it alone should be over.

19
MIRROR, MIRROR

Billie was still getting used to this place. When the blue door had opened and revealed an enormous room supported by several columns, she wasn't expecting to find an industrial lab complex complete with its own miniature air hanger. People in lab coats bustled to and fro, army personnel did likewise.

The man who had greeted them once they entered the room was named Tony Moore, a thin wiry man with a New Zealand accent. He identified himself as the head of these facilities, but Billie wasn't sure if that was true or not.

"What's that?" had been Sven's question more than once as Tony—*Doctor* Moore, as he preferred to be called—led them on a tour.

It turned out, Dr. Moore explained, the notion of military personnel having been completely wiped out when fighting the undead was a complete fabrication. Whether one constructed by the military themselves or just misinformed hearsay, he didn't say. Regardless, he explained that all over the world secret bunkers were abuzz with activity, with weapons of old being modified to withstand the threat of an enemy that could not die unless by specific means. The difficulty in conquering the undead was in ensuring they could be *completely* wiped out. All it took was one straggler that could infect another and the whole event could start all over again.

Billie understood, but as admirable and important as the work of these scientists and military men were—not to mention turning an underground parkade into a generator-powered near-state-of-the-art facility—they did not know they were going against a threat which went beyond the borders of the earthly realm. Heck, even she was still trying to wrap her head around that. She considered telling Dr. Moore about the angels and demons, but wasn't quite sure how to approach it so decided to wait for the right opening in their conversation.

"And over here we have Jetliers," Moore said, pointing to a row of motorcycles that had flat bottoms more like snowmobiles instead of wheels. Alongside each of the Jetliers was a set of doors that lifted up vertically like a Lamborghini so that once one was inside, they would be completely protected. "Each is armed with a Gatling gun, shot-blasters on the sides—think big, powerful buck shots—as well as heat detectors, cool-body read-outs, and bulletproof glass."

"Sounds impressive," Bastian said.

"It is."

Dr. Moore then led them over past a row of metallic silver weapons, each appearing to be a suped-up version of familiar military firearms: long-range rifles, machine guns, handguns, grenades. Even a bazooka. The handles on each looked to have a slot for one's hands to protect them from bites. All also had long-range scopes, even the handguns.

Billie considered the crystals embedded in the stone on her bracelet and expected there to be one here as well. She still couldn't figure out what they were for.

Dr. Moore took them past a set of doors, and like the other strongholds she and the others had visited, this one extended beyond the regular borders of the building above. As she, Dr. Moore, Sven and Bastian moved down the hallway, a strong sense of unease crept up her spine.

"Where are we going?" Billie asked.

"To the vault," Dr. Moore replied.

"What's in it?"

"You'll see."

She glanced back at Sven and gave him a look she hoped read: *I don't like the sound of that.*

At the end of the hallway was a single door, which Dr. Moore opened after using a key. The room was dark. Billie and the others stood outside the doorway.

"There's no way I'm going in there," she said.

"Why not?"

"Turn the lights on and we'll talk."

Dr. Moore frowned, then reached inside the door and flicked a switch. The lights flickered on, revealing a plain room with light gray walls, a large set of gray blinds on each except for the wall with the door, an eight-foot table in the middle, a chair on each side.

Dr. Moore gestured to the chairs. "Come, sit."

Billie eyed him quizzically then entered, Sven and Bastian behind her. They each grabbed a spot at the table; Billie was thankful to sit down after being on her feet most of the day.

Dr. Moore stood at the door to the room, looking past the doorframe as if talking to someone just outside it. Billie didn't know who could possibly be there as no one had been there when they first came

REDEMPTION OF THE DEAD

down the hallway, and the walls on each side didn't bear any doors.

"Something's not right," Billie said.

"What?" asked Sven.

She got up from the table and started toward the door. Dr. Moore gave her a quick glance, smiled, then closed the door. She ran up to it, turned the knob and pulled. Locked.

"Hey!" she shouted and smacked the door with an open-palm.

Behind her the chairs scraped along the floor as the two men got out from their seats.

"Open up!" she said, hitting the door again. She pulled and pulled on the door, but to no avail.

Sven put a hand on her shoulder and gave her a gentle push back to give him some room. "Open the door!" he bellowed and smacked it with the side of his fist.

Bastian pulled and tugged on the door knob. "Nothing."

Sven tried the doorknob, too, with the same result.

The two men kicked and beat at it until they turned away, sweating and panting, realizing there was no use.

Billie could only look at them with puzzlement.

What the heck was going on?

Over an hour passed. The trio sat around the table. Billie rested her head in her hand. Sven and Bastian each had their arms folded and heads down on the table. Every so often Sven let out a huge snore; for some reason She found it cute.

How long were they going to stay here? What was the point of coming here only to be locked up in a room?

Her stomach growled and she looked forward to having another taste of Sven's cooking. The big man let out another loud snore.

The sudden snap of the blinds on the three walls as they shot up gave Billie a jolt. She jerked against the table, the quick movement rousing Sven and Bastian. Heart racing, she saw the three walls each held a large mirror beneath the blinds. All three of them were on the alert, each looking at a separate mirror.

Whispers rose on the air, foreign whispers, a smooth rhythmic language. After a couple phrases, Billie recognized it was the same language that hovered on the air during the Storm of Skulls.

"We got to get out of here NOW!" Billie jumped over the table and ran to the door. She kicked it and pounded it with all her might. "No!"

Sven came up behind and put a hand on her shoulder. "What? Why?"

She spun around to face him. "Don't you hear that?"

"I hear it, but I don't know what it means?"

"It's a trap! We're in a trap!"

Finally, Bastian shot up from the table and came over to them. "Trap? What kind of trap? Are we going to die?"

Billie pressed her lips together, debating whether she should tell him the truth, that unless they acted, yes, they were going to die.

Sven gently nudged Billie aside and with a nod to his brother, he and Bastian went to work banging on the door and looking for a way to take it down. Billie knew that if the door was supernaturally sealed, their efforts would be useless.

The voices on the air rose in volume. She slowly turned around and her breath caught in her throat when she saw in the mirror opposite the door that her, Sven's and Bastian's reflections were gone.

"Uh . . . guys . . ." She didn't think they heard her above their thunderous thuds against the door.

She checked the other two mirrors. The one on the right bore the same thing, but the one on the left took her by surprise. Her visage in the mirror had changed. She was no longer the young, happy-go-lucky computer nerd she once was. Instead, a woman stood by Sven and Bastian, a tall woman with long, spindly limbs, pale translucent skin, sunken cheeks bones and dark eyes. Her hair was pale ginger, long and scraggly, hanging well past her waist. The woman's clothes were in tatters, mere ribbons of what must have been at one point a beautiful golden gown.

Trembling, she reached for Sven, tugging on his arm, the woman in the mirror copying her movement. He spun around and backhanded her, sending her across the room.

Billie lay on the floor, shaking, her face throbbing from the impact, her nose alight with fiery pain. He must've broke it.

Sven stormed over to her. "Where is she!"

"Where's—Sven, it's me. It's Billie!"

"Liar!"

He picked her up and slammed her down on the table. The shock of the impact rattled every bone in her body, dazing her. Sven leaned over her, eyeing her with such hate she didn't know if he was even who she thought he was. Perhaps he was one of the shape-shifting zombies and this whole thing had been a ruse, right from the cottage all the way through to this place. Had Nathaniel simply sent her off to die? Or had the angel been deceived and thought he had put her on a special assignment which, in reality, was devised by Hell?

REDEMPTION OF THE DEAD

Eyes watering, Billie said, "Please, Sven . . . don't . . ."

Sven cocked his fist. "Don't say my—" He looked forward to somewhere past her, maybe at the mirror across the way, and his expression went from raging mad to one of sheer shock and terror. He immediately collapsed beside the table and started retching on all fours. Bastian ran to his side only to be shoved away.

Sven got to his feet and began stumbling around the room, tearing out clumps of his gorgeous blond hair, ripping his outfit. Bastian shouted at him in German though Billie didn't understand the words except "dummkopf," which basically meant "stupid person."

Bastian once more tried to console his brother only to receive a violent kick to the groin that immediately sent Bastian to his knees. Now kneeling before another mirror, Bastian's body began to quake and Billie could only assume he saw himself in another way, too.

"Oh no . . ." she groaned.

Bastian shakily got to his feet and ran at the mirror. He crashed into it, the mirror cracking. Right after, he braced himself against it with both palms and started hitting his head into the mirror, sending out shards of it streaked with his blood.

"Bastian, stop!" Billie screamed, then bit back her tongue, thinking maybe he'd suddenly turn on her and assault her like her brother did.

Sven.

He paced back and forth near the corner of the room, arms outspread, screaming and cursing, occasionally taking swings at an opponent that wasn't there.

Billie tried to get off the table. The moment she raised her head, a bolt of nausea punched her in the stomach and she had to put her head down on her arm for a moment before trying again. Summoning her strength, she slowly rose up and was able to sit on the table. She deliberately kept her eyes off the mirror, only aware of the mirrors in her peripheral.

It's the mirrors that are messing up Sven and his brother because they keep looking at them. I don't want to see that woman I saw again, whoever she is. Oh no! Is it me? Maybe even the real me? She shook her head. *No, don't let them play mind games with you. Stay focused. You've been in deadly situations before. Keep a level head like Joe does. It's the only reason we lasted as long as we did. Is he okay? Oh, Joe, don't be dead.* She shoved the thought from her mind. *Mirrors. Mirrors, mirrors, mirrors.*

Billie hopped off the table, keeping her head bowed. She grabbed the nearest chair and took it to the mirror on her right. The first blow sent a

119

spider web across it. The second turned the spider web into a mosaic. The third shattered the mirror, the pieces falling off the wall, revealing glowing occult symbols underneath.

Ignoring the sudden rush of evil that permeated her being, she cautiously approached the mirror near Sven.

Please don't lash out, please don't lash out. Deciding to move and hit as hard and as fast as she could, she raised the chair and quickly smashed it into the mirror. Sven roared. She got in a second shot. Sven turned toward her, feral. Billie threw the chair again against the mirror, bringing it down, revealing similar glowing symbols on the wall beneath.

Bastian. Where was Bastian?

He came in from the side and took her to the ground.

"No!" she shrieked.

Bastian had his hands around her throat, his eyes coated over in black, reminding her of purple olives. Snarling, he squeezed, the pressure on her throat throwing her body into a panic.

Something shattered by her. Another crash followed by another, then a deep, hoarse roar. Sven flew in from the side, tackling his brother and getting him off her. He beat down on his brother without restraint, shouting at him in German.

Coughing, Billie rolled on her side, reached her hand out toward Sven. "St—stop . . ."

He struck Bastian again.

"Stop . . . Sven . . . stop . . ."

Panting and sweating, Sven finally let up, leaving his brother rolling beneath him, moaning with his hands to his face. Sven looked at her with sad eyes, then got up and went to the other side of the room.

Billie lay on the ground, catching her breath. *Oh God, have mercy.* She managed to slow her breathing enough so she could get up and start pacing, walking off some of the dizziness and sore limbs. Her nose still hurt like all get out and for a brief second she wanted a mirror to check it, then was quickly thankful there was none.

The room went dark; the glowing symbols on the wall increased their brightness. Soon the haunting colors of red and orange filled the room, reminding her of a photo lab. The voices resumed their chant on the air. The strong, disturbing power of evil dripped off the walls, causing her to shudder without meaning to.

It wasn't over.

20
HONESTY

THE TREK BACK to the safe house had only grown busy every twenty minutes or so, with a pack of the undead emerging from behind corners and back lots. Joe, Tracy and Felix took them down with ease, and despite her bumps with Felix in the past, Tracy noticed the three of them had a certain chemistry that seemed to work when taking on the undead.

Now below ground in the safe house, Felix went back to his book, leaving Joe and Tracy alone by the kitchenette. As Joe fixed himself something to eat—more than once saying how hungry he was and even a lame joke about there better not be any chickpeas around—Tracy simply watched him, wondering what their next move was, both professionally and personally.

Joe pieced together a small meal of canned corn, tuna and a pack of Raman noodles, which he didn't bother adding water to but instead simply sprinkled the seasoning on—chicken—and ate them like a bag of chips. He washed it down with a glass of water.

The two sat on opposite sides of the table, Tracy eyeing him with squinted eyes, already upset at him for being so preoccupied with his food that it served him as a good excuse to not immediately start talking. Joe kept his eyes to his plate, shoveling the food into his mouth then seemingly to consciously slow down as if trying to prolong his meal.

Just. Eat. The. Stupid. Food, Tracy thought, trying to project her thoughts across the table into Joe's head.

He just ate and drank, her "telepathic powers" not making a dent. When he finally finished, he sat back, arms folded across his belly, and let out a suppressed burp. "Sorry." It was only then since he first sat down did he raise his eyes to hers. The two stared at each other a long moment; she was fully aware he didn't want to be the one to break the ice because neither did she.

She crossed her arms and took a deep breath, prolonging the exhale, buying herself as much time as possible. *Fine. I'll do it.* "So?" she said just as Joe opened his mouth as if to say the same thing.

"Um . . ."

"What, were you going to say something?"

"No."

121

She arched an eyebrow.

"I mean, yes, I was, but you spoke first so go."

"I spoke first because you were just sitting there."

"Sorry for eating."

"You should be."

"What does that mean?"

She shook her head. "Never mind."

He glanced to the side, sighed, then said, "Look, I'm sorry, all right?"

Now we're getting somewhere. She stared at him, hoping to give the impression she was expecting him to say more.

Joe leaned forward and put his elbows on the table. Maybe she *was* telepathic?

He peered up at her with sincere eyes. "I'm sorry." He paused. "I'm sorry for leaving the house when I shouldn't have. You were right. I had some stuff to work out."

She kept her voice soft. "I know."

"You do, too, you know?" he said.

"Don't. This isn't about me right now. There'll be time for that later."

Joe waited a moment before speaking. "I had to go see if April was still alive."

Tracy's eyes widened at this. Though it was what she'd thought he was doing, to actually hear it was something different and she felt ashamed that it bothered her.

"I had to make sure. I went to her apartment, or at least where it was in my world. At that apartment, she didn't live there. I know this because the place had pictures of a completely different family. I mean, she" —he swallowed— "she could've maybe married someone and went by that name. I don't know. It'd be impossible to find out. I didn't see a single living soul out there, which makes it very, very clear that whoever's here in this place" —he glanced around, gesturing to the safe house— "are the very few who are left. I didn't see April at the Hub. She's not here. I even looked when we got back." He sighed. "I just had to know. I had to try."

It was hard to hear, but it was something she had to take in. She and Joe had talked about their exes in the past, but never got it out in the open that the pain and longing were still oh so real. His story confirmed it.

Joe nervously tapped his fingers on the table. He looked like he wanted to say something, but was too scared to.

REDEMPTION OF THE DEAD

Tracy reached across the table and grabbed his hand, folding it in both of hers. She looked into his eyes. "I'm sorry for being so mad at you. I was being selfish."

"No, you weren't—"

"Yes, I was. I was so selfish that I'm . . . I'm jealous."

His expression changed, slightly surprised.

She smiled a little. "You know that I understand where you're coming from. I understand that pain and what it's like to have a hopeful future ripped away from you, one that even goes beyond what happened to the world, to suddenly go from being at the threshold of heaven to being in the pit of hell. I thought maybe—"

"Tracy, I'm scared to death."

"Scared?"

"My whole life since losing April, first in my world simply on the day she left me that one weekend, to finding her as one of the creatures and killing her myself, to coming here and thinking maybe, just maybe, she was out there, that hope—I'm used to hiding, to keeping everyone else in the dark while keeping April in the light of my heart. Laying it flat out before you, Tracy, I miss her like crazy."

She winced at hearing that, but understood completely and her heart went out to him.

"And I've been so focused on her that it's wrecked so many things. To even possibly have a life—what I mean is, I" —he paused, licked his lips— "I met you and for the first time, that hope of a future returned, that amazing hope that seemed forever lost had returned."

She couldn't help but let her eyes water at hearing that. She gave his hand a gentle squeeze.

"Somewhere along the way, you got to me, inside, where it counts. A part of me wishes I told you sooner, but I'm also glad that I had a chance to confirm some things, check things through, settle something."

"Is it settled?"

"I'd be lying if I said yes."

"Oh."

"But I'd be telling the truth when I say that even if I find out she's alive, even if I talked to her, when all is said and done—I'd want to come home to you, if you'd let me."

Tracy withdrew her hands and brought them to her face. The tears poured out, overpowering emotions of gentleness, kindness and relief consuming her. Inside, her heart ached but not for hurt. It ached for him, for his pain that she shared because of Josh, the boy her future had once rested upon, for the fearful thought of letting herself fall into Joe's arms and run the risk of losing him to someone she had never even met despite what he just said—to the amazing and comforting peace that came with those same words. Though she refused to say it now, she knew that she loved him.

Gentle hands came around her shoulders then moved to her wrists to remove her hands from her face. She was embarrassed to look up at him with red eyes and tear-stained cheeks, but by the way he looked at her, she was comforted knowing that he didn't care.

Joe took her by the hands and brought her to her feet so they stood in front of each other. Oh so softly, he reached up and cupped her face in his hands all the while looking deep into her eyes. With gentle strokes of his thumb, he wiped her tears away, then pulled her in and kissed her.

ONE YEAR AGO...

Lucifer sat on his throne of stones and worms amidst the platform amidst the Lake of Fire. Though he could place his throne wherever pleased in Hell, it was here that brought him the most satisfaction for it was the screams of those he deceived that filled the pit. Each shriek of pain and terror the damned emitted was a pleasure and a reminder of victory against the One he swore war against. Now, with the portal having served its purpose, an ultimate final victory was assured.

The devil had known his minions would traverse the portal twice. It was inevitable for the One above always had a contingency plan. When the demons first went through, no doubt they thought all would go smoothly in the Earthly realm. Transforming to a downpour, the evil spirits were able to rain upon mankind and possess every soul that came in contact with it. Only those indoors or remained completely untouched by the rain were not taken over, but to do so would be easy as each spirit had the ability to infect another. Despite not being able to leave the body they possessed nor divide itself in two . . . the demon still retained influence over those they infected, depositing a little bit of their power into the ones they bit. Not all the infected would be as strong or stable as the others as a result, but the ability to encompass the globe in darkness would be achieved.

When the demons returned through the portal, they came right after their departure for in Hell there is no Time, only a single moment. This realm like its counterpart existed outside what was perceived as Time. Only when a demon or even the devil himself visited the Earth did the awareness of Time surface.

One of the demons—Forthinus—reported the angel Nathaniel was on his way to Hell to rescue a human who had fallen through the Earth to the realm beneath. Nathaniel had been gifted with foresight and long-range vision. He no doubt had witnessed the portal in use and thus would be able to recruit those among both angel and men who could counter their attack. The only choice was to return, re-enter, give an infusion of some of the devil's power into the portal itself, affecting all going through, transforming them into something stronger, and for some of his devotees, something larger.

Nathaniel wouldn't risk bringing the host of angelic warriors down to Hell to do battle and thus leave the Earth unprotected. Sure, those believers in the One above would survive, but those whom the angels had an interest in outside of those believers would be left wide open for immediate attack. What Nathaniel didn't know, was whether they were there or not, a mass possession was inevitable. It would happen too fast for them to counter and so they would be at a loss.

In time—Earth Time—Lucifer would step through a portal himself, a different portal, the one created the day he fell like lightning from Heaven.

21
THE LIE

The zombie horde led by Dr. Moore poured into the room, at least a dozen undead.

"Kill them," was all Dr. Moore said, gesturing to Billie, Sven and Bastian. The doctor's face distorted and turned dark gray, his hair falling off in patches, his clothes growing baggy and filthy, hanging off a loose, skeletal frame.

With arms raised, the doctor led the charge against Billie and her friends. The two German brothers immediately went to work taking on the dead hand-to-hand, breaking necks when possible.

Billie grabbed one of the chairs from off the floor and swung it at the doctor. Dr. Moore managed to weave his arm in and around the legs, locking it in place then yanking the chair away from her. He reached out to grab her. Billie ducked and rolled along the floor, then stood with a long shard of broken mirror in her hand. Even just touching the mirror and knowing the evil it showcased made her cringe, but she didn't have a choice.

Dr. Moore moved in; she lunged forward and jabbed the shard of mirror into the side of the doctor's neck, creating a geyser of smelly, black blood.

She heard Sven and Bastian's shouts and grunts of combat as they fought the creatures. Out of the corner of her eye she noticed Sven had picked up a shard of mirror, too, his even longer and more jagged than hers. She wasn't sure what Bastian was using for a weapon and it was difficult to see with all the bodies in the room.

Dr. Moore grabbed hold of her by the shoulders and lifted her off her feet. Quickly, Billie jerked out the shard sticking out of the doctor's neck and brought it down into his mouth just as he opened it in a moaning shriek. The shard penetrated through the back of the doctor's throat, popping through on the other side. Billie drew up her legs and kicked against the doctor's chest, releasing his grip and sending herself flying backward in the air, then landing hard on the floor. The back of her skull hit the ground on impact and stars danced before her vision. A big hand reached down and grabbed her by the middle of her shirt, lifting her to her feet. She shrieked, thinking it was one of the creatures, but was relieved to see it was Sven at her side.

REDEMPTION OF THE DEAD

Four more zombies remained.

Sven pounced at the nearest one, using his heavy weight to knock the creature straight over and drive the long shard of mirror through its skull. Another two came at Bastian, who dispatched the most rotten of the two by getting behind it and ripping its head from its body. The other he took out by kicking it to the floor then jumping high up and landing on its head, crushing its skull.

The final zombie stood there swaying as if not knowing what to do. Trying to ignore the headache setting in, Billie again went for the chair, picked it up, and brought it down across the creature's back, sending the thing to the ground. Once it lay there, she aimed her shot, used the chair leg like a spear and drove it down into the back of the creature's skull like a javelin finding its mark.

The three stood panting; Billie's nose was bleeding again so she pulled up the collar of her shirt, pinched it off and leaned her head back, not caring her middle was showing.

"Too many dead people," Bastian said.

"Yah," said Sven.

Billie sneezed, getting a spatter of blood all over her hands and inside her shirt. Embarrassed, she adjusted her makeshift tissue and pinched her nose even harder.

Sven was at her side, and she turned away so he couldn't see her in this state. He didn't say anything.

Taking the lead, Billie started toward the door, this time her head bowed and looking forward for any sign of more creatures.

Bodies shuffled behind her. She turned around and Dr. Moore was back on his feet. Snarling, Sven dove on top of the doctor and with his palm further slammed the shard of mirror through Dr. Moore's throat. He then took his own makeshift blade and brought down into the doctor's eye. The undead doctor stopped twitching.

Sven and Bastian joined Billie by the door and the three proceeded down the hallway.

"We need weapons, real weapons," Sven said.

"Yah," Bastian said.

Billie caught herself saying "Yah," too, and felt like a goon.

The three continued down the hallway, guard up.

"It doesn't make sense," Billie said.

Sven said, "Mm hm."

Having been in a similar situation before with August back when they had been taken to what they thought was a stronghold in a forest, but turned out to be a den of zombies, she cursed herself for not being more careful when it came to trusting anyone, even Sven or Bastian or Isabel. They could still be part of some great deception that would be hatched in its own time. She suddenly felt uneasy about her companions.

Keeping her voice to a whisper, she said, "Stop." The two men obeyed. "Keep an eye out, but we need a plan. We also just got thrown for a major loop."

"Thrown for loop?" Bastian asked, clearly not understanding the metaphor.

"We thought we were experiencing one thing with a certain kind of people then it turned out that wasn't the case."

"Ah."

"Let's talk this out: why would a zombie doctor take us through a storehouse filled with weapons that are meant to fight the undead, actually show us these things and explain them, then take us to a room and nearly kill us?"

The two men—always so alike—kept their eyes to the ground, the mental wheels turning.

"The guy at the beginning, the elevators of zombies so we had to take the stairs, the walk-through, weapons—The mirror! Opposites. That's it. Yes!" Billie hopped on her toes then had to quickly stop when her nose lit with a fresh blast of pain. "Ow."

"What did you think?" Sven asked.

"Okay, here's what I'm thinking—obviously they were trying to kill us. That just happened, but somehow they knew we were coming, so either they have really good intel or someone told them."

"What's 'intel'?"

"Just let me finish."

Sven closed his mouth.

To herself: "It can't be that easy, can it?" To the others: "If everyone we encountered were actually shape shifters, they are either brilliant shape-shifting zombies that can create amazing tech for war, *or* they came here and took the place of those who had."

"I don't understand words," Bastian said.

"We didn't use the elevators for a reason and clearly this place has power running via generators so the elevators could have easily worked. The guy that led us down here said there were zombies in the elevators. I'm thinking not. I'm thinking the contents of the elevators were concealed from us because they contain people, real people."

"People?"

REDEMPTION OF THE DEAD

"Yah," she said, this time with a wink. Sven grinned. "Here's what we do."

After she gave them the run-down of what she was thinking, the three headed toward the main room. Billie eyed the Jetliers as she walked past them and she noticed Sven do the same.

Concealing themselves behind desks and worktables so as not to be seen by any of the dead, she led the other two to the wall of gleaming metal weapons.

"Take one," she whispered.

The German boys grinned. Sven took the rifle, Bastian the machine gun. Billie grabbed a couple of handguns and a few grenades. She put the guns behind her back in the waistband and stuffed her pockets with the grenades while keeping the other gun at the ready.

Joe would have a field day with this, she thought. She hoped she would see him again and soon.

Now armed, the three moved through the room. A few of the undead milled about, a couple of them completely lost in their own zoned-out world. They were quickly dropped before a handful of others appeared and headed toward Billie and her friends.

The two German boys made quick work of sending the creatures to the ground.

"Stay ready," she said, still pinching her nose, making her voice come out nasally. "Any more out there will come as they would've heard the shots."

The three moved throughout the rest of the floor, taking out anything rotten that appeared in their way.

As they turned the corner which, according to the sign on the wall would lead to the elevators, they stopped when a row of feral-looking undead stood before them. Not wasting any time, Billie raised her gun and shot two in the head, the tops of their skulls bursting from the impact. Sven held up the rifle, expertly balanced it, and fire off a round of his own, dropping another. The creatures came forward and began crowding in on them. Sven used the butt of the rifle to smash open the head of one, while Bastian used the machine gun to cut through at least a half dozen of them on the right. Heads shot to pieces, the undead fell. Bastian turned his attention toward Billie and Sven.

"Be careful!" Billie shouted, referring to him firing that machine gun, but she wasn't sure if he understood the intent.

Rapid shots rang out, their thundering sound echoing inside the small space. Broken bits of floor and ceiling shot through the air every time a

129

stray bullet hit them. Two zombies honed in on Billie and were nearly right up against her, reaching out to take a firm hold. She popped one in the face and the other in the forehead. The creatures hit the ground and she did the same thing to the two behind.

Sven fired, a zombie fell; he took aim, fired again, another one fell; over and over. The guy was good, precise.

Billie had a half-second moment of "That's my man," before dismissing the notion and popping another couple of bullets into the face of an old walking dead guy.

The ring of fired bullets echoed on the air as the three stood with weapons poised amongst a pile of rotting dead bodies. The room was clear.

"Sven," Billie said, thumbing toward the elevator door. He came over, tried the elevator controls and when those didn't work, he motioned to Bastian and said something in German. The two got to work trying to pry the elevator doors open.

Billie looked around, trying to find something to use as a pry. Not finding one, she told the boys she'd be back in a minute and returned into the weapons room. She scanned the room, the floor, the desks. To the right, a zombie shambled toward her. She shot it in the head then went back to looking. With all the excitement, she forgot about her nose and hadn't kept the collar of her shirt in place. She was relieved the bleeding had stopped though it still hurt like the dickens when she touched it; she didn't care about her shirt being covered in blood.

After checking a couple more worktables, she found a large heavy pry bar and quickly brought it to Sven. The big man had got the door open a few inches, but judging by the deep purple grooves on his palms, it hadn't been easy work.

"Here," she said and handed him the pry bar.

"Danke." He took it and jammed it in between the doors and pried it open, the metal doors releasing a profound screech on their tracks.

The elevator shaft was empty save for the cabling which took the car up and down the building. Billie peered in and got a clear view to the shaft beside it; that car wasn't there either.

"We need to find out what floor they're stuck on. You guys don't have a flashlight, by chance, do you?"

The boys shook their heads.

"Okay, back to the other room and let's get looking. We need to know what's in those elevators even if it turns out they're empty, but if there is someone in there who can help us, it's worth risking our lives for."

22
ROOFTOP GATHERING

Joe and Tracy lay together on a cot in one of the small rooms, his arms wrapped around her, her body snug against his, her legs around him.

He wasn't sure if she was asleep, but kissed the top of her head anyway. He thought he felt her smile when her cheek shifted against his chest.

Things didn't progress any further than the kitchen and the two lay clothed on the cot minus their weapons and boots. They just wanted to lie there together, comforted, safe, a year's worth of pain finally melting away.

Joe remembered that April and him had done the same thing the night she stayed over at his place. There was something profound about just sleeping next to someone instead of it always being about sex. To his surprise, the memory of once doing this with April didn't bother him and instead just became a highlight of his past and nothing more. Was it possible it was finally over? Had he actually moved on? He hoped he had and gave Tracy another squeeze. She squeezed him back.

So she is awake. "How long do you want to sleep for?" he asked.

She shrugged. "At least four or five hours for sure. Be amazing if we can get in seven or eight, but I'm not used to sleeping that long unless I completely crash."

"Me neither."

"What do you want to do when we get up?"

"Well, how about have something to eat, get cleaned up a bit, then take it from there?"

She sighed. "I feel the same way. A part of me would be fine just staying in now instead of getting out there hunting."

"Me, too. It's like I just simply need to take a break, a *real* break."

After a few seconds, she said, "The thing is we know we can't. We are still going to need to do some scavenging, remain on the alert. It's so dangerous out there and given what happened at the Hub, I don't want the same thing to happen here. Would feel like if I left them—not saying we need to go somewhere else, just saying in general—that I'd be betraying them. There's few of us left and if we separate, unless we align with a new group of survivors, we won't have any hope."

"No, you're right. At one point, sure, maybe we can look at going somewhere or even—just mentioning it—we might be able to actually find someplace for us, someplace nice, maybe even a place that's normal. But, yeah, we need to stay put. In the city, I mean. I know that I have to stay because of . . . of Billie and August. They'll come back here looking for me, which means I have to be here. They have no idea what this version of Winnipeg is like as they were taken pretty much when we arrived. Unless they're already back and trying to find me, they don't know what to expect."

"They're from your world, I understand," she said.

The two remained quiet for a moment, then Joe said, "Thanks for being here with me tonight, Tracy. This means everything to me."

She hugged him tight. "Yeah, me, too. Feels so good to be in your arms." She looked up at him, eyes hopeful.

He brought his lips to hers and kissed her ever so gently and as affectionately as he possibly could. Unable to pull away, he leaned in further, the angle slightly uncomfortable. Tracy must have sensed it because she adjusted herself and came on top of him, pressing her lips hard against his, pulling him so close and so tight he could barely breathe.

He didn't care.

Tracy.

He was so lost in her touch, when Felix shouted into the room, it caused him to grab her by the shoulders and swiftly role her off him as if getting caught by a parent.

"What?" Tracy asked, running a hand through her hair.

Hope this doesn't turn into anything, Joe thought. Sure, Felix had been with Tracy when he met them on the road, but there wasn't—rather, *hadn't*—been anything between them so far as he knew.

"Something's not right outside," Felix said.

Joe's heart sank with relief.

"What is it?" Tracy said.

"The creatures. One of the scouts came in and said the giants are forming rank and the smaller ones are doing the same."

"Forming rank?" Joe said.

"Some sort of aligning of themselves, not in straight lines like soldiers, but not in a big mob either. They seem to be making a precise formation but until we can get a look from the air, there's no way to tell what it is, if anything at all."

"Am I supposed to do something?" Tracy asked.

"You're being called to the fore. You know why. Get yourselves together and we'll go upstairs." Felix left.

Tracy sat on the edge of the cot and rubbed her face.

"Why do they need you up there?" Joe asked.

"I'm a good shot, and they value my assessment of the creatures given all my time out on the field."

"I'm going with you."

She smiled and gave him a peck on the lips. "You better."

After getting their gear together and a quick bathroom break, she led him to the back corner of the safe house. There was a single red cubicle divider adjacent to another wall with a matching red door.

"Didn't see this earlier," Joe said, nodding toward the door.

"Usually it's covered with this thing." She gave a quick kick to the cubicle wall. She pulled out her keys and unlocked the door, which led to a hallway. Tracy fired up the flashlight; her and Joe entered. "This is an emergency exit-slash-roof access passageway we created when this place came down. The building underneath has collapsed, but those who built this place—so the story goes—adjusted the rubble above and between layering slabs of concrete on an angle and building a similarly-angled passageway beneath, it's given us access to the roof of the building beside it, which also has a fire escape."

"Just in case the safe house gets infiltrated."

"Exactly. Despite the fights and arguments that sometimes broke out at the Hub, one thing everyone could agree on was safety and contingency plans to ensure that."

Joe thought of the safe house being invaded by the giant undead and wondered if they'd had a contingency plan for that. He wouldn't ask Tracy, though, at least not right now lest he struck a nerve.

At the end of the hallway there was a left turn that led to a series of plywood slats that lined another hallway, but this one was clearly makeshift given how uneven the floor was and how the walls seemed to angle in or out at times instead of standing straight. The hallway was short, which made the climb steep. His foot slipped.

"Watch it," Tracy said. "It was built that way on purpose. People can figure out how to climb up something, takes the undead longer."

At the top was a door and again she produced her keys, put the flashlight in her mouth, and shone it at the knob as she unlocked it.

"Certainly a lot of keys," Joe said.

She took the flashlight from her mouth. "Can't leave doors open if you're on the escape."

Tracy turned the knob and opened the door. A handful of people were on the roof. Quickly, a man with gray hair came over to her.

"Joe, this is Dean," Tracy said.

Joe shook the man's hand.

Dean led her by the arm to the ledge; Joe followed, surprised at his jealousy of seeing another man touch what he supposed he should start calling his girlfriend.

Joe came to the ledge and looked out. Most of downtown was in shambles, with several of the buildings crumbled into heaps, others standing partially erect, partially demolished. The damage in this world was much worse than that of his own.

Felix had been right, however. At least a half dozen streets over, the giant undead had gathered together and stood side-by-side. The regular-sized zombies roamed the streets below, coming in from all directions and heading toward their giant counterparts. Joe eyed them intently, trying to discern between the ones already lined up in the distance and the ones approaching and the direction they were travelling.

"The scout that reported this—you know Dale—also reported he had been no more than five feet from one of the rotters and the creature just looked at him then continued on its way."

"Either something was wrong with that zombie or it knew exactly what it was doing," Tracy said.

"They don't think," Joe said, "but they do seem to have an understanding of their role, of what they do. Maybe even *why* they do it, for all we know. I've never known a zombie to pass up a meal unless it was physically incapable of attaining it, and even then . . . I don't know what's scarier."

The two eyed the walking deceased in the distance. Thanks to some of the buildings having been leveled, it made line-of-sight much easier to watch the creatures. From what Joe could see, the things streamed forward to the giants' feet then, as if hitting an invisible wall, spread out lengthwise. Others came in behind those zombies and did the same, but Felix was right in saying they weren't forming perfect lines.

"The only unusual behavior I've witnessed was," Joe said, putting Tracy's and Dean's attention on him, "where I come from, they move en masse from one area to another, actually emptying the place they just left." He couldn't help but wonder if his world was still living on somehow and if the undead had now completely overrun the Haven and downtown had become the safe zone. He supposed he'd never know.

"Where was this?" Dean asked.

Tracy covered for him and said, "How long has this been going on,

REDEMPTION OF THE DEAD

this formation of the dead?"

Dean thought for a moment. "Dale came in not long ago, like twenty minutes, but he said he'd been observing it for over an hour."

"Have the creatures ever exhibited any behavior like this before?" Joe asked.

"No," Tracy said, "nothing he would be considered 'out of the ordinary' for them. There's a strategy here."

"That's impossible," Dean said, "those creatures can't think."

"Apparently they can," Joe said, "but not the way you and I do. Their behavior both where I come from, and here, shows very clearly they are aware of what they are doing. They might not understand it or even care, but they all have one goal, right? Kill us, convert us, or eat us. Each of those three things require three specific sets of actions. Unless those three events have been happening by fluke and that's all these creatures are or ever would be capable of, then what you're looking at clearly shows something else at play, an aspect about them that we never understood before." He looked to Tracy. She gave him an approving grin.

"Well, you certainly seem to know a lot about this," Dean said. "Any advice."

Joe simply deferred to Tracy.

She said, "Right now, stay put, stay hidden. The undead haven't given any indication to us in the past or even now they know where we are. No sense drawing attention to ourselves if we don't have to."

"Agreed," Joe said.

More of the dead filled the street, their vast numbers suggesting many had remained hidden until now or were trapped and had just gotten out.

The undead took rank amongst their kin, the giants looking off into the distance as if waiting for something, as if *planning* for something.

23
ELEVATORS

With Sven holding her steady while Billie partly leaned into the elevator shaft, she looked up and counted the visible exterior doors from within and determined the elevator on the left was lodged on the seventeenth floor. Upon confirming the find on the eleventh floor, they were able to ascertain the second car was stuck up on the twenty-fifth.

Now on the seventeenth, it was the moment of truth. Sven was in charge of prying open the doors; Bastian had his machine gun at the ready, aimed squarely at the opening; Billie stood against the wall on the side, gun ready to shoot down anything that came out groaning or growling.

Billie nodded at Sven.

"Guten tag," Sven said loud and clear, giving the door a hard *whap* with the palm of his hand.

The three waited for a response, then muffled from within, "Hello?"

Sven smacked the door again. "Guten tag."

From inside: "Hello? Who's there?"

Billie's heart sank with relief, but this was only the first part of the plan. For all they knew, this was yet another trap and those "stuck" within the elevator were shape shifters.

Sven pried the door open only a couple of inches, just enough to clear the path of communication.

"How many are you?" Sven asked.

"Fourteen," came the male voice from within.

That's got to be cramped, Billie thought.

"Show me face," Sven said.

There was shuffling and bumping in behind the door, then Sven took a step back.

He looked at Billie. "He look okay."

"Only one," Billie said.

"Step back from door. Only one person come out. Anymore get shot, okay?" Sven said.

He pried the door open enough so a single person could squeeze through sideways. The moment the male in the white lab coat was pulled through, shouts arose from within along with demands to let them out.

REDEMPTION OF THE DEAD

Sven said something, but Billie couldn't make it out above the din.

"Tell them to be quiet," she said though it was clear Sven couldn't hear her either.

A series of rapid gunshots made her jump and the voices ceased. The man in the lab coat raised his hands in surrender. Bastian lowered his weapon as dust and debris from the ceiling settled at his feet.

"Better quiet," he said. He said something in German to his brother.

"Yah," was all Sven said.

He's going to have to teach me some of that one of these days, she thought. Billie kept her gun trained squarely at the man in the lab coat's head. "You have the barrel of a gun aimed at your temple, you have man in front of you with a machine gun, and the man who just let you out holds a giant crowbar not to mention he could break your neck faster than you could scream," she said. "Just letting you know who's in charge."

The scientist—a young man with messy brown hair, at least three or four days' worth of stubble, and a set of out-of-place-amazingly-blue eyes—simply nodded.

It was decided before they opened the door that Billie would do most of the talking because of Sven and Bastian's thick accents. "I want your name, who those people are, and how you got in there to start. Got it?"

The man nodded, his hands still raised. She wasn't about to tell him to put them down. "My name is Greg Undersall, engineer. Those people in there are my team. We were put in there by these men, strange men. They looked like people, but there was something about them that made everyone uncomfortable. Once one of them . . ." He bowed his head.

"Once one of them . . .?"

"He was able to control one of my assistants. Not like a robot, but he had this influence on her that was unlike anything I'd ever seen before." Greg nervously glanced at the elevator, then back at Billie.

"What?" she asked.

He didn't speak.

Billie nodded to Sven, who quickly wrapped his big fingers around the back of Greg's neck and squeezed.

"Okay, okay," Greg said, "tell him to stop. I'll tell you."

Billie let Sven hang on a moment longer then told the gentle giant to let him go.

After gasping for air and catching his breath, Greg said, "There's . . ."

From inside the elevator. "Don't say it!"

Billie scowled.

Greg shifted uncomfortably on his feet. "There's a body. One of my

137

group, his name was Steven, started to lose it after being trapped. He wouldn't . . . wouldn't stop screaming and pushing against everyone else. Eventually he got violent and" —she gave him a moment to take a breath before finishing— "things got out of hand and we—and I mean *we* as we all decided to take responsibility—ended up smothering him, our own safety our only concern. It was wrong. I'm haunted by it. He came back and immediately went on the attack, but we wrestled him down and broke his neck. Don't know why I just told you that straight up. I'm sorry."

"Don't say sorry to me," Billie said. "Back to the matter at hand: those men who trapped you, what did they look like?" She simply needed confirmation that those they encountered in the lab below were the same despite the connection being obvious. If being a computer enthusiast had taught her anything in her old life, it was that information was valuable and there was no such thing as too much of it, even redundancies.

Greg went on to describe Dr. Moore along with several others that matched the hairs and outfits some of the other zombies had.

"Those men weren't what they seemed," Billie said.

"You're telling me. So, what now?"

"I ask the questions."

He sighed and rolled his eyes. Apparently his newfound freedom was making him cocky.

"Put him back in," Billie told Sven.

Sven grabbed Greg on either side of his coat collar and shoved him toward the door.

"No, wait! I'm sorry. Don't put me back!"

People called from inside the elevator, begging to be released.

"Stop," she told Sven. "Listen, Greg, the three of us here don't have time for games or some sort of stupid power struggle. We're the ones in charge. Either you and your people get with that or we throw you back."

"Okay," he said softly, "okay. You win. I'm sorry."

"Good. What about the people in the other elevator, or were you fourteen it?"

"You're right. There was more than fourteen of us, nineteen, actually—and I'm talking about those of us involved with the underground research here since the creatures took over—but we had some military people here, too, overseeing what we were doing and coordinating."

"Coordinating what?"

"That's classified."

REDEMPTION OF THE DEAD

"You're about to become classified if you don't speak up."

Sven shoved Greg against the door, slamming him into it hard. Too hard, Billie thought, but was glad for Sven's support. Greg rubbed his shoulder. She could tell he wanted to take a swing at Sven, but it was also apparent it didn't take much for the engineer to hold himself back from going up against such a big guy. "You guys don't let up, do you?"

"Nope," Billie said with a grin. *Really getting used to this gun thing.*

"There are plans for an attack underway. Those are the things we were working on."

From inside the elevator, a female said to those within, "He told them."

Greg didn't seem to pay her any mind. "I don't have all the details as our job was simply to keep our heads down, work, and come up with ideas for items that would be more effective against the creatures given the resources we have, which aren't many."

Not many? she thought, recalling the amazing facility downstairs. *Perhaps compared to what you were used to before all this.*

Billie took it all in, then told Sven to close the elevator door. He did despite the shouts of protest from within.

"Okay," Billie said, "you come with us and we corroborate your story. We've encountered our quota of liars for the day and we're not about to exceed it."

Sven took a firm hold on Greg and the four of them went into the stairwell and climbed the eight flights to the twenty-fifth floor. Once there, they followed the same plan except Greg was the one to speak through the door and get the attention of those inside.

"We heard gunfire, what happened?" said a gruff voice from the other side of the doors.

"I'll let these people explain," Greg said and was tossed over to Bastian, who held him fast while Sven worked the door.

Sven suddenly stopped and shouted through the crack between the doors. "Put weapon down or we shoot, okay?"

The big guy waited a moment and, seemingly satisfied with the compliance from within, he opened the doors like before, only enough room for one person to squeeze through. He grabbed Greg; Bastian stood before the door with his machine gun.

"Back down, stay calm," Bastian said. "This be over in minute."

A man, who was at least in his forties, wore military fatigues and had leathery skin like someone who'd spent way too much time in the sun, came out. "What in the blue blazes is going on here, Undersall?"

Billie gave Greg a hard glare.

Greg said, "I'll just defer to the young lady here."

The man eyed Billie up and down. "You're takin' orders from a kid? Because I sure as heck ain't."

Sven stepped forward.

The man said: "Intimidation doesn't work with me, son. Try something new."

Sven snapped out his arms lightning quick and grabbed the man by the ears, lifting him off his feet. The guy screeched like a cat in water. Sven set him down.

"Wanna try again?" Billie said.

The man held his ears like they would fall off, and judging by how big Sven's grin was, she thought they just might.

"Let's start with your name."

"Lieutenant . . . Lieutenant John Nole."

"And those are your men inside there?"

He nodded.

This makes it easy. "Greg here told me about you guys coordinating an attack. I need to know more."

"And why's that, young lady?" the man said in between winces.

Because I know who *you're going to try and fight and you have no idea what you're getting yourself into.* She decided to keep the supernatural side of the equation to herself for now. "When was this attack going to take place?"

Nole eyed Sven, who held the pry bar aloft against his shoulder. "We didn't finalize a date, but we were looking into a fifty-to-sixty-day timeframe."

Too long. "Why do you need to wait so long?"

"Why do you need know?"

Sven reached with one hand for the lieutenant's ear.

Nole sidestepped a couple feet. "Okay, okay, easy. Some of the weapons are complete, others in the prototype stage."

"We saw them below."

"You did?" He looked to Greg for confirmation, who gave it. "And those who put us in the elevators?"

"Dead," Billie said. "By us, I might add. We also hold the key to your freedom so if anything, you owe us your allegiance." The statement sounded a little too video game-ish, but she'd played more than her fair share of them in her day so it was to be expected.

"How did you take them down?"

She gave the boys a wink. "We've been at this a long time. That's all you need to know."

They all stood in silence for a few moments.

Nole asked, "What's next? Any more pertinent questions or are you guys going to let the others out? They're thirsty, starving, and there's a bathroom issue you don't want to know about."

Billie slowly shook her head. "Not yet. We don't trust you and we're not going to trust you, and we're especially not about to let a whole lot of you out until you show me you're willing to comply with our demands."

Nole was clearly getting impatient, but was keeping himself in check lest Sven tear his ears off for real this time. "What are your demands?"

"I need to know more about this attack."

"I can help with that," Greg said.

"You're not saying anything," Nole replied.

"We don't have a choice, Lieutenant," the engineer said. "Let the tough guy thing go or, if not, we can just go back in the elevator and wait for the next group of people to come waltzing through here to let us out. If they even find us, that is, and you know full well aside from those who trapped us, we've been alone in this building for over a month with no one in or out."

Lieutenant Nole crossed his arms, and said to Billie, "Okay, lead the way."

"No," she said, "you lead. I need a shield in case any of those monsters surface."

24
SPILL IT

AFTER BEING ON the roof, Joe, Tracy and the others returned inside. First order of business was inventory, and though there was a record of what came in and what went out, everything was thoroughly double checked. Weapons were plenty for the amount of people there; there was also body armor, enough for one piece of protection per person. It was better than nothing. The intel from Dale, who periodically went up to the roof to check on the undead gathering beyond, said they were still coming together as of twenty minutes ago. It was difficult to say how long it would be until the undead force was at its peak.

Dean assembled everyone, filling the kitchenette completely. He stood on the countertop so everyone could see him. Joe and Tracy stood on the ground on either side.

"We don't know what the creatures are doing," he said, "but it's clear they're doing *something*. I know that some of us are strangers, which is fine, but when it comes to this place and to each of our own safety, we are friends. We have to be. I will pair you off and whoever you end up with will be your partner until I say otherwise. Tracy, fill them in."

She switched places with Dean, and Joe did his best not to stare up at her like a love-struck fool, but instead put his game face on so everyone knew that she meant business. Ah, but to see such a strong woman up there made him want to take her down and back to their little room.

"My name is Tracy, and I was appointed head of this operation. What is it, especially if we don't know what the creatures are doing? Simple: we are to be ready for any event, anything, no matter what. It is clear that something is about to happen. Maybe it'll be a miracle and those giants and the other ones out there are getting together just so they could leave. Or maybe it's going to be a lot worse and what we've known of the creatures over the past year was only part of the story."

"So what're we going to do?" a guy asked from amongst the crowd.

"I'll answer questions in a moment. First order of business has been taken care of. We know where we stand with firepower, who is here and what their skills are. You have been paired together according to those skills to complement each other. Do not deviate from your partner, and if you and your team are paired with another, this is also coordinated so that both teams will work fluently together based on your skill set. Next, safety. Everyone has been assigned a piece of body armor—all we have—again based on your talents. Third, right now this safe house is indeed what its name says it is. We are safe here and we will stay here despite what we hear outside, if something goes down. At no time will we leave this place until commanded to, or until you are the only survivor and you have no choice but to leave. Should we be discovered and an attack on the safe house takes place, we have created a roster and set of orders of door watchers and what to do in that event. Again, both you and your partner will work together." She lowered her voice a little. "At the same time, I understand some of you have been down here for a long time and the thought of possibly going topside to fight is frightening. I want you to try and relax and take comfort in your safety down here; just don't take it for granted and remain on the alert. Should you fight, you know the rules: only use bullets when necessary in an effort to conserve ammo. Always, always, always go for the head by killing the brain. Decapitation is fine, too. Try to keep shots and-or blows to the body minimal unless it's a means of self-defense. Speaking of which, these two gentlemen here" —she pointed to two large black guys—Hal and Rob— in grungy sweat suits off to the side— "will be coming up to pairs starting now and throughout the night to give a refresher on how to take a zombie down. Any questions?"

"What if we don't want to fight?" someone asked.

"Are you serious?" Tracy said. "If you choose not to fight, don't count on anyone to defend you. If you are not willing to stand beside your fellow man now, then get out. We have no room for you and are much safer without you."

"What if we run out of ammo?" someone else said.

"Then see if your partner has enough to spare. If not, you're going hand-to-hand."

"Are we really going to battle?" asked another.

"Weren't you just listening? We are staying here and are hoping for the best, but are preparing for the worst."

Tracy answered a few more questions then hopped down off the counter as Dean dismissed everyone.

"Nice job," Joe said.

"Can't believe some of the people here," she said.

"Don't hold it against them."

"Don't go soft on me." Her voice was firm. She looked him deadset in the eye. "Despite this thing we got going, I need you to stay as you are, don't change. Not for me, not for them. And I mean that, Joe. Don't compromise anything for me because I sure as heck am not going to compromise anything for you." She headed off down the hallway, leaving him with a twinge in his heart and a head that felt like it was being filled with sand.

"Maybe I'm wrong about this whole thing," he said. *Or maybe she's right. This isn't the time to think about "us." If we go to war, it's about more than a relationship. It's about the survival of a species.* Still, the thought didn't bring him much comfort.

Billie tried to hide her yawn from Lieutenant Nole unless she wanted to show weakness. She was in dire need of a nap, even a full-night's sleep, but until this issue about the forthcoming strike against the dead was settled, she was going to stay awake. Her headache didn't help any either. Now down in the lab room in the basement, Greg and Nole stood with them around a large table after securing the room that had the mirrors on the off chance the deceased creatures within somehow came back to life.

"The strike's codename is Operation Romero. Think what you want, but it seems fitting," Nole said. "It's about getting at the root cause of this, we hope."

Billie wasn't completely sure it would be, though. She knew what really lied beneath the rotten visage of each creature: a blood thirsty demon whose first allegiance was to the devil and to bring victory to their fallen angel leader in a pre-emptive strike before Armageddon. At some point she knew she was going to have to come clean about it, but she also needed to understand the supposed plan of attack first. She wished Nathaniel was here to help guide her.

"Operation Romero is being coordinated with remaining military agencies around the world," Nole said. "Once our preliminary attacks failed against the undead—and you need to understand that we certainly could have come in and nuked the bastards, but if we did, the fallout would make this planet inhabitable well beyond any survivor's lifetime; in fact, some raids needed to be conducted to stop certain parties from doing just that—anyway, listen, when the preliminary attacks failed, we tried again and made some headway, but eventually the sheer number of the things was enough to trump even our most sophisticated weapons.

REDEMPTION OF THE DEAD

One of the challenges was controlling the outbreak, not after the Rain because that caused its own chaos, but once that was over and we learned what was happening and how one could be infected—by the time procedures that were in place for the plague were activated, it was too late. It's not a one-man operation and it takes plenty of people. They were all changed over to be like those creatures faster than we could replace them. A retreat was the only option." He cleared his throat. "Correction: a *feigned* retreat. Over time, we were able to reestablish connections via radio communications, power generators, and the like. Human beings are not that incompetent to not to keep a few mechanisms running even in total chaos."

Greg said, "Don't mean to interject, but I don't know if she really cares about all that stuff."

"I do," she said, "but I also want to know precisely what you guys were doing down here."

"I'll say it again, little lady," Nole said. "I don't know why this is such a big deal to you—"

"If you keep talking, I might tell you and believe me it's news you want to hear."

That seemed to get his attention because Nole's face quickly went serious, and she knew she had him interested to give information in exchange for receiving some. He said, "We needed to find weapons that worked against them quickly and effectively. We needed to find competent people to man those weapons. We even decided we needed to make some new ones."

Billie flashed back to some of the other secret bases she visited and the amazing tech they were producing. "I'm aware of some of those."

"You are? Name one."

"Try the D-K-Fourteen-P-Two-X," she said, referring to that amazing exoskeleton she saw.

Nole's eyes widened then squinted with complete suspicion. "Who are you, really?"

"Just a kid, like you said, but I'm also a kid who knows stuff and stuff you need to know if you have any hope of surviving this attack."

"Yeah, like what?"

"You finish talking and if I like what I hear, I might say a thing or two, too."

Greg said, "I think we should listen. We got nothing to gain by holding back now. She obviously knows about one of our most secret projects. She's already seen the place. Even if she told people out there,

there's not enough of us to defend the fort anyway."

Nole put his hands on his hips. "So you're saying we should just let this chick tell us what to do and hope for the best? Since when did you grow a spine and tell me what to do?"

"Since I realized that if these folks could take out our captors and found us after so long without human contact aside from ourselves, they are people to be trusted, even just superficially to start."

Nole seemed to think it over. "I'll make you a deal, kid."

"I thought I was a *chick*," Billie said.

"Sorry. I'll make you a deal, Miss—"

"Call me B."

"Fine. B. Whatever. You give me a piece of info, I give you one of mine, and back and forth we go."

"How about you start and we'll go from there? You don't really have a choice."

He sighed. "What you're wanting me to divulge is classified information which could jeopardize an operation months in the making and coordinated around the globe. Do you get that?"

"I get it, and what you don't understand is you can tell me everything you know and the conversation will still end with, 'It's not going to work,' because I know something you don't and I'm not bluffing. I have a piece of intel you won't believe to be true, but it is, and unless that piece of info is factored into your game plan, you, your men, even me and mine, won't have a prayer out there for much longer."

"Much longer?"

"Yeah, Lieutenant, not much longer because a real bad guy has come to town and, you could say, is even the one responsible for what you see out there."

"Tell me!"

"You first."

Checkmate. Billie kept a straight face, didn't even blink.

"Those men in the other room," Greg said, "they forced us to show them how our weapons worked. And we did. We had no choice because, like I said before, they had a way of making a person do what they wanted them to, so we showed them. Those who refused were killed and came back as one of those creatures. The weird part was, those men didn't kill those that returned and told us not to as well. Instead, they wanted to find a way to make those creatures immune to our weapons. They asked us to make those walking dead things invincible."

"You didn't figure it out, did you?" she asked.

He slowly shook his head. "Not quite. We had ideas, even a few tests, but the decaying tissue was too fragile. Even those who were once with us, who died then came back, they started to decay rapidly compared to how long it would normally take for a human being to decompose, and that's just a human in the air, not in the ground where there's all sorts of aids to break them down quickly."

"Why did they lock you in elevator?" Sven asked.

"Part of it was simply to threaten us," Nole said. "They couldn't kill everybody otherwise they'd have no one to work for them. They started locking us up one by one. It worked for a few people and they complied without question. A few others tried to secretly come up with a plan to get out. That didn't turn out so well either. Those ones were killed and, like the others, came back and were used in experiments. Dr. Moore was different, though, wasn't he, Greg?"

"Oh yeah."

"Go ahead, tell them."

"Moore was one of my colleagues and a genius at coming up with really strange ideas, but every one of them was solidly backed up by science. It was more an issue of if it could be done or built versus looking good on paper. Just because the background facts add up doesn't mean what you try to do with them will."

"Get on with it," Nole said.

"Moore was there when the first men went down. He was the only one called forth to conduct the early experiments. We didn't see him for hours on that day, but when he returned, he was different. Sometimes he'd act like himself, other times he was a completely different person. Some days I thought maybe he'd been abducted by aliens or something and had been replaced."

That's pretty close to the truth, Billie thought, but kept it to herself.

"Moore quickly started taking charge and asking us to do more and more bizarre things, even bizarre dissections with one of the creatures and one of the people *while they were alive*, and try and crossbreed them. I mean, Moore knew full well we didn't have the equipment for that kind of thing down here, but he insisted we make do with what we had and assured us that conventional scientific method might not be needed for working with a new species. Eventually, it was clear Dr. Moore had sided with our captors. They even answered to him. I couldn't dwell on it all the time. I was run ragged enough as it was. So was Nole here. We all were. Like I said, we basically were told to keep our heads down and work."

"That all changed when I guess it was realized that Dr. Undersall, myself and the others had done all we could, so we were all thrown into those elevators. I even asked Moore why they didn't kill us and he said that our services might still be required. That was the last we saw of him or those other men. A few days later, you guys showed up."

It was a lot to take in, but it was clear the demons were attempting to create an invincible army by any means necessary. Billie wasn't sure if it was completely meant for a battle with man and then another means would be used for a battle with the angels, or perhaps even an attempt to become impervious to *any* assault was the end goal.

"The weapons," she said, "are they functional?"

"If they hadn't changed anything since a few days back, yes," Greg said, "but not all of the prototypes have been tested."

"All right, Lieutenant," Billie said, "you held up your end of the bargain so I'll hold up mine. This attack you're planning? It has to happen now."

"Oh yeah, why's that?"

"Because this isn't about killing zombies anymore. This about taking on the armies of Hell itself."

All four of the men looked at her with uncertainty.

"I think you're too tired, Billie," Sven said. "You don't know what you mean."

"I'm fine," she said. "Lieutenant Nole, I can quickly create a briefing for you if you give me something to write on. You can relay that info to all parties that you are working with. I know I sound crazy, but we're also living in a crazy world at the moment. I know that you and Greg didn't tell me about the mirrors."

Both men's eyes widened with surprise.

"You know about those?" Greg said.

"That's what you were referring to when you said they 'had a way' of controlling your people."

He nodded. "How did—"

"I fought the mirrors, these guys, too. That's when Moore came in. He changed form, gentlemen, went from the man you knew to one of those disgusting creatures. I also know why you were told to do the experiments you were. The undead aren't merely people risen from the grave. They are people who are possessed with hell spawn." The elation of sudden revelation buoyed her spirits. "Why do you think people began to decay faster than normal once they returned? If you have death itself inside you, there is only one result." Had she said too much? She decided it best to keep her mouth shut until she felt it was appropriate to say more.

The four men stood there, silent. Billie glanced over to Sven, who returned her gaze with a look of pity.

Please don't think I'm crazy, she thought. *I'm telling the truth. I'll show you somehow. Just don't push away whatever it was you thought about me before, I . . . I began to like it.*

After a long moment, she said, "What's our next move?"

Nole glanced at Greg, and after a sigh, said, "Know any good priests?"

*T*he Present...

    It had come to fruition as Lucifer planned. The Earth had fallen, humanity possessed. Only a few small pockets of resistance remained. Even the angelic presence that used to be so common on Earth was now whittled down to very few.
    The greeting at the lakeside had been commendable and it was there the devil got to see these new creations—these undead creatures—for the first time. They were beautiful and grew even more gorgeous by the second as he absorbed the damage they had done to humanity.
    After speaking with them and ordering them to sniff out every last human soul on the planet, he spread his own wings and ascended into the sky and flew over the land, taking in the ravaged cities, the fields of bodies, the infected animals, the dead trees and grass, even the dead fish in the lakes. Though it wouldn't affect him, the toxicity in the air would take its part on killing all that remained with its poison. The canopy above of gray clouds and brown sky further reduced any interference from life-giving water and the sun's healing and growth-giving rays. The Earth was rotting and it didn't take eons to bring it to the brink; only a single year.
    The smell of death lingered on every molecule of air, exciting the devil as he flew. Even the ocean as he soared over it at incredible speed looked chalky and stale. With no sun, the water didn't evaporate and just stayed there to stew with the awesome amount of dead sea creatures within.
    It had all come to pass perfectly.
    Once humanity was absent and his army complete, the invitation to battle would be sent to Heaven's gates and, outnumbered, the Golden City would be overrun by demon and possessed human alike, and finally—after eons of waiting—the enormous throne in its center would be his.
    The devil flew on, a grin creasing his face.
    However, he needed one last item to ensure victory.

25
DEMONS

Joe laid alone on the cot. He had looked around for Tracy and, not finding her, started to panic, thinking maybe she was more mad at him than he realized and had taken off into the streets, but when he saw her talking to one of the trainers he sighed with relief. He wanted to go up to her and ask her if she was coming to bed, even waited around for over twenty minutes, trying to look like he was occupied inspecting the floor, but when she didn't look his way he cut his losses and went back to what was supposed to be *their* room. Alone.

Now, laying there with his arms folded across his chest, no blanket, it felt like old times again. No girl. Just him. Always alone. The difference was, now he knew better than to base his identity on a girl and instead tried to be himself. He was most certainly not his old, old self. That man—that boy—had died the day of the Rain. He was becoming something new, but he was also aware he had to suppress this new side of him for the time being, and not only at Tracy's command of doing so, but for the good of himself and any he might have a chance of influencing. With a possible war coming up soon, he couldn't lose his edge.

He hoped Tracy would take the time to lie down even if it was not with him. She needed to rest, too, and it scared him to think he'd have to compensate for both of them in battle if she wasn't functioning properly.

He closed his eyes.

When he opened them again, he knew he had dozed off because he felt the heaviness of sleep inside his head. He didn't know what time it was, but the whole place was darker and quieter. A few snores floated down the hallway.

One little one rose up beside him.

Tracy.

He was relieved to see her and chastised himself for jumping to conclusions over where he stood with her. He owed her more trust and respect than that. Joe leaned over and kissed her forehead before rolling onto his side and falling back asleep.

"Forty hours, are you crazy?" Lieutenant Nole screamed into the radio receiver.

"*I didn't make the planes, I fly them,*" came the voice through the other end. "*They only go so fast.*"

"Look, we have over a hundred different sites and over a five hundred new weapons. We need to share the wealth!"

"*Obviously, but I can't magically transport the stuff over, I'm sorry. You're asking us for the Rendezvous months ahead of schedule, disperse our assets, then transport said assets back to the individual sites in less than twenty-four hours. Can't be done.*"

Nole pinched the bridge of his nose. "I know, look. Just get it done as soon as possible. We need to work fast. Intel has already come in. The creatures are acting strange, even the big ones. It'd be one thing if it was isolated, but it's in every location we have eyes and ears in. Something's going down."

"*I'll be on it, Lieutenant. I promise.*"

"Good. Thanks. Nole out." He hung up the radio receiver.

"That didn't sound good," Billie said from behind him.

"You been standing there the whole time?"

"Yeah."

"You should be sleeping with the others."

"Couldn't."

"Oh yeah? Why not? Don't got your teddy bear?"

"Don't start with me. Just because you're a grouch doesn't mean you have to turn everyone into one, too." She sat down on the chair across from him, hugged her elbows and crossed her legs. "Did you get an ETA?"

"Forty hours. They'll try, anyway. Forty-eight or forty-nine, even fifty, would be more accurate."

"That's up to two days. That might not be enough time."

"We don't have a choice. This is crash planning. The gentleman I spoke to is the lead on a team of organizers whose job it is to coordinate the drop of our shared tech to each of our predetermined locations."

"Which are?"

"There's over a hundred of 'em."

"Oh."

"We got a guy coming to pick up what we got here and what we got in a warehouse not far from here. Some stays with us, the rest goes out. We stand our ground once the rest of the weaponry arrives."

"What if things start before then?"

"Then we make our stand. Won't have a choice."

"Hide out here?"

"If possible, but you never know. Doesn't hurt to be ready."

"Yeah." She closed her eyes a moment then opened them.

"You okay?"

Was Nole actually being *nice* to her? *Weird.* "Just miss my friends."

"Where're you from?"

"Winnipeg."

"Where?"

She wasn't surprised Nole hadn't heard of it. It wasn't exactly a popular city, though it was easily the best place in Canada to live without going broke. "Central Canada, right above North Dakota."

"You guys got polar bears there, right?"

"Yeah, and penguins on every corner."

Nole chuckled.

She looked him in the eye. "I need to get home."

He sighed. "I don't know what to tell ya, B. You're on the other side of the world. There ain't exactly an airport around the corner where you can just hop on a plane."

"No, but you guys got planes."

"Military planes. Some of them are jets."

"But some have to be carriers if you're going transport all that gear around."

His expression straightened. "Not happening, kid."

"You owe me, John."

"Oh, so we're on a first name bases now?"

She shook her head, disbelief that this guy was actually military. "You don't know my first name."

"Think so? How's 'Billie' for ya?"

"What? How?"

"I'm not as stupid as you might think and I know how to talk to people."

Sven. Wait, maybe it was Bastian. Either way, those guys are gonna get it. "I really need this, *Lieutenant.*"

He glanced to the floor, then back up and pointed his finger at her. "No guarantees, okay?"

She couldn't help but smile. "Thanks."

"Now go to bed."

"Yes, Dad," she said and left.

As Billie returned to the small room off to the side, her bracelet lit white. She immediately checked the range and stopped when it cast a rainbow in a halo around her wrist, each crystal emitting its own light. Like always, the bracelet vibrated and a few moments later, crackles of amethyst-colored energy rose from the floor and embedded itself in the bracelet, filling in the last of the clear stone.

"Am I done?" she said quietly. "At least this thing looks like it is." She stared at it, waited for it to do something, but nothing happened. "In time, always in time."

When Tracy woke up, Joe was no longer beside her. Before, she had considered finding a cozy spot of her own, but thought better of it and snuggled up beside him instead. It had been the better choice, she told herself when she sat up and stretched.

The rich scent of freshly-brewed coffee floated down the hallway to her room. Screw the bathroom. Coffee came first. Thank God for battery-powered coffeemakers. When she went into the kitchenette, she smiled when she saw Joe sitting at the table, cup of coffee in one hand, his new .9mm in the other.

He looked up at her and gestured to the gun. "It isn't the X-09, but it'll do. Maybe with a few modifications . . ."

"Leave it," she said as she poured herself a cup. She sat down beside him. They both took their coffee black.

"Sleep okay?" he asked.

"Kind of. The sleep part. The dream part was messed up, though."

"Want to share?"

"It's all a fog, but I remember clear images of bullfrogs with purple skin, and something about jack-o'-lanterns being good for you."

"Maybe as pie."

"Maybe." She took a sip of her coffee. "What time did you get up?"

"You know, I didn't even look at the clock. I don't really care. Ever since this all started—well, I sort of had a schedule when this all started, but since things got crazy and I came here—yeah, just whatever. Sleep when tired. Don't when not." He took a sip from his own cup. "Was up on the roof. Dean was up there. Does that guy ever sleep?"

"Wouldn't know."

"The dead had finished formation."

"Already?"

"Yeah. Until we can get really high up, we don't know exactly what the formation is, but there is actual form to it. Looks like a triangle to me."

"Really?"

"Not a perfect one, but yeah. Got the big guys in the front, then all the other ones gathering behind them, but not in equal rows. Looks like the rows get shorter and shorter the further back they go. Looks like a triangle to me."

"What do you think it means?"

He sighed then took another sip. "I think this is going to go beyond what anyone expects or even what anyone here might even be hoping for." He leaned forward and put his elbows on the table, cup between his hands. "Before I came here, my friends and I took a helicopter off the roof of the Richardson Building—*our* Richardson Building—and we were in that storm I mentioned a while back."

She remembered, and she believed him.

"When we came through the other side of the storm, the sun was shining and the city was intact. People were walking on the sidewalks, cars were driving down the streets. It was beautiful, so amazing to see after a whole year under a sky that looks like a foggy beer bottle. We landed in a bank's parking lot, of all places. We went in. The people inside didn't see us. This was me, Billie and August, by the way. We lost Des . . . he didn't make it to the chopper and was something else when we returned but I'm getting ahead of myself. At the bank, the people couldn't see us, couldn't hear us. We separated and as I made my way down the stairs to the basement, I fell through the floor, actually *fell* through it and was engulfed in total darkness. I fell for a long, long time and at ripping fast speed. To be honest, I don't know how long it took, but I landed on stone and it started to get hot, real hot. In the distance I saw this enormous lake of flames."

"I remember you saying you went to . . . you know."

"I was in Hell, Tracy. *The* Hell."

Her heart pounded and even though Joe was safe here with her now, she was terrified for him.

He took another sip. She wanted one of her own, but right now even the heat off the coffee didn't sit right.

He said, "These creatures, these awful creatures attacked me. I tried to defend myself but it was next to impossible. These things—compared to them? I'd take fighting the undead all day every day if there was a choice." Quietly, he said, "There might not be a choice soon."

"What?"

"Down there, I thought that was it. I had died or something and was in the place every person dreads to go even if they don't believe in it, and I tell you, you better believe in it if you don't because I was there and that place is very real. So these creatures attacked me and I would've been doomed had not this angel come down in in this crazy brilliant blaze of white and golden light, sword in hand, and saved me from those things. He took me back to the surface, back into the bank, but by then it was too late. The bank's floor looked smashed and ripped open and after we came out, all those terrible creatures came out after us and started attacking my friends and I. The angel defended us, but also told us to go. We did, made it to the helicopter despite being attacked again. The storm started up again, this time at ground level. We wound up back in the storm then came through and were in the air. We landed back on the same roof and, well, you know the rest." He finished his coffee. "This thing happening outside, those creatures aren't stupid. You know as well as I do that, yes, some are as brain dead as this cup, but others show more cunning. I think those evil spirits inside them are limited in that they can use the body, but can't operate it at its full potential, yet need that body to take over everything first."

"Which they've pretty much done."

"I don't know how many of us are out there, but compared to the seven billion or so people that used to be on this planet? I can't see there being more than a hundred thousand, two hundred thousand tops left. It might sound like a lot, but that's really next to nothing. That's worldwide. I won't claim to be an expert at this, but I'm guessing that phase one of their plan is pretty much complete and the only way to finish us off is to go to phase two."

"Which is?"

"Who knows, but that triangle thing they got going outside? That's got to be part of it. The undead don't just all get together and wait around. They're always moving, even the ones that can barely walk."

She took a minute to soak it all in and finish her own cup of coffee. If what Joe was saying was right or even partly accurate, their little band of people at the safe house wouldn't stand a chance in a fight. Though Dean would probably feel otherwise, it seemed the safest choice was to hightail it out of town and not look back. "What're we going to tell Dean?"

REDEMPTION OF THE DEAD

"This is his house, so he's got to know, but as inspiring as your guys' speech had been, it's not going to do much good out there. You need to talk to him, warn him."

"What about the others?"

"I don't know. Pros and cons. Do whichever outweighs the other after you talk to Dean."

"Okay." She took his hand in hers, his warm fingers comforting after what he just said. She kissed his hand, then got up and left the table. "Don't go anywhere."

"Don't plan on it," he said as she left the room.

After heading to the bathroom then tracking down Dean, who had finally gone to bed after having probably been up all night, she hated to wake him but gave him a nudge anyway.

"Hm? What?" he said, mouth half-closed.

"It's Tracy. I need you to wake up."

"What time is it?"

"I don't know."

"Is it important?"

"Very."

He blinked his eyes open, yawned. She caught a whiff of stale coffee breath. It didn't bother her as much as it used to, not since living in a city with the unrelenting stench of decay on the air.

She laid it out plain as day for him. Dean simply sat on the edge of his bed, eyes to the floor, listening. When she was done, he said, "You realize that guy's crazy, right?"

"Stop it."

"He is."

"No, he's not. I've known him a long time."

"How long?"

"Long enough to know he's not nuts. Look, you have to trust me. I know it sounds farfetched, but we also live in a world where the dead have come back to life, and if you believe that, then you have to believe what is clearly the cause of the madness. Don't brush me off, Dean. You've known me to be completely level-headed, dedicated, and hardworking. Why would I come to you with a fairytale unless it's real?"

"You're serious."

"More than."

"Then this is something that I have no idea how to handle."

"Few do."

"Will our weapons work?"

157

"I don't know. They have, so far so unless something drastic changes, they should still be effective."

Dean sighed.

"We're running out of time."

"I don't think we should tell the others," he said.

"Because?"

"Because either one of two things will happen: they'll simply not believe you and you'll be a laughing stock, or they will and" —he lowered his voice— "some of these guys are already on the edge of crazy. Do you want to be the one to push them over?"

"Those who aren't have a right to know. Imagine if we're out there fighting and suddenly these things transform, then what?"

"Maybe they'll panic and attack out of survival instinct?"

"Or maybe they'll curl up in a ball and get slaughtered."

"Okay, fine. I'll give you a list of names of people *not* to tell. Everyone else, take aside privately, take Joe with you just in case someone overreacts. Bring up to one more with you—whoever of whom you tell, but only one—and use them as 'helpful reassurance' or something as you break the news to people. If they have questions, send them to me."

"But you don't have answers."

"Neither do you, not completely, but we need to help each other out so I'll handle that side of it, or pretend to. It's my duty, anyway." He yawned. "We're doing this now?"

"There might not be a later."

26
LEAVING

BILLIE SAT IN the belly of a cargo aircraft, arms crossed, knees drawn up, just waiting out the flight. Few personnel were with her aside from the pilot and co-pilot. She was told to remain in her seat at all times. She didn't mind. She was dead dog tired, but the extreme noise of the plane made it difficult to sleep soundly. At best she'd been able to doze off and on since they departed. She checked with a short guy who was writing something down on a clipboard what time it was and he replied 4:42 in the morning, but didn't make clear which time zone.

Not as bad as I thought. Been in the air for seven hours already. Still a long way to go, though. Nole had pulled some strings and got her onto the cargo plane headed for Wales where they'd offload most of the cargo and reloaded it with an array of weapons from the other underground tech labs at the rendezvous point. Only cities with great infestations *and* the giants were to receive the cargo, the plan being to hit hard where the biggest threat was first and, if successful, branch out and eradicate the easier threats.

Sven and Bastian were with her, Sven refusing to leave her side and Bastian refusing to leave his. She thought it was sweet and was actually looking forward to getting to know Sven better. Never thought she'd be into a foreign guy, but here she was.

Billie eyed the bracelet. "Going to be home soon," she quietly said. *Home. Hope Joe's still alive.* Last she saw him was when the biplane that rescued her and August flew away without him. She'd have to tell him about August and assure him their friend and mentor didn't die in vain. Billie knew Joe'd feel guilty over it despite anything she might say, but she had to tell him anyway.

When they eventually landed back home, she didn't know how she react or how bad it might've gotten, but thankfully she had Sven and Bastian to keep her company until things got sorted out. She did make one definite decision though: once back, she would never leave the city again.

Tracy looked wearied when she came up to Joe and he was about to prescribe her a nap when she said, "Well, I told people. Not everyone, but most. Some thought I was crazy, others didn't care—can you believe that?—and others looked at me with such doughy-eyed wonder that I was the one that felt like I was getting the weird news."

"At least you told them."

"That's all I can do."

"You look tired."

"It's not that. Just worn out in general. Like waiting for summer vacation, but when it comes, you got to figure out what to do with all that time and you wish you could stay in school."

"You wished that?"

"So I'm a bookworm. Sue me."

He smiled. "One of these days I'll track down copies of my comics or something and give them to you, see what you think."

"Might not be a good idea. I'm very picky."

"That's fine. I've had my fair share of bad reviews so I got a thick skin. Besides, after the past year, everyone in the world could hate me and I'd be fine with it."

"Better not put me on that list."

"Naw, you're on a different one."

"Which one?"

"Ask me when this is all over."

"*If* it ever is all over."

We'll see.

Someone screamed down the hallway; Joe and Tracy immediately ran toward the sound.

A skinny Asian girl stood by the main entrance, back to the door, her knees bent and legs planted as if she was actually trying to hold it up.

Another woman ran up to her. "What? It's okay. What happened?"

From the other side of the door: "Hey, let me in!"

"Who is it?" the woman said.

"It's Jerry," the voice said. "Open the door! He's going to bi—" Jerry's scream was hoarse.

The woman shoved the Asian girl out of the way; Tracy caught her.

"What's going on?" Tracy asked.

The girl's tears ran into her mouth as she spoke through them. "We went out on a quick scout of the perimeter. We were followed, couldn't close the entrance in time. I saw them grab him. He might be bit. Don't let him in."

Jerry's scream was louder and when Joe looked up, the woman had the door open and Jerry's body fell into the room, a row of gutmunchers behind him, one of them attached to his leg.

Joe whipped out his gun and popped the creature in the head before taking the lead and helping the woman pull Jerry in by his blood-soaked hands. He fired off a couple more shots, dropping the nearest advancing undead, then slammed the door, locked it.

"No one comes in or out, understand!" he shouted.

A couple of people nodded. Others were too wrapped up in the pandemonium to hear him or care.

Back at Jerry's side, the heavyset man with the shaved head roiled in pain on the ground, kicking both legs, the one with the bite spattering blood on the wall.

"Hey . . . hey!" the woman said, Jerry's head in her hands. "Wake up, Jer. Wake up!"

Jerry's eyes were half-closed.

"He's losing a ton of blood." Joe leaned closer to the wound and just as he got a good look at the torn, blood-drenched flesh, a loud gunshot went off and blood sprayed him. Shocked, he looked down the length of Jerry's body and saw his head had been blown open, bone and brain all over the place. Just beyond the body was another of the men who called the safe house home, a gun in his hands, smoking snaking out of the barrel, body trembling.

The room went silent except for the sound of undead hands pawing against the other side of the door.

Tracy snapped the gun out of the man's hands; he grabbed her and Joe immediately lunged over Jerry's body toward them. Tracy hooked the guy in the head. He teetered and she came in again from the other side, dropping him.

Joe jumped on top of him, wrestled him over, and held his hands behind his back. "What's the matter with you? That guy could've survived!"

"Not after being bit," the man shouted. "I just saved us all."

"You don't know that. We could've saved him."

"You owe me. You all owe me!"

Joe shoved his forearm against the base of the guy's neck, keeping the man's head down and hopefully his mouth shut. The man started wailing and bawling into the floor.

To the side, Tracy ensured the Asian girl was in the proper care, while everyone else gave Jerry's body some room, even the woman who had tried to bring him around. Joe simply laid his weight into the guy who killed Jerry and kept him down. Once the man began to settle, he was passed off to Rob and Hal.

Getting up, Joe asked Tracy, "What're they going to do with him?"

"I don't know. This kind of thing happens once in a while and they're each dealt with case-by-case. Odds are they're going to take him somewhere where he can't hurt anyone else, get him to calm right down and, maybe, work it out."

"They can't take him out of here. You saw the creatures."

"No, they'll find a spot here."

The zombies still beat on the door. The safe house was compromised.

"Jerry's an idiot," Tracy said.

"He's dead, show some respect."

"I *am*. I know he's dead, but he's an idiot for letting them follow him. He would've known the protocol. Even getting in here is *not* easy. Either he panicked or something worse happened and he did the best he could. Probably a bit of both."

"Still not an idiot."

"I'd call you the same if you led a horde of them in here."

"You can call me what you want, but, man, that guy's dead. Slow it down."

She looked away.

What's her problem? Maybe she is worn out, like she said. Patience is at an end. "Look, everyone's already getting together. It's time to come up with a plan, and fast."

27
ON THE STREET

JOE AND TRACY moved through the back corridor of the safe house, taking up the lead with Dean. Behind them were the two trainers, the guy who shot Jerry in between them, followed by everyone else. Fully-armed with flashlights lit, the group negotiated the corridor, which was about thirty meters long, until they emerged from another door that led into a small alcove beneath one more pile of rubble.

"That big one, there," Dean said, pointing at a slab of concrete about three feet by four.

"Right," Joe said, and the two men went and pushed against it. The big slab of concrete fell forward and slid slightly down a small hill of more rubble, a crashed car, and the remainder of a bus bench with a broken realtor's ad.

After checking the coast was clear, Joe and Dean hopped out. Dean drew his glock and kept watch while Joe helped the others through hole.

"Okay, where to?" Joe asked, trying to ignore the groans of the gathered dead not far from where they stood.

"I'm thinking Cityplace would be our best bet. It's underground," Dean said.

"Not all of it."

"Most of it. The buildings above are some of the few that haven't yet been demolished, but we could get in there and, provided the rotter population is minimal, we could clear it out and lock it up."

Joe looked to Tracy.

"We don't have a lot of options," she said. "We basically go high up or low down, low down being the ideal."

She was right. As much as being above street level would provide protection from the creatures roaming the streets, once the giants got active again, it would only be a matter of time before one would knock something down.

"So be it," Joe said.

Word spread backward throughout the group.

"Everyone stay together," Dean said. "Ready?"

Everyone nodded.

"Then we move."

The group stayed huddled together as one, eleven in all. Packing up to leave was limited to getting armed, a few basic supplies like canned beans, soups, cans of Coke, and everyone's single piece of armor. Joe's was an arm guard for his forearm. Tracy had on a shin pad. Dean wore a chest pad. One of the trainers had a helmet. The others wore similar items.

The streets were empty, but not leaving anything to chance, all walked with their weapons at the ready. No one talked as per instruction and were only allowed to speak if they spotted one of the creatures.

After crossing the street, they turned north on the sidewalk, sidestepping any obstacles and abandoned, rotting body parts. Joe stepped over someone's hand. Coming up behind an old rusty Camaro, the group stopped, tightened up together, and scanned the area.

"If we continue that way" —Dean pointed past a fallen billboard sign— "we'll come up next to the MTS Centre and then, if all is clear, we'll go along the building opposite, locate the doors and assess."

"How badly damaged is it over there?" Joe asked.

"Haven't been in a long time, but last I saw it, the entrance to Cityplace was still there. That could be different now, though, just a heads up."

Dean waved for the group to continue on as they stayed out of sight as best they could while also taking a round-about way to their destination so as to sidestep the gathered dead beyond.

The group moved and any time someone spoke, they were shushed. A couple of times they stopped and listened close for shuffling footsteps, but heard none. The groans filling the air were growing louder, which Joe didn't understand. Zombies rarely increased their volume. During an attack it might happen as their aggression sometimes came out through their groans, but a genuine crescendo didn't make sense.

"I don't like this," Tracy said.

"Me neither," said Joe.

"Shush," came someone from behind.

They kept on . . . and a haunting feeling crawled up Joe's spine, over his chest and heart, and settled in his stomach. His ears picked up a rough scraping sound, like sandpaper over very coarse wood. It wasn't singular either. It was a chorus of them.

"We got to move," Joe said and got in front of Dean, taking the lead.

"What're you—"

"Take up the rear, guard the back."

"You're not in charge."

"We're about to have a real big problem; someone skilled and who knows these people should take up the rearguard. Tracy and I will cover the front. You got those two big guys—Rob and somebody—to cover the middle." He nodded toward the trainers.

It was clear Dean didn't want to. Tracy put a hand on his shoulder and gently said, "Please?"

He looked into her eyes, clearly displeased, but nodded and headed toward the back.

There were a few murmurs amongst the group asking what was going on.

The scraping sounds slightly faded.

Joe led the group down the same route Dean would've, his .9mm always at the ready. *Really wish I had the X-09 right now. Really miss that thing.* That gun, his own design and build, was like an extra limb for him, an extension of himself. The .9mm, though effective, felt like he was trying to play ball with someone else's glove.

They came in behind the MTS Centre, the large parking lot in the back covered in a mash of cars, twisted metal and plastic, chunks of the ground churned up from the giants.

"We cross here," Joe said, "then headed over to the building across the way. Turn right and we'll check the doors."

"Should send scouts," Tracy said.

"We need to stick together."

"What if the doors are completely smashed in? Be nice to know, don't you think?"

"We stick together."

"Don't think it's a good idea, not sending a couple of guys."

"I hear you, I really do, but the last thing we need is for anyone to get separated." He knew that she knew he was right in that regard; at the same time, Tracy was right, too.

The scraping sounds returned.

She said, "They're all gathered, last we saw. Unless . . ."

Joe looked her in the eyes and hoped his gaze told her his fear.

"We better get a move on," she said.

The group traversed the parking lot at a brisk jog; almost at the other side and Joe spread out his arms to hold up the group.

"Hold on a sec," he said and ran off to the side.

"What're you doing?" Tracy called after him. A few of the other folks chimed in as well.

Joe reached the far edge of the lot, near the corner. Coming up Main by the train station was an army of the dead. He couldn't see the end of the horde because of a building in the way, but of the ones he did see he estimated there were at least thirty of them. As tightly-packed as the throng of the dead was, they didn't move in one big block, but instead were loose in their approach and some started to drift down the same street as the entrance to Cityplace.

Joe ran back to the group. "We need another way in. There's a plethora of them on Main, probably heading toward the gathering, but some are moving this way. If they see us, we could have an army of them on our tail."

Tracy passed on the news to Dean. A woman beside him said, "Where's Jessica?"

Joe heard the question and looked around. Jessica, the same Asian girl that had refused to let Jerry in, had gone over to where Joe saw the dead. She must've heard him and separated, unnoticed.

To Tracy, he said, "I'll grab her. You and Dean lead them to another way in."

"If there is no other way, if everything's blocked?"

"Let's hope it doesn't come to that." Joe ran off. When he caught up to Jessica, he said, "Come on, let's go," and grabbed her by the hand.

"No," she said and started walking forward toward the zombie horde.

Joe pulled her back. "Are you crazy? They'll kill you or make you one of them."

"I deserve it," she said. "I deserve to die. It's my fault Jerry's dead. He died because I didn't let him in."

With a hard tug, he pulled her toward the group. Even when she tried to pull away, he kept his hold on her.

"You're hurting me," she said.

"You're hurting yourself if you think walking into a pack of those monsters is going to make amends for what you think you did, which was nothing, by the way."

"I know. I did nothing."

"I meant you didn't do anything wrong. You acted in what you thought would be best to keep the group safe."

"Let me go," she said, then jerked her hand away and started to run.

Joe took a few large strides, caught her, lifted her up and put her over his shoulder.

"Put me down!" she screamed. "Put me doooowwwwnnn!"

"Quiet. They'll hear you." He turned around.

The undead had and a few were already starting in their direction.

"Are we there yet?" Billie asked Sven.

"Not yet. At least two more hours yet. Go back to sleep." He put his arm around her; she didn't mind.

"This is boring," she said, but knew she needed the rest, her body and mind in dire need of some catch-up. Her headache had alleviated some, however. "I hope it doesn't take too long when we get there. Is it cold in Wales? Wait, never mind. The weather is the same everywhere."

She checked out the crates of weapons. Some were small, the size of a TV, but others stood large, some the size of a refrigerator or deep freezer. The Jetliers were in some of those crates. She wondered which ones held those silver weapons. She hadn't minded the handguns she used when getting Greg and Nole from the elevators.

The downtime on the flight had given her some time to think. Heading back home would also mean heading back to the place she lost Des. *Her* Des, not the one that was a monster in disguise. The guy had been a hardcore gamer, an ear, and a good friend. Though the two were never together in the official sense, Billie always considered her and Des a couple in terms of best friends. Man, she missed him.

"Really wish you were alive," she said softly, the sickening feeling that she hadn't even taken the time to properly mourn him settling in her gut. "I'm sorry we let you die."

Putting her arm around Sven's middle and gripping him hard, she put her face into his chest and started to cry.

The group was already moving closer to the north side of the MTS Centre when Joe and Jessica caught up with them.

"What happened?" Tracy asked.

"Later." He adjusted Jessica on his shoulder, but didn't put her down. She was too busy crying to fight anymore anyway. "We got some stragglers headed our way. I counted five. Hopefully there's no more."

The undead turned the corner and were coming toward the parking lot. A couple of them moved fairly slowly, but the remainder must've still had their ankles intact as they walked quickly and firmly.

Tracy faced them. They were at least thirty or forty feet away. She raised her gun, took aim, and fired. The first zombie took a bullet to the head. She fired again and dropped a second. The one further back she hit in the shoulder. It stopped for a second then kept on. Her next shot took it down.

"That's enough," Joe said. "Save it."

At least she got them some distance from the remainder. Back with the group, they kept on until they hit the street and saw another crowd of the creatures, most of them making their way to the gathering, but another group of rotters saw them and started heading their way.

Guns went off immediately as a couple in the group started to take shots, dropping only three of a procession of nine coming their way.

"Man, where'd you learn how to shoot?" said Rob. "This is how it's done." He took aim and popped a zombie in the head. He did the same to another.

Past the group on the other side, more of the creatures came, three sides out of four now covered. They had no choice but to go back the way they came.

They retraced their steps, this time not as organized. An undead male came in from the side and took hold of one of the ladies. He was already biting her by the time she shrieked. Before the person next to her was able to aim their weapon, the zombie had taken the woman down and ripping her flesh with his teeth. The shots rang out, two of them. The zombie on top of the woman fell flat. When Rob came to pull their friend away, he stopped, let the person's arm fall to the ground, and said, "Bullet went right through this rotter. Hit her in the chest. She's dead." He aimed down at the woman and waited. Moments later, she started to twitch and he put a bullet in her head.

As they moved, Joe shot down a couple of zombies; Tracy, too. Dean had only fired once. Maybe he was one of those guys who was careful with bullets, which was a good thing, Joe thought.

The undead started to come out, the noise of the scuffle tipping them off. With no place to go, he wasn't sure how long their group would survive.

28
NEW PLACE

TRACY TOOK AIM and brought down an undead teen girl wearing a black T-shirt and ripped jeans headed there way. She took out another teen girl in a blue T-shirt a moment later.

Since they had no choice but to go back the way they came, their best bet would be to get to the safe house's back entrance and try and hold up in the area between the door and the safe house proper. If the dead had somehow got through the front door, odds of them finding the back door and getting through that in this short a time was minimal.

Not everyone in the group were warriors. One of the men started to panic and kept tripping over his feet. Hal came in and picked him up while firing a shot off into the head of an approaching zombie. Another of the creatures came in from behind and took the trainer out at the knees, its rotten mouth attached to the trainer's calves. Amidst the shouts of pain, two folks surrounding them tried to rescue him, but were mauled themselves. Dean shot down the attacking zombies, then ran up to Tracy.

"You can't leave them," she said.

"They're bit, all of them. They'll either turn fast or, if we carry them, it'll slow the rest of us down or they could turn."

"Can't risk it."

Joe said, "I'm going to—" Just as he stepped forward, presumably to see if he could save the others, more of the dead drew closer. He shot down a few before quickly being preoccupied with a screaming Jessica on his shoulder.

Everyone running, they managed to sidestep a handful of creatures then hit the nearest alleyway. One of the people jumped into a dumpster, while the others kept going.

Is he crazy? Tracy thought. To Joe: "I'll get him."

She ran to the dumpster and saw Cameron, a middle-aged dude with a gentle demeanor, huddled up in the corner. She reached out her hand, glanced up and saw Joe and the others disappear around a corner. "Cam, give me your hand. You can't stay here. They'll climb over and you'll be dead or worse."

"They can't smell me in here. It stinks so bad that I'm going to hurl."

He let rip into the corner he was huddled against.

Perfect, she thought. The undead were getting closer. They had about ten seconds to act or there was going to be a fight. Cam took her hand, coating it in puke.

"Thanks a lot," she said, and pulled him to the edge of the dumpster, tugging on his shirt as he started to climb over.

Once his feet hit the ground, the two made a break for it. Tracy fired off a shot behind her and took out the monster nearest them. Heading the same way Joe did, she had to stop when a couple of other rotters came around the same corner. She shot them down, went after Joe, who was with the others who were already up ahead a solid two sidewalk lengths.

"Let's go, Cam," she said and tugged on his sleeve.

He stared at her and only when the blood poured from his mouth did he fall forward, a zombie on his back biting deep into his neck. Tracy sent a bullet into the creature's head, then kept on to avoid the others nearing.

Sorry I couldn't stop you from changing, Cam. If only she had some extra time, but how much she would've needed varied. Some people came back from the dead right away; others took days, some even longer.

She ran to catch up, not having to fire a single shot after managing to dodge around a couple of the creatures that tried to grab her. She ran past a body and saw it was Gail, another of the group. She, too, hadn't turned yet.

Once back together again, they did a headcount: five. Her, Joe, Dean, Jessica and Rob.

The swarms were growing thick and time was of the essence. The group continued as one down the sidewalk, moving quickly, but not at an all-out run lest somebody tire and fall behind.

"We've lost half already," Joe said when she caught up to him. "We just left."

"I know."

"There might be too many this time. Far too many. Unless we stay ahead, that's it."

"Don't think like that."

"It's reality, Tracy."

"Doesn't have to be. Remember, I need you to be strong right now. If this thing between you and me is softening you up—"

"Don't tell me that. I've heard enough of that before all this. Trust me, I was fully immersed in nice guys finishing last. I was a master at it."

REDEMPTION OF THE DEAD

"Okay, sorry." *Touchy. This isn't the time to let your relationship screw up everything. Why did I even bring it up? I'm such an idiot. Can I have it that bad that I've just been fighting what I know to be true: that I actually have a chance at happiness and I'm trying to be all tough by shutting it down even though, technically, it's already underway? Come on, Tracy, you're crazy. You're in a life-or-death situation, a major one, and you're thinking about a boy. This is so not you.* She basically had the same conversation with herself in her head three more times before she decided: *Swallow it. Shut up. Just shut up, forget about it and stay one hundred percent on the present. That stuff doesn't matter. It just doesn't.*

Turning at the next corner, options were slim.

"There," Joe said, pointing to a set of cement steps that led to the basement of Johnny G's.

"How did we end up here? We were totally going in the opposite direction," Tracy said.

"Weren't you paying attention? We basically more than double backed. Was the only way to stay ahead of them. They're going to the inner city, we start backing out."

He was right. Her mind had been elsewhere. Completely. *Stupid!*

The five headed down the steps. The basement door to the place was a faux door, once used but no longer. Joe kicked against it and beat it with his fists. It didn't budge.

Rob squeezed in between them. "Let me." He shoved Joe aside and railed into the door with his shoulder. He did it two more times then took out his gun and shot the lock off the handle and also the two hinges on the left side. With a yank on the handle, he ripped the door away, the door itself remaining intact but the frame of wood around it that had secured it to the one inside was in splinters.

"How did you—" Tracy started.

"Strategic shooting," Rob said as he waved everyone in. "Kidding. Just weakened the framing enough so we could get in. Besides, your boyfriend here was hitting against it instead of pulling." Rob winked.

Tracy couldn't help but laugh.

"Okay, funny, ha ha," Joe said. "Besides, so were you." He went inside.

Rob rolled his eyes and waved Tracy in with a "lady's first" gesture.

From inside the door, Joe said, "Come on, Tracy."

She went in, Rob behind. Once in, Dean and Rob went to work getting the door up, while Joe went and started grabbing chairs from the tables in the billiard room they found themselves in.

Rob and Dean talked quietly by the door.

"I think we're okay," Rob said.

"We need to hammer this down," Dean said.

Joe stacked chairs beside the door but not in front of it. He gestured to them and said, "For later," before going off to get some more.

Using her flashlight to find her away around in the dark, Tracy followed the side wall of the billiard room until she found the stairs that led up to the main lounge and restaurant. There was a door at the top, still closed. She drew her gun and cautiously approached it. She tested the handle. Locked. Good. She quietly went down the stairs.

The men were scouring the room, the bar, beneath stools and tables, presumably looking for something to secure the door with.

Tracy went over to Jessica. "How are you holding up?"

The thin girl stood there, hands wrapped around her elbows. "I feel stupid and terrible. Look what I did!"

"Shhh, keep your voice low."

Jessica broke down. Tracy put her arm around her and brought her over to one of the cushioned benches on the side. Jessica wouldn't stop crying. All Tracy could do was wait it out. In the meantime, she hoped Joe and the guys would figure out how to ensure the door was locked in place.

29
THE WAR BEGINS

MANY HOURS LATER...

The loud echoing sound of a plane was heard even down in the billiard room of Johnny G's. Joe sat at the pool table on one of the benches, the table lined with bullets and guns, everyone having disarmed shortly after they got here, a chance to take inventory.

"A plane," Joe said. *Really?* He got up from the table and got close to the door, which had since been boarded over using planks from the handful of cushioned benches down here. With the cushions removed, they had been able to get at the joints where the seat met the legs and through prying and patience, were able to get the planks off while retaining the anchoring nails. They used the butt of a gun to hammer them in place and all was well.

Joe put his ear to the door and listened closely.

Tracy was suddenly beside him. She had a way to sneak up on someone and whether she just did it now intentionally or not, it didn't matter. She was amazing.

"Shhh," Joe said. "Listen."

Tracy leaned her ear closer to the door. They waited. The sound returned, this time louder than before. Tracy's eyes went wide. Joe smiled.

"They're probably flying over," she said.

"I know. They're not here for us, but if they're flying over, they'll see the legions of the dead outside. That's got to count for something, especially if it's connected in some way."

Jessica came up to the door, too.

"Going to tell Dean and Rob," Tracy said.

"Sure," Joe replied.

Jessica stood with him, quiet.

Tracy had been able to talk to her, she later said, and was able to give the young girl some perspective and help alleviate the guilt. Tracy's wisdom worked so much that Jessica had taken Joe privately aside and apologized for putting him and the others in jeopardy earlier.

The sound of the plane returned and this time didn't fade out. It got louder and louder and the idea it was going down and crash right near them flashed inside Joe's mind. He listened some more. It wasn't going down, but it *was* close.

Dean and Rob came by to listen, too.

"What do you think?" Rob asked Dean.

Dean had to raise his voice to be heard above the sound of the plane. "That big thing that we figured was happening?"

"Yeah?"

"It's happening. That's not one plane. That's three of them, if not four. And big suckers, too."

All looked at him with surprise.

"Trust me. Been a plane fanatic my whole life." His face went white. "They better not bomb us."

Joe's heart skipped a beat at that one. If indeed those were military planes—and big ones, like Dean said—they could be bombers and there was no way to know what they were carrying onboard. The zombie giants couldn't be taken down by conventional means, at least the means that most everyone had. They'd have to come down with missiles, even flat out bombs. So far as Joe knew, Canada didn't have any nukes, and if it did, they kept it a well-locked secret. Even then, the logistics involved in that. He also remembered this wasn't his city, even his Earth. Things were different here and nuclear technology and who had what could be one of them.

"We stay in for now," Joe said, "and lay low. We listen and we wait. We have to."

"Are you sure you're ready for this, Billie?" she asked herself as she sat in the cockpit of DK-14-P2-X Mech. Personnel were few, but she got a crash course on the twelve-hour flight over.

The aircraft was going to touch down on the Legislative grounds, the Legislature Building and surrounding structures destroyed, leaving a nice wide open space. Her, Sven—who had a Jetlier—and Bastian—who opted for a M-16 Harness—were to stick together. There were five planes in all, each loaded with weaponry from the pick up at Wales. From the air, Billie and the rest of the crew got a good look at what was going on below. The giants—all ten of them—had gathered in twos side-by-side, each duo facing the other in a kind of circle, behind them a vast army of zombies assembled like a pyramid, the combined effect creating a pentagram. Billie didn't have to guess the reason for that specific formation. Most likely it was a calling card, even an access point. What might come through that access point, well, she only hoped that it wouldn't come to that.

The whole plane shook as it hit the ground. These things were designed for quick touch down and gos. It didn't need much to slow down before stopping. When the plane stopped moving, the giant doors to the rear of the plane opened, revealing an expanse of chewed-up lawn covered in brown and yellow dead grass.

Home sweet home, she thought.

A voice came through the comm. inside the mech. *"B-8, this is squad leader, do you read me, over?"*

"Got you loud and clear," she said, then placed her hands inside the control cylinders beside her. Inside the cylinders were grips and handles for her fingers, like bicycle handles only smaller, and instead of one brake on each handle, there were four small ones, each with their own function. In front of her about flush with her stomach was a control box with more buttons. She stood in the mech like wearing an oversized ski suit, her feet and legs stopping around the knee of the exoskeleton. There was a slight cushioned ridge to support her backside. The front was covered over in a bulletproof shield with a small view window so she could see. The mech's giant hands and arms were controlled by her hands inside the cylinders. There was a gas pedal by her right foot, a brake with the other to make the mech walk or stop. With another switch, she could fold the legs and use the wheels on their sides like a car. Turning was operated via a small joystick by each of her thumbs, one for pivoting side-to-side, the other to go up-and-down.

The squad leader checked in with all units through the comm. link then said, *"Move out. Cut down anything that moves. Try to keep civilians casualties to a minimum. According to B-8, there is at least one survivor. Hopefully they are indoors. If transformation occurs, fire."*

Billie smiled at the mention of Joe. The poor guy had been left alone this whole time.

"Copy that," she said and set the mech in motion. Bastian was on her side at ground level, M-16 harness strapped over him, which enabled him to carry the equivalent of four machine guns at once along with streams of ammo to last all four plenty. Sven pulled out in front of her in the Jetlier. She couldn't see him because of the canopy over the vehicle, but she was proud to envision him ready to go to battle and help reclaim the Earth.

The other squads moved out as well. Billie headed toward Portage Avenue. From down here on the street, she saw how enormous the undead giants truly were for the first time, around fifteen stories. They'd been ordered to leave the giants alone as much as possible and focus on clearing out the small ones. Two of the planes were going to come in and try to shoot them down with a barrage of missiles. This would wait, however, until most of the regular-sized dead were destroyed so the units could move out of the attack zone and minimize the risk of injury or fatality to the squads.

Crowds of the dead were gathered. Some turned and looked at her with blank stares; others remained facing the other way as if in some kind of trance.

"Now we send you back to Hell," Billie said and opened fire. The DK-14-P2-X—or DK-14 as she called it for short—raised its arms. Alongside each was a Gatling gun. She mashed down on the triggers and the guns opened fire. A barrage of bullets went straight into the horde of the dead in front of her. She tried aiming for their heads, but it was easier said than done from inside the mech. The undead fell down in waves before her, their bodies jerking and twitching at rapid speed as they were riddled with bullets. Heads were blown off some, simple shots, even ricochets hitting others in the skull. Billie released the triggers and set the mech in motion to get closer. The DK-14 rocked as it stepped on the bodies of the undead, its shocks and balancing mechanisms kicking in to keep it from tipping.

The vast horde of the dead in front of her started moving toward them. Bastian had opened fire beside her. Sven was shooting from inside the Jetlier in complete rapid fire. Billie got to work and started up the Gatlings again. The power of the DK-14 was unbridled. If only they had something like this a year ago then maybe victory would've been theirs and all the pain and torment wouldn't have happened.

Bullets flew. Zombies were torn apart in shreds of flesh, bone, brain—payback.

The nonstop cracks of gunfire sent everyone in the billiard room to the door again. Joe couldn't believe the sound. It was a cacophony of gunshots, grenades, shouts and screams.

"It's a warzone," Tracy said.

"Maybe it's a rescue mission," he said, "or a liberation mission. I thought the army was totally down."

"They're supposed to be," Tracy said.

Judging by the immense amount of heavy gunfire and how, by the way the ground started to shake, the giant zombies had gotten mobile again, he worried the battle would come to their front door.

"Ears open at all times," Dean said.

"Agreed," Tracy replied.

"Just let me out and I'll join them," Rob said and smacked his fist into his palm.

"No," Joe said, "we lay low as planned. We have to. You go out there, you're a dead man. Are you listening to this? I have to raise my voice just so you can hear me. We stay here and if or when we have to move, we stay together. We've lost enough people today already."

30
GETTING OUT

BILLIE'S SQUAD HAD been the first dropped off. Others were coming in, but due to space issues, they had to land further away.

The Gatling guns rattled the DK-14 as she fired. Every so often she'd stop, take the mech over near a larger group of the dead and opened fire again.

The ground shook as the giants started moving. One threw a fit and brought its hands into the side of a building, wailing on it and bringing it down, creating a whirlwind storm of dust and debris. One of the others had stormed over to a line of ATVs that had been packed full of guns and cannons, not caring if it stepped on its small counterparts. It brought its foot down on an ATV and squashed it in a violent smash of metal and explosion of flame. The giant's foot caught ablaze. As it stomped on the other ATVs, the vehicles exploded, taking out men and zombie alike.

"We got to keep on the move unless we meet the same fate," Billie said into the comm. "What's the ETA on the bombers?"

"*Fourteen minutes,*" came the squad leader.

"Roger." *Love it.* She blasted away at the dead, dismantling them bullet by bullet, skull by skull.

Peeking off to the side, she saw Sven take the Jetlier up on a sidewalk and bulldoze a couple of rotters before opening fire on a rank of them. When they started to swarm his vehicle, her heart picked up pace, but he managed to turn it around and get away.

One of the other platoons must've arrived because she saw a crowd of them blasting machine guns and hurling grenades while other mechs fought the dead.

Bastian seemed to be having a heyday beside her. She didn't think he had stopped pulling the trigger since he first opened fire.

Billie progressed forward then suddenly tipped to the side when the ground shook the same time the DK-14 stepped on a fallen body. The balancing systems prevented her from falling over, thank goodness.

Signaling to Bastian and Sven: "B-6, B-7, we're going to back it up, go left, then come in from the side. Copy?"

"*Yah.*"

"*Yah.*"

REDEMPTION OF THE DEAD

Billie turned the mech around and proceeded as planned. A sudden boom rocked the DK-14 and the entire unit pitched forward, sending her DK to the ground face first.

Over the comm., Bastian screamed then went into radio silence.

"*Bastian!*" It was Sven.

Oh no, Billie thought. "Sven!"

"*Big trouble,*" came his voice. "*Bastian is . . .*" His voice broke at the end.

"Don't get out of the Jetlier, Sven. You can't or—" The mech lifted off the ground and Billie was suddenly airborne inside the cockpit, the sudden change in inertia lifting her backside from the cushion; even her hands and feet rose from where they were supposed to be. Through the window, the brown and gray of the sky was changing places with the pavement and—dark yellow of dead grass raced up to meet her.

A giant. Hate those, she thought.

Once again face first, she settled herself back where she was supposed to be inside the cockpit.

"Sven, do you copy?"

"*Use proper name protocol, B-8,*" came the squad leader.

A few panicked screams came through the comm. right after.

"Bastian's down," she said, tears welling in her eyes.

"*I said—*"

"Shut up! Who cares about stupid protocol? Someone just . . . died."

"*We're in a war, B-8. Get used to it.*"

How could anyone be so cold? Furious, Billie got to work manipulating the controls so the mech could right itself and get moving again, all the while checking in with "B-6" —Sven.

Finally he came through after she got the DK-14 upright. "*Sorry, fräulein. I'm okay on outside, but not inside.*"

"Oh Sv—B-6—I'm so sorry." She desperately wanted to give him a hug and take care of him so he could grieve, but as she looked out the mech's window, she couldn't see him. "Where are you, B-6?" No answer. More chatter came through the comm. Another soldier was being eaten alive in front of her. "B-6? B-6!"

Sven remained quiet.

179

The entire place was beginning to rattle. Joe and the others were gathered around the pool table, each re-arming themselves. They were well-stocked, no doubt about it. Everyone's weapons were arranged in their own square on the table. Joe had his .9mm and a belt full of clips. Tracy the same. Dean had his glock, with a series of magazines, but not in the same volume as Joe and Tracy. He stuffed his pockets with them. Rob had a rifle, two boxes of bullets, and a simple handgun, one he'd been carrying since all this began. Unfortunately, he ran out of bullets for it a long time ago and only hung onto it for sentimental reasons. Jessica didn't have anything, and so two of the pool cues were refashioned for her, each having been broken in the middle, creating jagged points and carved to be sharp and useable thanks to the knives at the bar.

A loud, deep boom made everyone pause for a moment before they finished loading up.

Outside, the sounds of war increased even more.

A loud explosion followed by a thundering crash made everyone hold onto the edge of the pool table. The ground shook and rumbled so bad that Jessica lost her footing and fell; Rob slipped, too, but managed to retain his balance.

More crashes and booms until a violent crack echoed through the room. The concrete wall by the door split, a giant jagged gash running from floor to ceiling. Joe also noticed the boards against the door had gone partly loose, some of them cracked as well.

Something hit the building and crashed through the window upstairs, creating a series of smacks and bangs as whatever came through bulldozed everything in its path.

"Under the pool table," Rob said and went beneath it.

Joe figured might as well. If the place came down, they'd be squished, but if only part of the structure gave way, then having something above them to break the impact could mean the difference between life and death.

Outside, a violent storm of dust erupted into the air several streets over from where Billie shot the dead. The bombers had flown their first pass and had taken two of the giants out, their enormous heads exploding in a ghastly rain of bones, black blood, and gushes of sloppy gray brain matter. Even from Billie's distance, some of the gore had

REDEMPTION OF THE DEAD

landed on her mech. It didn't stop the undead though. Billie released the trigger and checked the ammo read-out on the console. She was down by a quarter and she must've fired off thousands of shots by now.

She turned the DK-14 and caught sight of a pack of zombies in the lower corner of her viewing window. Clunks and swats hit the mech as the undead tried to climb up it, bite it, grab it. Billie pressed down on the pedal and the mech started to move. Like a car, the harder she pressed the faster it went. Her legs were in it like a pair of stirrups that "rode" with the mech's movement. Her readout said she was doing about thirty. Most of the undead had let go. A couple held on. One was on the Gatling gun. Billie raised the right arm and opened fire, shredding the creature's legs that hung over the barrel. With the other arm, she wiped the half-torso off. The other zombie she managed to shake after running the mech a block. She backed up, stepped on its head, killing it.

She turned the DK-14 around and opened fire, marching on, back into battle.

When an enormous crash from upstairs sent a chunk of the ceiling down and just missing the pool table, Tracy was glad at Rob's suggestion of hiding out under here. She peeked out from beneath the side of the table and, with a chunk of the ceiling missing, was able to see into the restaurant above. Part of the front wall had come down along with one of the support beams by the main door. Already a thick cloud of dust had wafted into the restaurant and was sinking into the billiard room. If it got to dense, she and the others wouldn't be able to breathe.

Dean already had his hand over his mouth, using it as a filter.

The chalky taste of dust settled on Tracy's tongue. *That was quick.*

"We're getting a move on," Joe said. "There's a back door upstairs. I'm going to quickly check and if there are no creatures, we climb and go, get some distance so we can breathe. We won't last long down here."

"Good thinking," Dean said.

"I'm coming with you," Tracy said.

Joe shot her a look that said, *No, you stay here. I'll be back in a second.*

She ignored it and swatted him in the shoulder to get him moving.

The two climbed out from under the table and surveyed the damage to the room. A pile of rubble and debris from the fallen ceiling sat in a heap on the ground, but it wasn't high enough for either of them to climb and get up to the second level.

Joe nudged her forward, gun poised. "We'll go up on there, I'll lift you."

That was *not* a good idea. She might be rough-and-tumble around the edges, but a girl's weight was a girl's weight and she did not want Joe hoisting her. "Sorry," she said.

"Too bad. I've lifted you before. Doesn't matter."

Right. Forgot. They got up on the heap. He bent down and grabbed her just above the knees and hoisted her up. She leaned her backside against his shoulder for support and was able to see into the upstairs of the restaurant. There were no rotters from what she could see, but the place was trashed so she wasn't certain.

"Hard to tell. Everything's everywhere," she said. "Get closer. I might be able to climb up."

"No."

"Then I can't tell you if it's safe."

"Fine." He took a few steps closer, holstered his weapon, then with both hands gave her a big boost. Tracy was able to grab onto the broken corner of the ceiling, careful to take hold of where the flooring met the joists where possible for extra support. She pulled herself over the edge, rolled over once for safety, then stood. The noise from the battle outside was even louder up here, the dust worse as well. She covered her mouth; her eyes began to water. The entire restaurant was now a mess of tables and chairs. The bar up here was covered in broken booze bottles, the pictures from the walls on the seats beneath them. Even the awesome art piece of John Lennon, Bob Dylan, Mick Jagger, David Bowie and Neil Young on the wall was splattered with blood. Over her shoulder at the fore of the restaurant, through the broken wall, one of the giants lay in a heap on top of the partially-demolished parkade across the street. Its head was a giant crater of gore and bone; its huge hand was close to the front of the restaurant, its fingers still twitching.

A low rasp came from behind her.

"See anything?" Joe called from below.

"Hang on a sec."

She walked a few steps and saw a rotter behind the bar, a short one. It climbed over the bar, looking at her the whole time. It was a kid, probably four years old. Undead children were hard to face.

"Sorry," she said, lined up her shot, and took the young zombie down. She scanned the room again, then yelled down to Joe, "I think that's it."

REDEMPTION OF THE DEAD

The whistle of what had to be a missile sung through the air. The explosion and enormous crash afterward made Tracy instinctively throw her hands to her ears. The ground shook and she fell backward over a fallen chair and smacked her head on the overturned table beyond.

"Tracy?" Joe said from below.

"Fine," she said, but wasn't sure if it was loud enough. That bump on the head stung like the dickens.

"Tracy?"

"Coming," she said louder.

The ground shook some more. She went to the edge to climb back down to the billiard room. Joe was facing away from her, gun aimed. She leaned over the edge enough to see along his line of sight and saw there was a big hole along the wall that buckled and cracked when the ceiling came down.

Joe fired off a shot the moment a rotter stuck its head through the hole. It went limp, but already decaying gray hands were clawing past its fallen comrade and trying to get in. Joe shouted for the others to get out from under the pool table.

Over his shoulder, he called, "Tracy, help them up."

"I'll try, but you're going to have to boost Rob and Dean."

Joe fired off another shot.

The rest of the group gathered around him.

"There's lots," Joe said.

Tracy looked up to the broken wall toward the front. Fortunately, the main restaurant was a good ten feet above street level so at least the dead didn't have direct access to it. It wouldn't be long until they started climbing, though.

"Hurry it up," she said.

Rob lifted Jessica and Tracy pulled her over the edge. Below, Rob told Joe to just keep an eye on the hole and he'd lift Dean. He did and Tracy had to dig in with her legs and back up as she held onto Dean's wrists and pulled him up.

Rob turned around and Tracy thought he was going to tell Joe it was time to go, but instead the big man spun Joe around and started lifting him to the edge.

"What are you doing?" Joe asked.

"You go first."

"Stop it." But it was too late. Joe was already in position to grab the ceiling. With a grunt, he pulled himself over the edge and then got on his haunches and reached down to Rob. "Grab on!"

183

"You go," Rob said.

"What's the matter with you?" Tracy said. "This is no time to be a hero."

"I'll run interference. You guys go."

Undead faces started popping up near the open front wall.

Joe said, "We're running out of time. Grab on. Don't be a—"

"Go!" Rob disappeared from view.

Tracy called down, "We're going around the back."

Rob didn't reply.

Joe dropped onto his side and peered down into the hole. "Crap," he said and drew his gun and fired off a shot. "Idiot," he said quietly. He stood, took Tracy by the arm, and they started toward the back.

"Is he . . . ?" she asked.

"They grabbed him. I shot one. Was too late for the other."

"That's too bad. I liked him, from what I knew of him."

"Sorry, Tracy."

The back door was already open, probably having been kicked in at one point prior when the looters had their heyday. They went through. The back alley was clear. They headed straight across the alleyway and into the parking lot beyond. The dust on the air was so thick that Tracy couldn't wait to finally find a clearing.

After they traversed the lot, they hit the street beyond.

"Head down to the river," Dean said. "We'll follow that."

Tracy agreed. It was a safer route unless there was something there she wasn't expecting.

31
IT'S ABOUT TIME

THE DK-14 HAD been crowded by a horde of the dead again, nearly knocking it over. Billie had been able to shake most of them loose and shoot the others. For a short while there she let a few hang on and bite at the metallic hull, letting their rotted teeth crack and break until she was able to smash them against a wall or parked car.

The comm. had been quiet for the last ten minutes or so. She tried raising people on it, but was met with silence, even from the squad leader. As for Sven, her heart ached to think of what might have become of him. She was truly looking forward to getting to know him more and, maybe, dating him. Ignoring the forming tears, she motored on, shooting down every creature she set her eyes on.

Explosions and the whistles of missiles went off around her.

An enormous foot set down in front of her; the entire cockpit shook. She pressed down on the pedal and used the mech's momentum to climb up and over the giant's foot and land on the other side. She kept it going full throttle, the giant's hand just missing her as she maneuvered out of the way.

Another mech stepped in and opened fire on the giant.

"It's a waste," she said into the comm.

The mech kept shooting. The giant reached down, picked it up, and threw it like a baseball. It crashed into the remains of a fallen building.

Billie checked the ammo read-out. A little under half down. She'd purposefully stayed to the perimeter of the dead for easier targeting and her own safety, but it still looked like she hadn't made a dent in their numbers.

Loud booms from cannons thundered; her Gatling guns whirred at high pitch; the steady *rat-a-tat-tat-tat* of machine guns added to the din. Visibility low due to the enormous amount of dust on the air, she took the mech further away and hoped the excessive dust wouldn't interfere with the DK-14's performance. She hit a road gridlocked with abandoned vehicles. With a press of the pedal, she took the mech up and over the cars, leaping from one to the other, the mech's powerful mechanical legs making light work of the obstacles.

The next thing she knew, she found herself by what was left of Earl's Restaurant, and saw a pack of zombies beneath the neighboring railway bridge. Heading over there, she fired and killed them. There were more on the left a further ways down. She went over and did the same.

"This is for all the times you nearly killed me," she said. "This is for August and Des. This is for Sven and Bastian." *Oh Sven, I hope you're all right.*

The dead were obliterated by a maelstrom of bullets. Blood and flesh burst into the air like liquid fireworks. Billie kept on, shooting anything that moved. Everything. If it had legs—was that . . . people? Up ahead, coming out of the Exchange and heading toward the river? Hard to tell. She mashed down on the pedal to head over there, Gatlings at the ready in case they were a pack of monsters.

The chalky taste of dust in Joe's mouth made him yearn for a drink of water. He knew he wasn't the only one dying of thirst. They found a bit of booze at the billiard's bar, but nothing thirst-quenching. The little bit of Sailor Jerry rum he had took some of the edge off, though. Even made him feel pretty good. Too bad the river was polluted with all that gray rainwater.

Loud thunks thumped along the pavement, sending vibrations into his feet. Down the road was what looked like a huge robot barreling toward them. Was he seeing things? Did his body need water so bad he was starting to hallucinate?

He tapped Tracy on the shoulder and pointed toward the robot. "Tell me you don't see that."

"See what?" she said, then turned around. "Oh. That."

Joe held his gun aloft. Tracy did the same along with Dean. Jessica held her sticks out. Joe didn't have the heart to tell her they weren't going to help.

The big robot ran up to them, arms laden with—Gatling guns?—aimed right at them.

"Tell me I'm not seeing this," Dean said.

"You're seeing it," Jessica said.

The robot's arms lowered, followed by a mechanical whirring sound. The—what now Joe realized was a cockpit hatch—on the front torso of the thing opened. He squinted against the dust on the air, gun still ready to blast the head off of any—

"Joe?" came a female voice.

Me?

"Joe!" His name came out more like a shriek than his actual name. A short girl climbed out of the cockpit and came through the dust fog.

"Billie!" Joe said, dropped his gun and ran toward her. He wrapped his arms around her and picked her up and spun her around before setting her back down. "Are you serious? It's you?"

"I can't believe you're alive. I thought . . . maybe . . ."

"No, I made it."

"I'm stunned," she said, "but thank God."

"Yeah." Joe couldn't help but just stare at her. She was a different girl now. Her hair's natural color was showing at the roots—dark brown, it seemed—her glasses were gone, her face dirty, and she had a strength about her that she didn't have before. "What about August?"

Her eyes went soft and she pressed her lips together as she shook her head.

Joe's spirits sunk and a hollow hurt filled his heart. "How?"

"Not now," she said. "Please?"

He licked his lips, tasting the chalky dust anew. "Okay, later then. I just . . . I just can't believe he's gone. I held out hope for both of you."

She hugged him. "Thanks. Just know that . . . that he didn't die in vain."

It made him feel a little better, filled him with a sense of pride. A guy like August—wise, gentle, caring, a leader—he deserved a dignified death and Joe wasn't surprised in the least that that was how the man made his last stand.

"Come, meet the others," he said.

She sniffled, said okay, and he led her over to the group.

"Everyone, this is Billie." Gesturing to the others: "Tracy, Dean, Jessica."

Billie gave a small wave. "Hi."

Tracy said, "What is that thing?"

Billie looked back at the robot. "It's the DK-14-something-or-other. It's a mech exoskeleton. Super long story. I've been *everywhere*, and I'm not exaggerating." She didn't take her eyes off Joe.

"Okay, let's keep it simple. How'd you get here?" he said.

"There're planes over there" —she pointed— "and we had a couple thousand men battling the dead. I'm not alone. Lots of the men are dying. One of mine—two of mine—are gone. One for sure. I need to find the other. His name is Sven. He's huge, German, blond hair, driving what looks like an enclosed motorcycle."

Joe arched an eyebrow.

"Trust me, Joe."

"If you say so."

Billie thumbed back in the direction she came: "As you probably know, most of the horde is downtown—down-downtown—and the giants are being taken out, but Joe—you know there's more to this than what we see, right?"

He nodded. "Don't worry. I told them everything."

"Everything?"

"Everything-everything."

"Their formation had been a pentagram. I saw it from the sky when I first flew over."

"That thing flies?" he asked, pointing to the mech.

"No, the plane. Now listen. When we got separated, and after August—in the end, I met an angel—"

"The same one from before?" He was too overwhelmed to get excited, but was glad that at least there was a shining light to all this.

"Yeah, I should've said *our* angel. In the end—Joe, this is big: those zombies, those demons, they're not alone here anymore."

"What do you mean? What else happened?"

"I don't know how to say this so I'll just say it. Just brace yourself: I saw the devil, and he's here on Earth. He's behind it all."

A shockwave went through his body head-to-toe. His legs grew weak. The others stared at Billie in stunned silence.

"I saw him come through this portal," she said, "and I felt his evil even from where I stood, which was far away. I don't know where he is now. Frankly, I don't want to know, and I wasn't sure I was going to tell you if I saw you, but after seeing that pentagram from the sky . . . . We're in some serious trouble."

Heart beating rapidly, Joe was at a loss for words. It was to be expected, her news, but that she actually saw it—he flashed back to his time in Hell and shuddered at the memory. Now Hell had come to Earth, even worse than the zombie invasion which, it seemed, was actually a possession.

All he could say was, "Where's the plane?"

REDEMPTION OF THE DEAD

Billie led the procession in the direction of the large aircraft, shooting anything undead that came in front of them. A few gunshots echoed behind them as the others took up the rear.

It felt so, so good to see Joe again. His hair had grown since she last saw him, but she recognized that hard-edged face of his, one forged from hunting the undead, one carved from pain. Yet he now had this twinkle in his eye. Something had changed, but she wasn't sure what.

The trek to the aircraft was long and it got worse as they had to enter into the dust cloud. They kept to the peripheral as long as possible so they could see clearly and breathe better, then had to press in by the Canada Revenue office on Broadway. She told them before they left that it's not like they'll get to the plane, show their tickets and settle in for an in-flight movie. If anything, they'd be going there to hide out. The plane had been emptied when they landed, everyone taking up arms. Billie decided to try the plane's radio once on board.

Gunshots went off behind her then the sound of someone yelling. She turned the mech around to see Joe crouched over the Asian girl, four dead zombies lying around her. Joe glanced up at her and slowly shook his head.

Even though she never knew her, Billie's heart ached for the loss.

Emerging out of the dust, a Jetlier cut in front of her.

"Sven?"

The hatch opened and it was him.

Suddenly filled with excitement, Billie opened her cockpit, but stayed inside in case her guns were needed.

"Guten tag, fräulein," Sven said.

She smiled, too happy to say anything. She noticed the Jetlier was covered in blood and goopy, gray flesh.

He walked up to her and held out his hand. She took it. "Are you okay?" She could kiss him. "I'm okay. Are you?"

With a wink he said, "Fine on outside, not fine on inside."

"I know, sweetie. I'm so so sorry for your brother."

Tears glazed over his eyes. "Danke."

Joe came up. "Who's this?"

Roles now reversed, she said, "Joe, this is Sven. I met him in Austria."

"You met him in . . ." Joe's words came out slowly.

"Just say hi," Billie said.

Joe stuck out his hand and Sven swallowed it with his own.

"Guten tag."

189

"Guten—" He looked at Billie. "You were in Austria?"

"Later, remember?" she said.

The sound of bullets fired told her she'd been wrong about everyone being dead. A relief. A couple cannons went off. The ground shook as the remaining giants stomped around.

All of it was silenced when blasting shrieks cut through the air, the terrible sound sending her into a panic.

"No, please no," she said, her heart at a gallop. She knew those shrieks. She'd heard them before.

Demons.

Judging by the way Joe's eyes went impossibly wide, she knew he recognized that awful sound, too.

"Okay, time to go," Billie said.

Sven kissed her hand, then without a word went to the Jetlier.

"Meet at the plane," she called after him.

He raised his hand in a wave without turning around.

Billie closed up the mech and used the exoskeleton's huge arm to signal to the others to follow her. Gatlings raised again, she started firing when she saw shadows behind a veil of dust.

32
RETREAT

The DK-14 opened fired, sending round after round into the shadows in the dust. The bullets seemed to go right through them. Thinking she might have missed, Billie double checked the mech's Gatling alignments and opened fire again. Proceeding forward and seeing the same result, her breath caught in her throat when she saw it wasn't the undead coming toward her, but demons, already freed from their shells. That meant their metamorphosis was across the entire legion of the dead and the game had changed.

The others wouldn't stand a chance.

Sven sped ahead of her on the Jetlier, heading straight for the demons.

"No, don't!" she screamed into the comm., forgetting his comm. was probably down and that was why he hadn't responded to her the other times she tried to raise him.

The demons jumped on the Jetlier—one on top, one on the side, and another underneath—and catapulted it into the air, sending it flying to the side where it smashed into the roof of an abandoned car, tumbled across a handful of others and landed somewhere on the other side.

In a rage, Billie mashed down on the trigger and fired off a string of shots before changing course and taking the mech full throttle in the direction Sven had been thrown. The mech ran and leaped on top of the cars' roofs, jumping from one to the other before landing on the other side. Sven's Jetlier lay in a crumpled heap, its side and roofed smashed in.

Panicking, she came over to it and used the mech's powerful hands to grab hold of the bent door and pry it off. She threw it to the side and opened the cockpit. She jumped out and ran to Sven's broken body.

She fell to her knees at his side. "No, no, no. Not now. Not you."

Sven lay there, his legs twisted at the hips past their natural torque, one of his arms bent behind his back so far that the hand was visible beneath the opposite shoulder. His face was covered in blood from a severe bleeding nose and already the flesh around his eyes was swelling shut. "Fräulein . . ." The word was weak.

"Hang on, okay?" she said. "I'm going to get you out of this." She assessed the damage again and his body was so tangled up in the smashed

Jetlier that she didn't know where to start to even attempt to free him never mind gathering the courage to run the risk of accidentally moving something the wrong way and making it worse.

"Danke," he said.

She sniffled back the tears. "For what?"

"For letting me be friend to pretty girl like you."

She smiled and sniffled again. "Thank you for letting me *care* about a handsome man like you."

He smiled, too, his incredible green eyes looking into hers.

A loud thump shook the Jetlier; Sven's limp form rocked with the motion. Standing over him on the Jetlier's frame was a demon, its wings spread, mouth open, hissing.

Fear turning her limbs to jelly, Billie tried to back up, stumbled over her own feet and fell down. The demon eyed her. Billie looked at Sven.

"Go, fräulein," he said. "Ich liebe dich."

The demon pounced on Sven and got to work ripping him apart.

Screaming and cursing at the demon to stop, Billie stumbled backward and scrambled toward the mech, the tears so thick in her eyes everything was a blur. Once back inside, she closed the hatch, and fired at the creature. The bullets passed through it. It didn't even look over its bony shoulder.

"Joe . . ." she said, and turned the DK-14 around.

Joe fired round after round into the demon that had swooped low, grabbed Jessica, and taken her high into the air. His bullets didn't stop it.

Tracy and Dean were right behind him, tucked up against him so tight that if they pushed against him any harder they'd knock him forward.

Foul shrieks and haunting hisses emanated from all around. Joe instructed the others to stay with him and keep heading toward the plane.

Tracy and Dean fired their weapons behind him. Billie's mech emerged not far ahead and was firing a barrage of bullets in what seemed like all directions. The loud thunderous crash of a giant smashing a building made the ground rumble. Joe was able to see the creature's enormous form even from a few streets over as it drove its rotten fists into a building's roof before raising its giant arms to the sky. Bright red light shone from the top of its head and then made a fiery red lightning

REDEMPTION OF THE DEAD

bolt down its body. From the top of its head, huge scaly hands with long claws dug their way out and pushed down on its skull from either side, disrobing, revealing a massive demon with a wing span that covered three city blocks. The demon howled, and leaned back its dragon-like head, spewing forth flame, casting a fiery glow on everything.

"Head for cover!" Joe shouted. The three of them ran to the nearest building and burst through the doors. He didn't know where they were as the place was unrecognizable because of the damage. It did appear like a lounge of some kind, but most of the place was overturned, windows smashed, broken bottles and shattered picture frames everywhere.

A whirlwind kicked up outside as more howling shrieks filled the air, deafening booms and crashes making all three of them cover their ears in protest.

All the surviving giants must have transformed, Joe thought. How were they going to counter this? They wouldn't stand a chance.

Tracy took his hand in hers. "They can't find us. We need to hide."

"I know, but where? The only thing I think we can do is try to get to the plane and meet up with Billie. Maybe Dean here, being the airplane guy, maybe he can fly—"

A loud, deep *pop* sent a jolt through Joe. He and Tracy turned around and Dean was face first on the floor, a portion of his head missing, part of his brain on the ground. Blood poured from the wound, pooling around his head and upper body.

It took Joe a second to process what happened. He turned away. Tracy didn't.

"Couldn't take it," she said.

"I guess," he replied quietly. A well of anger bubbled within. He was mad at Dean for offing himself; was mad at the undead for not just today's losses, but *all* of them; was pissed April had been transformed and he accidentally killed her; was furious August was gone; despite not always getting along with him, he was even mad Des had been changed after they returned through the Storm of Skulls and was now dead as well. He was downright furious that this battle might claim Tracy, too.

Joe drew Tracy in and embraced her. "It's just you, me and Billie. That's it. We're of no more use here. Whatever plans might have been meant for us—not anymore. We run like heck to the plane, pray Billie's there, and hope for a miracle."

She nodded and grabbed his face between her hands and pressed her lips against his, one of fear, need and passion. When she released, she checked her firearm, loaded a new clip; Joe did the same regardless whether or not the bullets would be of any use anymore.

At the entrance to the building, they counted it off and ran into the dust cloud.

"I think it's over there," Joe shouted above the shrieks on the air. He hoped Tracy saw which way he pointed.

They ran through the cloud, the shrieks of demons overhead. Joe paused for a second then kept going after he felt this strange electric tingle on the air. Not far over to the left, he saw the aircraft.

"Billie!" he shouted, hoping to get her attention though he didn't know how well she could hear through the mech's cockpit shield.

Metallic thuds came from off to the side and Billie's mech came up beside them; all three headed in the same direction.

Her voice came through the speaker: *"Glad you guys are alive. I couldn't find you. We need to get to the plane. Does that girl know how to fly?"*

She meant Tracy. "No, she doesn't." He double checked: "Right?"

"Sadly, no."

"Meet us at the plane, Billie."

"I'll stay alongside."

They weaved in and around cars. A couple of the demons swooped low. They managed to evade them by ducking and suddenly stopping before adjusting their course.

The plane was now in view, maybe fifty yards off.

That same electric tingle returned, this time stronger, carrying with it the ability to send jolts of fear through whoever it contacted. Joe tried to ignore the hairs on the back of his neck standing on end and the sickening trepidation about things getting worse.

Wind blew through the dust, which caught him off guard as there hadn't been wind in the city for a year unless it was artificially created. The wind grew steadily warmer with each passing second until the heat became unbearable and sweat broke out all over his skin.

Tracy coughed.

They made it to the plane and were on their way to the back hatch when all the demons shrieked as one, then silenced at the same time.

"Joe . . ." Tracy said, her voice weak. He'd never heard an undertone of impotence in her voice before. She gestured to Billie's mech. Standing before it was a man in a dark purple button-down, black dress pants and shoes, clean-shaven with neat blond hair. The man reeked of sulfur and Joe had to put his hand over his mouth and nose.

As much as he willed his legs to move, fear kept them locked in place. The violent flapping of wings filled the air as hordes of demons came and occupied the area around them, and hovered above them.

Billie . . . "Billie!" Joe said.

The man turned to him. His eyes were black, cold. He held out one hand toward Joe, palm open, the other toward Billie, palm open as well. From the hand in front of Billie, red electric charges emanated from his fingertips, the red strings of energy dancing through the air until they connected with Billie's mech. He snapped his hand into a fist and the front hatch of the mech tore straight off, hovered midair before the man, then was cast to the side with a wave of his hand.

"Hello, Billie," he said.

She didn't speak.

Joe's heart raced and Tracy looked like she was in a state of disbelief. The guy's presence . . . there was something very wrong about it, something worse than the undead, small or large, even the demons. Then Joe understood.

It was the devil.

33
BATTLE OF THE ANGELS

BILLIE TREMBLED BEFORE the incarnation of evil in front of her. His pitch black eyes were as smooth as marble and as deep as the farthest reaches of space. He was alluring, she hated to even notice never mind admit, and could only assume the dark one's beauty was part of what made evil so attractive.

"I suppose I have you to thank for all this," he said.

"It was a mistake," she said, choking on the words.

"But you won't have the credit. I never share credit because this world has now become mine because of me and what I've done."

She didn't want to hear it. She considered trying to run, but it would spell her doom if she did. All she could do was remain before him, helpless.

"You have something I want, don't you?" the devil said.

"What do I have that you could possibly—" *The crystals*. If this guy wanted them, then they couldn't be something she could let go of; she would protect them with her life, if she had to.

He eyed her bracelet. "I see you wear the ornaments of another realm." He snarled. "Give them to me, Billie."

Joe and Tracy stood there, mouths slightly open, still seemingly stunned.

Billie's heart picked up pace and began slamming so hard in her chest she felt it in her throat. There was only one answer she could give him: "No."

"I see. And there's nothing I can do that would sway you?"

She shook her head.

The devil nodded as if he understood. "Very well." The hand facing Joe and Tracy suddenly elongated, the fingers turning into long, stringy tubes of scaly leather, with claw-like tips. They snapped out in an instant then snapped back and reentered his hand, his palm and fingers returning to normal.

Joe choked off to the side, his eyes wide, a hand to his throat. Blood bubbled out of his lips as he tried to speak, but all he could do was sway forward when Tracy caught him.

Screaming, Billie jumped out of the mech and started to run toward him when the devil caught her.

"The crystals, Billie," he hissed. "I want them, and I want them now."

REDEMPTION OF THE DEAD

Tears leaking from her eyes, Tracy lowered Joe to the ground, almost falling with him as his body went limp. She kneeled beside him and stroked his cheeks, his forehead. She removed his hand from his throat to reveal two large puncture wounds: one straight through the esophagus and trachea, the other perfectly aimed through the center of his aorta. She quickly put his hand back and pressed hers against his, trying to stop the blood that was gushing out between their fingers.

"Joe . . ." she said.

His green eyes looked at her and he tried to reach up to touch her face, but his hand barely lifted. She took it and put it to her cheek.

"Say something," she said.

His lips parted then closed slowly a couple of times, before he managed, "Tra—" His eyes went wide, as if looking at something majestic just past her. "Jesus forgive me . . ." The muscles in his face went slack and his head tilted to the side, his gaze vacant.

Sharp stabs of pain and grief piercing through her, she started to shake and furiously stroked his face and cheeks as if her touches of affection would revive him.

Her words barely dribbled between her tear-soaked lips. "No, not . . . Joe . . . don't leave me . . . not like this . . . not you. Anyone but you . . ." A full-on cry threatened to burst forth. Tracy summoned her training and stilled herself, biting back the tears, the pain, the excruciatingly sharp heartache that threatened to kill her.

She turned to the devil. "I'm going to kill you."

"With what, Tracy," he said.

She gently laid down Joe's head and stood, gun drawn. "Don't ever say my name."

Billie was clearly terrified, her eyes glazed over with tears, her gaze fixed on Joe's body.

Taking aim, Tracy was about to fire a shot when the whole area lit up in bright white light, the rays immediately causing her to squeeze her eyes shut.

Demons shrieked above and the thwapping of furiously flapping wings drummed in her ears. She blinked her eyes open and a man stood behind the devil, who was now growling against the intrusion. He still had Billie in his arms until the man behind him grabbed him and in a flurry of gold and white, sent Billie stumbling forward, free, with the man now standing in between the devil and the two girls.

The light faded, revealing the most beautiful sight Tracy had ever seen. He wore a golden robe, folded over and over as it draped on his muscular frame, with fiery hair, a silver shield on his back. Hanging off his golden belt was a scabbard with a large sword.

"Nathaniel . . ." Billie said quietly behind her.

The devil said, "Oh, it's you. You are of no concern."

Sword drawn, Nathaniel raised it, pointing its sharp tip at the devil's head. "Silence, snake. Your presence here is not welcome."

"You forget, Nathaniel, the Earth is mine, has been for many millennia."

"You are a defeated foe. The Host are here and your legion is falling."

The devil went to move to the side, but Nathaniel set his sword in his path, blocking him. "You really think you could beat me?" the devil said. "I know your role. You are not nearly powerful enough to stop me."

"He might not be," said a loud voice, "but I am." A man with enormous golden wings set down beside Nathaniel. He was dressed the same, but across his chest was a blood-red sash covered in beautiful golden symbols that shone like stars.

"Michael," the devil hissed.

Tracy was relieved that help was here even though she didn't believe she was seeing it. Two angels? That had to be what they were. They were amazing, full of light, huge wings, big, powerful. Even standing near them caused her to tremble. She hoped that indeed they were on the right side.

All around them the sounds of war rang out as angel clashed with demon both on the ground and in the air. Demons swarmed around Tracy and Billie, flying in with bared claws and mouths open with sharp fangs. The bright silver of sword blades burst through the demons' heads and chests, ripping through them and reducing them to ash.

Just beyond, Nathaniel and Michael had their swords drawn; the devil had one of his own and right when he drew his liquid black sword, he transformed into a tall beast with powerful muscles coated in dragon scales, his face dark like tar, his eyes black as pitch, wreathes of smoke and fire igniting and bursting all around him in a continuous cycle of flame. Large, leathery bat wings shot out of his back, their razor-sharp tips moving like an extra set of blades.

The devil moved lightning quick, the strikes of his sword deflected

REDEMPTION OF THE DEAD

and parried by Nathaniel and Michael, each of the angels moving around the devil in circles, keeping him contained, while also blocking blow after blow of the demonic sword. The devil tried to escape upward, but Nathaniel was quickly in the air above him, brought down his sword and sent the evil one back to the ground where Michael came in with a violent slash, narrowly missing the devil's chest just as he dodged it.

Foul screeches pierced Tracy's ears; Billie's face was scrunched up in a wince. The terrible demonic creatures kept trying to have at them, but it was as if there was a force field of golden light encasing the girls so they'd be safe. Tracy followed the speeding lights around her, occasionally catching a glimpse of a warrior angel in battle armor: ornate silver helmets, breastplates and leg guards, silver shields and silver swords. Their presence was a comfort amidst the air of evil.

The devil moved quickly to the side, able to twist around and get past Michael. He immediately went for the girls, his black sword coming in to cut them to pieces. Tracy wasn't sure the golden light field around them would hold. Nathaniel appeared in front of them, deflected the blow and kicked the devil back into Michael's arms. Contained, Michael was about to wrestle the devil to the ground when the evil one twirled like a tornado, jumped up, then slammed his sword into the ground. The earth rumbled and shook, the surrounding buildings immediately beginning to buckle and crumble from the earthquake.

Tracy and Billie lost their footing and landed on their hands and knees. Nathaniel came in beside them, scooped them up and took them into the air.

Below, the earth around the devil and Michael caved in like a funnel the size of a football field, the plane teetering on the edge of the dead grass and ground before falling into the chasm that kept growing and growing.

All around angels and demons clashed in the air in whirls of light and scales. Shrieks and powerful calls in a language Tracy didn't understand consumed the air.

Nathaniel rose high over the city, one girl in each arm.

"Thank ... thank you ..." Tracy said.

"You're welcome," the angel said, his voice authoritative but oh-so-soothing with gentleness and comfort.

"I'm so glad you came," Billie said. "Thanks for saving us." She took a deep breath, then said, "Joe ..."

The very mention of his name made the tears flow and Tracy looked away.

"I know," the angel said gently. "I'm sorry."

"Is he okay?" Billie asked.

"It's not for me to judge."

"Why couldn't you get here in time?" Tracy said, looking his way. "He died because you weren't here!"

"The battle was in motion even before you saw these creatures for what they were, before the dark one emerged."

"Quiet!" she snapped.

"Tracy!" Billie shouted. She shook her head slowly. "Don't." Her tone said she was dead serious.

"Tracy, all is not lost. Please be strong and please trust God to work this for good."

How dare he? Her heart beat in furious rage. "You want to start talking like that after what happened? Look!" She pointed down.

Below the dark chasm became a giant pit around which angels and demons fought toe-to-toe in a whirlwind of golden light, fire and black smoke.

She glanced back at Nathaniel and to Billie beyond. Billie's face was stern. Nathaniel's—it was hard to read him. His jaw was set firm, but his fiery eyes contained gentleness.

A fowl hollow screech filled the area and in a dark cyclone from below came the devil, his wings spread wide, flying at blinding speed toward them, Michael hot on his tail. Nathaniel turned on the air and bolted away while the devil gave chase.

"Come back!" he shouted.

"Set me down," Tracy said. "You can't use your sword otherwise."

Nathaniel squeezed her all the tighter and kept on. Behind them, the devil's hot breath burned at their feet, its heat quickly rising past their soles and up their legs until he had caught up and was right over them. With a feral growl he grabbed Billie straight out of Nathaniel's hands. Nathaniel arced up and snatched her back; Billie screamed and said something about her arm. Michael caught up, grabbed the devil and drove his sword into the evil one's wing, puncturing a hole.

The devil turned over and focused on Michael again, their swords clashing.

Nathaniel arced down toward the ground, getting distance.

"Put us down so you can get him," Billie said.

"No, we have something else to do. Michael will contain him. It was what he was created for. At the appropriate time, Lucifer will answer to One far greater and will pay dearly for his transgressions."

Below the amount of angels versus the amount of demons seemed to have increased.

We're winning, Tracy thought. *Wait, what is he doing?* "Hey!" she shouted.

"We will now set things right," Nathaniel said.

"I don't like it," Billie said and Tracy knew why. They were flying directly toward the enormous chasm in the ground.

They crossed the opening and were quickly engulfed in darkness except for the angel's glow.

"Are you crazy?" Tracy said. "Where are you taking us?"

The angel didn't reply.

34
IN HELL

The rush of wind as they sped deeper and deeper into the bowels of the earth grew warmer with each passing moment. Sweat had already begun to break out across Billie's skin, the wind from their fast descent not enough to cool her.

"You're taking us down to—" she started, but couldn't bring herself to finish the question.

"We must complete our mission. Mine was to set you on the right path, gather that which was sent out. Yours was to right your wrong," Nathaniel said.

Billie glanced behind herself. The entrance of the hole was nowhere in sight. In front of them, the hole was growing narrower with each moment. Soon they were rapidly descending down a rocky tube no more than a dozen feet in diameter and even that was growing smaller by the second.

"Um . . . Nathaniel?" Billie said.

The tunnel grew even thinner and Nathaniel changed position, switching his descent to feet first, Billie's stomach doing a flip from the change. She thought she heard Tracy yelp. In the ambient glow of the angel's light, the dark stony ground below rushed up to meet them as the walls grew impossibly close. If Billie reached out to touch them, they'd take her arm off. She hugged Nathaniel tight and saw Tracy do the same.

The walls of the tunnel closed in right around them and soon cast wide as they emerged in a massive, vacuous cavern.

The heat was severe and Billie turned her head, seeing what she knew she'd see: the Lake of Fire off in the distance. The haunting screams of the damned rose and filled her ears.

They touched down on the hot stone floor.

"Where are we?" Tracy asked, her body hunched over, probably from the oppressive atmosphere of this place.

Billie felt it, too. "The last place anyone would want to be."

"You mean?"

She slowly nodded.

The howls of the damned sent her on edge. The angel beside her was calm.

REDEMPTION OF THE DEAD

"Before we go on," he said, "we must cross the Lake. Do not look into the fire because what you will see will be very hard to forget."

"Why are we here?" Billie asked.

"We are outside of Time in the eternal realm. You and I have been here before and so we must come to find the portal and set things right." He turned to her. "Do you have the crystals?"

She showed him the bracelet. "I do. What are they?"

"They belong to this." Nathaniel reached into his golden robe and produced a pocket watch. *The* pocket watch, the one which determined the time of Armageddon. "When the watch did not reset, I kept it in my care. After pulling Joe from this place and we were under attack while the demons flooded the Earth, I dispersed the watch's contents—the crystals—and they landed in each of the places you visited. During the year since they were cast away, they acted like beacons and drew together forces for good to assemble and begin work on defending the Earth. It would have worked had Lucifer not manifested. I, however, have been too engaged in battle to retrieve them myself. We must return where we first met." He held out his hand. "Give me the stone."

Billie touched the crystal-filled stone, gave it a tug, and removed it from the bracelet. She handed it to him without reserve, frankly glad to be rid of the thing. Nathaniel opened the pocket watch, pressed a tiny lever and opened its face. Beneath was an intricate array of diamonds and indentations of different shapes that matched the crystals. He placed the stone on top of the diamond bed, and in a flash of golden light, the stone went clear, the crystals now in each of their respective cradles. He replaced the watch face, closed its cover and put it back in his robe.

Billie glanced around. "Did it work?"

"It will," he said.

"Did what work?" Tracy asked.

Nathaniel continued, "It must be returned to its appropriate point on the Timeline. We must be very precise."

In the distance, a bright red glow in the shape of a large oval lit up.

"We've already taken too much time." Nathaniel picked up both girls and sped off in the direction of the Lake of Fire.

Tracy held tight as Nathaniel flew them through the chasm of Hell. Demons were already on their tail, chasing after them. She produced her gun and fired off a couple of shots.

"It is a waste," Nathaniel said. "Natural weapons do not defeat a supernatural foe."

Now he tells me. She put the gun back in its holster and saw the Lake of Fire come up beneath them. She knew he said not to look. Billie had her face buried in the angel's golden robe. Curiosity getting the better of her, Tracy looked down. Millions of skeletons rose up above the flames, calling out to her and the angel as they flew overhead, begging to be rescued. Their bones were dry and cracked, ash-gray, their faces skulls, yet each distinct as if a reflection of the human being they once were. Their cries echoed from below and reverberated inside Tracy's soul. She pulled her gaze from the lake and saw the disappointment in Nathaniel's eyes when she looked at him.

"Sorry," she said.

He cast his eyes forward and kept flying.

Swarms of demons were nearly upon them before they suddenly switched course and headed downward toward a man . . . Joe!

"No!" she screamed. *He's here! He's in Hell!*

The demons closed in around Joe, hiding him from view.

"Do something!" she shouted.

"I will," he said, "but not yet."

"What do you mean 'not yet'?"

"We must use the accessway they've created." He flew them toward that glowing red object which was quickly coming into focus. It looked like a gateway of some sort. "I must vanish. Hold tight. I am here." His light extinguished and all went pitch black except for the glow coming off the lake and the gateway.

She felt a hard squeeze around her middle as if Nathaniel's way of reassuring her of his presence. It helped. A little. They swooped in low and began to fly so fast she couldn't breathe. As the last of the demons went through the portal, so did they . . . then flew past them at such speed she began hammering on Nathaniel, trying to tell him to slow down. Her stomach felt like it was in her feet and she couldn't get an ounce of air, couldn't even squeal. She couldn't see Billie. She couldn't see anything.

Until light shone above.

Billie screamed when a giant illuminated skull flashed in front her against a charcoal-gray sky. Lightning flashed, thunder crashed, whispers on the wind.

The Storm of Skulls.

"How are we back in the storm? I thought we were just in Hell?" Billie asked.

Nathaniel relit his glorious presence. "We were. The portal as it started triggered the Storm. It happened when the demons first rose. It happened again thus enabling your return and when they changed their plans. It's happening now because we were just outside of Time and are now entering what would be considered the *first* Storm. We must arrive ahead of the chopper that brought you, Joe and August."

"Joe?" Tracy said.

"How do we know where they are?" Billie asked.

"It's too difficult to say. We are between worlds, in the Storm."

Skulls flashed against the charcoal clouds; whispers in Aramaic haunted the air.

"Who is that? Who's talking?" Billie asked.

"It's a manifestation of the workings of the portal. It's speaking into the air, creating a path. This Storm is all over the Earth right now, but only in certain places and in certain quantities. Large groups of people are in the middle of it right now down below, where in other parts only a single person is immersed in it, ignorant of its occurrence. These are they, like you, who the Storm touched and thus made you immune to the effects of the rain."

As interesting as that was, Billie just wanted to get out of here and land at that stupid bank and—then what? Meet herself? Nathaniel said that was impossible, that she couldn't interact with herself on the same plane of existence.

Thunder crashed and lightning pierced the sky. Nathaniel aimed for one of the thunderbolts and in a blinding burst of light, the sky went blue and they were high in the air.

The angel shot down and the three landed in the back lane behind the bank. Quickly, Nathaniel transformed, but not to the old man that he was when she first met him, but the young man from the forest, the one that wore a gray turtleneck and jeans.

"You and your friends will emerge in a moment. We must hurry," he said and led them to the front of the bank. "Billie, you will stay with me. Tracy, you are the one now who must take this watch and wait until you give it to me, but I will be different. I will appear old. White velvet hat, white overcoat. He will know what to do when you give it to him."

He handed Tracy the watch.

"I thought I was the one that was supposed to fix this," Billie said.

"You have."

"I don't understand."

"You got the crystals and brought them to me. Now it's Tracy's turn. She has to because if the other you shows and sees you, then this mission won't be properly carried out."

"I don't get it," Tracy said. "Why doesn't she just stop herself from entering the bank thus stopping everything . . . else." She furrowed her brow. "Does that mean that all this is suddenly going to disappear, or we'll disappear, or—help me! Here, I don't want this." She gave the pocket watch back.

"How about just trust me?" he said calmly, and returned the watch to her.

"No," she said and tried giving it back, but Nathaniel withdrew his hand. "Seriously, take it."

"Please trust him," Billie said. "I know you're confused, I know this is confusing, but he knows what he's doing. He wouldn't have brought us here otherwise."

Tracy looked at the watch. "Fine. Just . . . whatever." She headed toward the bank's doors.

35
THE PAST

TRACY REACHED FOR the door handle and her hand passed through the metal. Thinking she was losing it, she tried again and the same thing happened.

"What is this, a hologram?" she said.

Someone else was coming up the steps behind her, a middle-aged man with dark gray hair.

"Can you open the—" she started, but he walked right through her, opened the door and went in. "What just happened?" She faced the door and tried touching it again. Like before, her hand went through the handle. Giving up, she said, "I'm not going to even ask anymore." Slowly, she stepped toward the door's glass and, bracing to smack her head into it, she instead passed smoothly through the glass and was in the bank's landing. "Whoa," she breathed and proceeded to the main entrance. She passed through it and was before the ATMs on the other side.

There were people all around. A security camera covered the front entrance. When she glanced up at its corresponding monitor, there was no one where she stood. She tried talking to the next person to pass her and was completely ignored. She went to touch them on the shoulder and her hand passed through them.

"This is cool in its own way, but you need to stay focused."

Outside, lightning flickered and a black helicopter emerged in the middle of the parking lot, not affecting any of the cars around it. A few moments later, an older man with long hair and beard followed by Billie and Joe came out.

"Joe . . ." she said. She stepped forward to run to him, but stopped herself despite her heart desperately telling her otherwise.

Outside through the window, the trio spoke before Billie fell forward and sank into the sidewalk. Joe pulled her up and she started freaking out.

Thank goodness that didn't happen to me, Tracy thought.

Soon Billie came in first and hid. Joe and August entered shortly after and started looking for her.

Joe was so handsome and put together, the long coat, the bald head with only a bit of stubble. He had a hard edge to him, the same he had when she first met him and saved his life. She wanted to go up to him, to wrap her arms around him and caution him of what was to come, but remembering the horrors of the demonic undead invasion, any wrong move on her part could destroy what she, Billie and Nathaniel came here to do. She could only hope and pray that what she was to do here would save his life in the end.

Tracy kept to herself near the brochures, pretending to be just another customer in case they saw her. She watched as Joe and August went around, looking for Billie. Joe called out her name. It was so good to hear his voice again.

An old man in a white fedora and overcoat was outside the bank, about to come in.

That's him! she thought and ran through the bank, through the doors, straight in front of him.

He didn't say anything, but she knew he saw her because he was looking directly into her eyes.

"Nathaniel?" she said.

He simply nodded.

"I have something for you." She pulled out the pocket watch and gave it to him.

He took it without reaction, tipped his hat, and walked on past into the bank.

"What?" she said. "No thank you?"

Billie came around the side of the bank, alone. She gave Tracy a wave. "Done already?"

Tracy did a quick replay of the pass-off in her mind's eye. "Yeah. Too easy. Just gave it to the old guy and—Where's Nathaniel?"

"Said he'd be right back, wanted to check on something." Billie's eyes went wide in apparent realization. "You don't think—"

"I guess we understand now, don't we."

"I guess, but if he has the watch and it's intact, what is the one inside the safety deposit box?"

"Safety deposit box?"

"Yeah, that's where the original pocket watch was, the one that he went into the private booth to reset and I interfered, thus him missing the reset time."

Tracy waved her hands. "Wait, wait, wait. What's that watch for?"

"You know, it's a long story, but in the end . . . I was told that by him resetting it, that that was his assignment. He comes in and resets it every

REDEMPTION OF THE DEAD

week and by doing so forbids the Doomsday Clock from rolling over and unleashing Armageddon."

"You mean *the* Armageddon?"

"That's the one."

A series of dark shadows rose over them and when Tracy looked up, she saw a host of demons on the bank's roof, looking right at them.

The forces of darkness upon the roof leered at them before swarming down and surrounding the girls. They had them trapped, each of the creatures hissing and snapping as they taunted.

Tracy already had her gun drawn. Billie wished she had one of her own, not that it would do anything, but at least she'd have *something*.

If it's my time to die, then I'd rather do it myself than them. "Tracy, shoot me," Billie said, suddenly feeling like a coward.

"What?"

"It's either us or them who decides how we die. Do you want to leave that choice in their hands?"

"Leave them in mine." A bright golden robe with enormous wings landed in front of them, sending the demons back a step. The angel drew his long sword and got to work cutting heads, wings and bodies. Each time one of the creatures came in, he countered their attack lightning quick and removed either a limb from their body or ended them entirely.

When the blur of golden motion was over, Billie saw who had rescued them.

Michael.

"My friend has other matters to attend to," he said.

Suddenly, scores of demons rose from the ground, weapons drawn. Michael immediately got at the ready. Surrounded by a multitude of them, Billie didn't know if they'd make it.

From the sky, an army of angels descended and instantly the battle began.

Running for their lives, Billie and Tracy headed back into the bank and she jerked Tracy out of the way when she saw her other self pass through the wall into the booth where Nathaniel was about to reset the watch.

Not long after, her counterpart emerged with Nathaniel forcing her along, the ground shaking. The angel passed her off to August. A moment later, the two started running. At the same time the ground split open and demons began to funnel out like bees escaping a packed hive.

"We're too late," Billie said. The same thing that happened before was happening again. It wasn't supposed to be like this. Nathaniel was supposed to have it all in hand. Where was he? She bolted toward the privacy booth and was quickly mauled by a demon that swooped in low and fast.

She scrambled, trying to get away from its grip. Tracy fired round after round into the creature, the bullets not making a difference. Tracy hurled the gun at it in frustration.

The foul demon's claws pierced Billie's legs; she screamed, and in an instant the evil creature swallowed up her body underneath.

Hissing, it whispered its victory, then ran its claws through her neck.

Landing on the demon's back, Tracy beat on it. "Get off her!"

Billie's limp form lay beneath the creature, most of her head detached from her body. The demon fluttered its leathery wings and sent her flying off its back into the air, and into Nathaniel, who had now changed into his angelic form and was fighting off the demons.

He pulled her to her feet, but her shaking legs gave out and she collapsed.

"Billie . . ." she said, looking into the angel's eyes.

With a look of sadness which quickly turned to red-hot fury, Nathaniel fought through the packs of demons, Michael coming to join him, the large angel cutting at the swarm of demons flying through the hole in the bank floor, through the walls and into the world.

The Rain. "Joe," Tracy said quietly.

"Gone already," Nathaniel said, running a demon through with a sword to its face.

"And me?"

"Help me." He swiftly came beside her and stuffed something into her hand then dove right back into the fray. She opened her fingers and had the pocket watch.

"Hold it as close to the opening as possible," he said.

The demons started to rise in a tornado, their flapping wings creating a whirlwind she was having a hard time fighting through.

REDEMPTION OF THE DEAD

"Open the watch and wind it back!" Nathaniel shouted as the demonic assault grew larger.

"Wind it back? How far?"

"Look at it!"

She read the clock's face. It had hands like any other watch, but it wasn't measured in minutes. It was measured in months, weeks, days. It seemed one full wind back would count for one year, but an odd three-hundred-and-sixty-day-year. "All the way?"

"All the—" A demon pounced on him and took him down. On his back, Nathaniel ran the creature through and chopped the head off another that quickly got closer.

Tracy wound back the hands. The watch face glowed white. She assumed that once she suppressed the winder, something would—she was brought down from behind, the watch falling on the floor and sliding away.

She rolled over.

The devil stood above her.

"Tracy . . ." he hissed, his black eyes filled with malice. He drew his liquid black sword and pointed it at her throat. "I lost Joe to my Adversary. I'm not going to lose you." With a snarl, he lashed out. The blade was deflected just inches from her face by a silver flash.

Nathaniel kicked the devil back then locked swords. "Get the watch!"

Tracy scrambled to her feet and scampered toward where the watch had slid under a chair.

A series of whooshes rose on the air then a searing pain pierced her lower back straight through to her gut. She looked down and saw almost half of the devil's blade protruding from her abdomen. Falling on her knees, the blade causing her muscles to start locking, she strove forward inch by painful inch along the floor toward the watch.

It was in view. Hot pain ignited in her feet as a pair of sharp teeth dug into her legs. One of the demons had her.

"Help . . ." she wheezed and was alarmed when she had difficulty breathing in.

Her fingertips touched the watch as the demon crawled up her body. She pulled the watch into her hand and instantly the demon's weight lifted. Had she suppressed the winder? She checked and it still was out, the watch face glowing. Hot pain fired up in her back and mid-section again as the sword was yanked from her body. Her blood gushed out and she could barely move. The devil stood over her and just as he reached for the pocket watch, both Nathaniel and Michael flew in from the side and pulled him away. Both the devil and the angels disappeared through the wall beside her.

Hands shaking, she pulled herself along the floor, blood filling her mouth. She coughed then gagged, and darkness started to invade her vision. Near the hole, the demonic swarm poured out, but seemed to be thinner in numbers.

Tracy reached as far forward as she could and pressed the winder.

EPILOGUE
ALTERATIONS

SIX MONTHS LATER...

Tracy walked down Main, Nathaniel guised as a young man beside her. She wore a black T-shirt, black jeans, the color something she refused to give up after what happened at the bank six months ago. As the two walked through the crowd of people, even now she still saw the city she once knew, the one ravaged and broken, with the undead at every corner. The pain, the suffering, the blood. The brown and gray sky.

And Joe. Her Joe.

After she passed out at the bank and came to later in an odd realm of golden light, she'd been told the pocket watch activated a temporal vortex which drew the demons back to the Pit, sealing them in once more. Billie hadn't survived.

Amidst the heartache over losing her, it was a relief to know that because the timer had been reset, none of it had ever happened. Joe was alive, so was Billie—her counterpart that was not present at the bank—August, even Des, though she never met the last two.

Nathaniel had kept her company every day since the bank, had helped her heal. Aside from Michael, Nathaniel was her only friend. Once she had been feeling better, she asked specific questions about stopping the demonic assault on the Earth. She wanted to know if she was able to finally lead a normal life, even right some wrongs. It was then she found out the horrible truth.

She would never have a normal life because she never returned to her own Time. No human would ever see or hear her again. She begged Nathaniel to fly her back to Hell so they could somehow get back to their own time, activate that portal which in turn would cause the Storm of Skulls and lead her back to *her* present.

"It can't be so," he had said. "To activate the portal fueled by their evil is abominable. Lucifer was the one that powered it. Even if we did, it would quickly lead to all that we just fought to prevent."

"Couldn't you and your army just go down there and stop them from entering?"

"It's not our time to fight them, not the one ordained. That is still a

213

little ways off yet. Besides, that portal has been destroyed as was its maker after Michael and his archangels took the devil back to where he belonged. It won't happen again."

"What about me? Life?"

"It is the cost of changing the course of history, in your case, getting history back on course."

"I'm doomed?"

"No, but chosen, and one day you will be rewarded by the King for your sacrifice and service. He won't forget you, Tracy. He loves you and will one day restore you. Until then, I will remain with you until we received word as to where we are called next."

After that conversation, she spent many nights weeping, thinking of Joe and the life they could've had, the bitter thought that maybe he was now with April. She couldn't bring herself to check on him. She mourned for her family and friends who she'd never speak to again. She was assured there was a version of her here and now living in the natural realm. What that woman was doing, she wasn't yet prepared to face. Maybe in time, maybe when things healed.

Now, looking up at the sun shining overhead, she longed to feel its warmth. Instead, she had to rely on the warmth of promise and of one day being restored. Until then, she had to bear the pain and carry her cross.

They turned a corner and started heading to the railway bridge underpass. A glimmer of gold caught her eye and she looked up. Michael stood on the bridge overhead, sword drawn, fire in his eyes.

"Come, he has been located," Michael said.

Tracy looked at Nathaniel. "Who?"

Nathaniel's eyes lit with a fresh burst of holy fire. "The Antichrist."

As the angel changed form beside her, Tracy reached back over her shoulder and drew her own sword. Its energy passed through her and liquid silver armor formed over her body, delicate scripts and glyphs surfacing right after. She turned to Nathaniel, who asked, "Ready?"

"Ready," she said, then spread her wings and rose into the air.

ABOUT THE AUTHOR

A.P. Fuchs is the author of many novels and short stories, most of which have been published. His most recent books are *Redemption of the Dead*, the third book in his zombie trilogy, *Undead World*; *Axiom-man: City of Ruin*; the paranormal romance series *Blood of my World*; and *Zombie Fight Night: Battles of the Dead*, in which zombies fight such classic monsters as werewolves, vampires, Bigfoot, and even go up against awesome foes like pirates, ninjas, and Bruce Lee.

Also a cartoonist, he is known for his superhero series, *The Axiom-man Saga*, both in novel and comic book format.

Please see **www.axiom-man.com** for more on this series.

Fuchs lives and writes in Winnipeg, Manitoba, and barely ever leaves the house.

Visit him on the Web at **www.canisterx.com** and follow him on Twitter at **www.twitter.com/ap_fuchs**

Thrillers, Suspense, Horror...

...this is what we do.

Browse our Catalog at Coscom Entertainment Online
Bringing You the Very Best in Quality Fiction
www.coscomentertainment.com

All books available in paperback and eBook at your favorite
online retailer like Amazon.com

BE SURE TO

CHECK OUT THE

Axiom-Man™

COMIC BOOKS

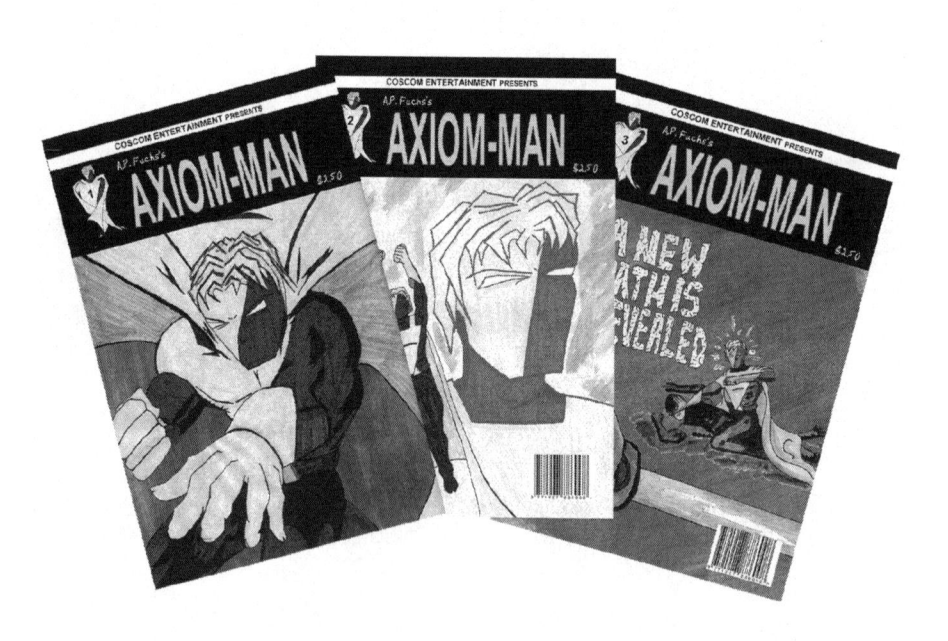

AT

WWW.AXIOM-MAN.COM

More from the World of
A.P. FUCHS
WWW.CANISTERX.COM